Tears of Betrayal

Meleigha
Happy Reading
Sherry B.

Sherry A. Burton

Published by Dorry Press
Edited by Michelle Johnson
Digital layout by www.formatting4U.com

For more information on the author and her works, please see www.SherryABurton.com.

Chapter One

Sitting at her vanity, Amber gazed at her reflection in the mirror; her deep, nearly black eyes stared back at her.

Her mom had always said, "Your eyes Amber, they're very special, they capture people. There won't be a man alive who will be able to resist you when he looks into those eyes of yours."

Jeff, her husband, had told her that her eyes had drawn him to her. He said he liked the way he could see his reflection in them.

Amber studied herself in the mirror. She was glad the wrinkles had not yet taken up residence on her face. Her eyebrows had an enviable natural arch and thankfully, she had inherited her mother's nose. Not too big or too small, it was just right. Behind her full lips were straight, white teeth, making the three years of braces nearly worth it. She winced, remembering all the relentless teasing. Being referred to as "metal mouth," "zipper mouth," or "tin grin" was hard, especially combined with the small mole, which lay just to the left of her upper lip.

"Just like a movie star," her mom would say. "Don't worry about those kids, they're just jealous that they don't look like movie stars too." No matter the dilemma – real or imagined – her mom always found a way to make her smile and see the bright side.

I wish you were here, Mom, Amber thought. *I sure*

could use some of your happy thoughts.

As she pulled a hairbrush through her silky black hair, she let her mind wander. Surely Jeff would notice her weight loss tonight. Amber had been losing weight steadily for the past few months, but to her disappointment, her husband hadn't uttered a word about it. Not that she had ever been heavy; she was simply trying everything she could think of to get her husband's attention.

"Enough of this pity party," she chided as she placed the hairbrush on the counter.

With a sigh, she headed down stairs for her morning cup of coffee. A cold breeze stung her face as she swung open the door and scooped up the morning paper. She hurried to shut out the ever-present Michigan wind, and headed down the hall toward the kitchen. The kitchen was filled with golden rays of warm sunshine, streaming in from the sliding glass doors. The large back yard was lined with pine trees, which blocked the brutal winter winds. They also added privacy from the prying eyes of nosy neighbors.

Sadly, the same could not be said about the front yard. No, that yard had plenty of eyes watching every movement - one of the drawbacks of living in a small town. Amber loved having the curtains open and wished they had lined the front with pine trees as well.

She turned on the coffee pot and sat on a stool, crossed her legs then leafed through the paper until she found the horoscope page. She folded the paper backwards then in half again as was her morning ritual.

"The time for romance is near," it read. "Take the time to see things as they really are."

Amber's eyes rolled upward. "Yeah right," she laughed. The last time Jeff was romantic was when he landed the highway repair contract in the city. That was seven years ago. Since then he had practically lived there, coming home on Friday and leaving again on Sunday. Lately, even that wasn't a given. His idea of romance these days was a six-pack and a blowjob.

When the gurgling of the coffee machine subsided, Amber poured herself a cup and reached for the sugar. Scooping up the white crystals, she watched as they dissolved into the depths of the brown liquid. As she sat stirring her coffee, her thoughts turned inward.

I know Jeff is a good provider. Hell, most people would kill to have a house and car that's paid for. And he is quite the looker – even if he is a tad vain. She shook her head as she pictured Jeff primping in front of the mirror. It was common knowledge that he spent more time getting ready in the morning than did she.

Then there's Julie, she thought, smiling at the thought of their only daughter. *Sure, she can be a pain, can't all children? But as teenagers go, we're very lucky. The happy little family...*

Amber's dark eyes filled with tears. *If we're so happy, then why am I so damn miserable?*

She watched the coffee swirl around in the cup, the perfect metaphor for her inner turmoil.

It's because every day is just like the day before, Amber thought. *Is it so wrong to want to be loved or even be appreciated? Just to be told I look good, that I'm sexy or desirable.*

Don't start this again. She wiped the moisture from her eyes. You don't do yourself or anyone else any good when you get into one of your moods. She took a drink of her now-warm coffee.

The slamming of the front door startled her out of her funk.

"Mom! Clancy got loose again," Julie's annoyed voice shouted from the foyer. "I let him out to do his business; he saw something and took off running down the street, leash and all! I don't have time to go after him again. I have to finish getting ready for school."

Wonderful, Amber thought as she grabbed her coat and keys and headed for the car. *That damn dog is going to drive me crazy.*

Clancy, a large goofy boxer mix, was more trouble than he was worth sometimes but he never failed to let her know when someone was at the door. Plus, he kept her feet warm on those cold, northern nights. Jeff would have a conniption if he knew she let the dog sleep with her. As if Clancy knew, he never tried to get in bed with her if Jeff was home.

Amber scanned the neighbor's yards as she slowly maneuvered her car around the circle.

Nope. Not at the Johnson's, she thought. *Not at the Marshal's either.*

She headed toward the park. A black squirrel darted in front of her, followed by none other than Clancy. He dragged his leash in a dead run and was oblivious to everything but his mission at hand. Amber slammed on the brakes, just missing both of them. The squirrel scurried up a nearby tree and Clancy stopped. He looked bewildered; as if questioning why the fun had stopped so abruptly.

She curbed the car, opened the door and called for the dog. Clancy sniffed the base of the tree. As though realizing his defeat, he trotted to the car, jumped in and sat in the passenger seat. His tongue lolled from the corner of his mouth as he sat panting and looking quite pleased with himself.

"You rotten dog," Amber scolded. "One of these days I just might decide not to come looking for you."

Clancy leaned over and started licking her face. She pushed the slobbering muzzle away.

"Knock it off. You're not going to get on my good side that easy." To her amazement, Clancy sat back down and rested his head on his paws. Amber couldn't help but smile.

I think the little shit actually knows he's in trouble, she thought and patted his head.

"You better stop running off before you get yourself killed," she said sternly. Clancy wagged his short nub of a tail.

Turning the car around, she headed back the way she had come. As she pulled into her driveway, she noticed the curtains pulled back ever so slightly at the house next door. Karen, her nosy neighbor, was always keeping tabs on everything she did. She couldn't pass gas without worrying that Karen would run off and tell someone about it. Amber's face flushed.

Why don't you get a life? she thought. *You'd think she'd have better things to do*. The second Amber turned the car off Clancy jumped up.

"You'd better not take off," she said firmly. She opened the car door, grabbed his collar and led him into the house. Her daughter's voice called down from the middle of the stairs.

"Mom! Robin is on the phone."

Amber looked up to see the cordless phone sailing down from above, and reacted just in time to catch it. Julie was clad in jeans, an oversized Redwings sweatshirt, and wore one striped sock. The other was casually draped across her right shoulder. Julie's long brown hair hung loose, thick eyelashes accentuating the startling green eyes she had inherited from her father. A few blemishes that came with being a thirteen¬year-old dotted her cheerful face.

"Good, you found him. Come on Clancy," the teen called. He scrambled up the stairs behind the dark-haired girl.

Amber sighed. She pushed back her hair and placed the phone to her ear. "What's up Chickie?"

"Hey you," Robin greeted. "Julie told me the dog

took off again. Did you find him?"

"This time he found me," Amber laughed. "I nearly killed the crazy mutt. He was too busy chasing a squirrel to even care there was a car coming. It's a good thing I was driving slowly or I wouldn't have to worry about looking for him anymore."

"I don't know why you keep going after him."

Amber gazed out the window. "It gives me something to do. Besides, what would Karen have to look at if I didn't?"

"That old crone. Is she still spying on you?"

"Yeah. She doesn't think anyone can see her."

"Or she doesn't give a shit. Why don't you just wave at her and see what she does?"

"I did." Amber laughed. "She just moved to another window."

"You ought to give her something to really look at," Robin teased.

"Oh sure, like what?" Amber asked. "Some gorgeous blonde hunk of a man in tight jeans and leather boots?"

"Mmmm, works for me. Why not? You could use some excitement in your life. Speaking of excitement, when does the highway man get home?"

"About eight o'clock. Why?"

"I thought maybe we could go shopping or something."

"Not tonight. I thought I'd fix him something special for dinner."

"I don't know why you bother," Robin said. "He never appreciates it. Hell, he never appreciates anything you do. Did he even notice you lost weight?"

"Shit no!" Amber said in a voice so loud it surprised even her.

"How much have you lost all together?"

Amber sighed, knowing the weight loss wouldn't make a difference. "About twelve pounds."

"Wow! You better not lose any more or there won't be anything left of you."

"I know. I was hoping that just maybe this would be the thing to put the fire back in our marriage."

"If you ask me, the man is gay," Robin laughed. "Anyone that has a woman as sexy as you and doesn't want to be with you every minute he can, has to have a problem."

"Robin, you're not turning bi on me, are you?" Amber teased.

"I'm just saying you're a great looking lady and the man needs to have his head examined," Robin countered.

Amber's voice took on a serious tone. "You're my best friend Robin. I hope you know that."

Robin's voice brightened. "If I was bi we could really give Karen a show!"

"This is getting deep," Amber said with a laugh. "I best be getting off this phone. Clancy and I are going for our morning run; would you like to join us?"

"Me run? Yeah right! Besides, I have to be to work early this morning. I have to do the end of the month reports. Anyway, I think Clancy already had his morning run."

Amber laughed into the phone. "You really don't think that tired him out do you?"

"You always say he's a mixed breed. I think he's mixed with the energizer bunny."

"In more ways than one girlfriend," Amber chuckled. "He could give that bunny a run for his money. Listen, I've got to go. I need to light a fire under Julie before she's late for school."

"Okay. See ya lady!"

"Later." Amber turned off the receiver, walked to the base of the stairs and looked up. "Julie! You need to come down for breakfast!"

"I'll be down in a minute. I'm almost done," Julie

hollered through her door. Amber walked to the counter and folded the newspaper.

I don't know why I read these things, she mused. *Love, romance, that's just in the movies…*

"Mom, is it okay if I stay the night at Kelly's? Mom?"

"Huh?" Amber asked, suddenly aware the teen was in the room.

"Gosh, Mom, you looked like you were in a trance or something," Julie said, sounding edgy.

"Just daydreaming I guess. What did you want?"

"I wanted to know if I could spend the night with Kelly," she repeated, as she pulled her long brown hair up into a ponytail.

Amber's brow creased with a frown. "But honey. Your dad will be home tonight. Don't you want to see him?" She reached up, tucking in a narrow strand of Julie's hair that had managed to escape the grasp of the hair tie.

"I'll see him tomorrow. Besides, he won't miss me. He doesn't talk to me anymore either," Julie said, waving her hand to further express her point.

A look of confusion crossed Amber's face. "What do you mean, 'either?'"

"I'm not stupid, Mom. I watch talk shows. Dad is just using you."

Amber couldn't help but notice how much Julie reminded her of herself. Especially the way her eyes narrowed and her lips scrunched together when she was trying to make a point.

"I think you'd better lay off the talk shows, dear. You're reading too much into things," Amber said sternly.

"Denial. It's not a good state to be in," Julie said, giving her mom a big hug. "So? Can I go to Kelly's?"

"I guess so, but no more talk shows," Amber said, playfully swatting the teen's backside.

"Sure Mom. Anything you say." Julie turned to wink at her mom then headed to pack her things.

"Hurry up or you'll be late for school." A sudden sense of sadness washed over her as she watched her daughter trot back up the stairs with Clancy right behind her.

God, she's growing up, she thought, shaking her head. *I wonder if I was that perceptive at her age. Hell, who am I kidding? I'm not that perceptive at my age. She's right though, Jeff doesn't notice either one of us anymore. Maybe I should start watching those damn talk shows. Maybe they would teach me a thing or two.*

Julie called down the stairs. "Mom, have you seen my new Lady Gaga CD?"

"Sure. I listen to it all the time. I keep it right next to my Alan Jackson collection," Amber teased. "Try cleaning your room, you might just find it."

Julie flew down the stairs with Clancy hot on her heels. Zipping her backpack, she snatched up her lunch money and rushed towards the door. She reached for the doorknob and used her leg to block Clancy. "I'll clean my room tomorrow Mom, I promise."

"Jeez, don't I even get a kiss goodbye?" Amber asked, faking insult. "What about breakfast?"

Julie gave her mom a quick peck on the cheek. "Don't worry, Mom. I have a granola bar. I'll see you tomorrow. Tell Dad I said hi." She slammed the door behind her.

Amber looked down at Clancy. "Well boy, I guess it's just you and me now. How 'bout we go for our run?"

Amber picked up the leash, sending Clancy into a frenzy of eager barking and jumping.

"Okay, calm down," she fussed as she strained to fasten the leash. Locking the door, Amber headed out with Clancy for their morning four-mile jog.

Chapter Two

Dalton Renfro led his sweaty horse to the stable after his morning ride. He was met at the door by a tall, lanky teen with curly red hair.

"Morning, Boss. How was your ride?" he asked, giving the steamy chestnut mare a loving pat.

"Not bad, Jake," Dalton handed the reins to the youth. "She's coming along nicely. Cool her down thoroughly before you put her back in the stall."

"You got it, Boss." Taking the reins, he turned, leading the horse down the well-worn path.

Dalton watched as the young boy easily led the big mare away. At sixteen, Jake was better with horses than most people who have worked with them all of their lives.

A natural gift with animals, Dalton thought, turning toward the house.

He gazed at the big house. A wide, covered porch supported by thick white pillars ran completely around the stately dwelling. Black shutters accented each of the massive windows, offsetting the white. Large black ceiling fans that were strategically placed all along the porch added to the stark look and offered a much-needed breeze during the scorching days of summer.

A true Southern home if ever there were one, he thought approvingly.

Dalton had his dream house built years ago in the heart of Kentucky horse country, overseeing every detail himself. It was an impressive home with five large bedrooms and six and a half bathrooms.

A house big enough for a huge family, Dalton thought with a sudden wave of emptiness. A bright red truck rolled up beside him, interrupting his thoughts.

"There you are, Dalton; I've been looking for you," the older, pepper-haired man said as he slid out of the truck. A hand-rolled cigarette perched in the corner of his mouth. Striking a match with his yellowed fingers, he lit the cigarette and inhaled deeply. Carl – a true cowboy – rolled his own cigarettes, refused to use lighters and slept under the stars whenever he got the notion.

"What's up Carl?" Dalton asked, looking into the man's tobacco stained grin.

"I just got a call from old man Patterson. He agreed to your offer on that stallion. Do you want me to pick him up before he changes his mind?"

Dalton's boyish face brightened, lending a twinkle to his crystal blue eyes. "Well it's about dang time. Old man Patterson drives a hard bargain, but I think that horse will be worth it." Dalton lifted his black cowboy hat, ran a hand through his thick wavy black hair then replaced his hat and glanced toward the barn. "Why don't you take Jake with you? That stallion can be a handful."

"You're right," Carl said as he took another draw from his cigarette. "If anyone can calm a horse, it's that boy. I have to admit I had my doubts when you first hired him, him being so young and all, but he sure has pulled his weight."

"He's not so young," Dalton countered. "He's sixteen. Shoot, I had my first job when I was only ten years old. I got paid fifty cents an hour to stack hay in old man Shiller's barn."

Carl took one last drag, dropped it to the ground then crushed it out with the toe of his boot. "Oh no, here we go again. Next you'll be telling me, yet again, how you bought your first five acres with the money you earned."

"Laugh if you want to Carl, but hard work never hurt anyone. Besides, if it weren't for my hard work, I wouldn't be needing your ornery ass working here as my head foreman."

Carl dropped to his knees, closed his eyes and clasped his hands as if in prayer. "Oh forgive me, Sir, I forgot to be grateful," he sang out. Carl opened one eye to judge the reaction of his boss.

"Very funny," Dalton responded, a slight red tingeing his cheeks. "You better take Jake and go get that stallion before I decide to give that boy your job."

Carl rose, took off his cowboy hat and extended it, then bent at the waist into a playful bow. "Yes Sir, Boss, anything you say, Boss." He stood up and returned to his pickup truck. He gave Dalton a playful wink and drove off toward the barn.

Dalton watched him go.

Best damn foreman a man could ever have, he thought. *Even if he is a smart ass*.

As Dalton neared the house, the glorious smell of bacon cooking wafted over him. He had just reached the porch when the door burst open. A rotund older woman, with tightly curled black peppered hair, met him at the door.

"There you are. I thought I was going to have to come looking for you. Breakfast is going to get cold if you don't hurry up," chided the older lady. "Katie Mae will be right down. I sent her up to get dressed while we were waiting on you."

"Sorry Maggie," Dalton said. He took off his cowboy hat and dutifully followed the woman as she waddled toward the kitchen.

"Carl stopped me out by the barn. Seems like old man Patterson finally agreed to my price on that stallion."

"Land sakes, it's about time. I think it's a shame the

way he keeps you waiting like he does." Maggie picked up a bowl of fresh, homemade biscuits and placed them on the table. "He was probably okay with the price all along, he just wanted to get you all worked up."

"I know, but he's like that. He has to let you know he is the decision maker. Let me wash my hands and I'll be right in."

"Hurry up, young man. I didn't slave over this stove all morning just to have you eat cold eggs." She wiped beads of sweat from her round face with the ends of her orange apron.

"I'll hurry," Dalton replied, playfully swatting the old woman on her rear. "But cold or not, you're still the best cook in the county."

Maggie chuckled and began putting the rest of the food on the table. As she set the fried potatoes down, Dalton came back into the room.

"Boy Maggie, you sure do know how to lay out a spread. I think I might just have to marry you someday."

Maggie became flustered. "Now you cut that out, Dalton. You know I'm old enough to be your grandmother."

"Yeah, I know. But they say age doesn't make a difference"

"Well I don't know who "they" are, but I think in this case they would reconsider," the lady replied with a wheeze. "Besides, I think it's far past time you find you a pretty lady of your own age to settle down with."

"Don't start playing match-maker, Maggie. Carl does enough of that already."

"Now Dalton, you know Carl means well. Besides, I'm sure he has some really nice friends."

"Don't get me started on Carl's friends," Dalton huffed. "The last girl he set me up with proposed marriage halfway through the first date."

Maggie smiled. "I guess that's the price you pay for

your rugged good looks and your strong, healthy body."

Dalton's face turned crimson. Just as he was about to open his mouth in response a small voice pierced the air.

"Daddy!"

He turned, scooping up the pigtailed girl as she ran into the room.

"Hello, Little Bit," he said, kissing each of her deeply dimpled cheeks. He tenderly brushed her dark bangs out of her eyes. "How's Daddy's little sunshine today?"

"I'm not so little, Daddy. I'm four," the brown-eyed girl adamantly shook her head.

"So you are, honey," Dalton said, lowering her to the chair. "So you are."

Maggie lowered herself into her usual seat and reached for the biscuits. "Well if no one else is going to eat, I am. I didn't cook all this food only to have it go to waste."

Dalton fixed a plate and set it in front of the little girl sitting at his side.

"Here you go, Katie Mae. You eat this before Miss Maggie has a cow," he said with a wink.

The little girl snickered and tried to return her father's wink.

Dalton smiled in return, piling an extra high helping onto his plate to try to appease the woman he held so dear.

"It nearly slipped my mind! Lana called this morning," Maggie said, interrupting his thoughts.

"Lana? What on earth did she want?" Dalton asked frowning. He glanced at his daughter. She had strawberry jam all down the front of her shirt and her jet-black bangs had drifted back into her face. He made a mental note to trim them. Her big brown eyes smiled back at him, her cheeks showcasing the dimples she had inherited from her mother.

Maggie's voice penetrated his thoughts. "She said she wanted your help with a present for Kelly's birthday."

Dalton looked relieved. He loved his sister, but when it came to Katie Mae, they just didn't see eye to eye. Because of that they hadn't spoken, except for holidays, in nearly four years. If she wanted his help with his niece, however, that he could do. "I wonder what kind of present she has in mind. Did she say?"

The older woman shook her head. "No, she just said she didn't know who else to ask but you."

Katie Mae reached over and touched his arm. "Can I help with the present too, Daddy?"

Dalton wiped the strawberry jam from her face. "Of course you can, Little Bit, of course you can." He wiped his own mouth with his napkin and pushed his chair away from the table. "Good God, Maggie, if you keep laying out a spread like this, none of us will ever get any work done around this place. Speaking of work, I have plenty to do this morning with both Carl and Jake gone. I will have my cell phone with me if you need anything."

He kissed Maggie on her forehead, then leaned down and picked Katie Mae up for a big hug. "You be a good girl for Miss Maggie, okay?"

She wrapped her arms around him squeezing tightly. "Okay, Daddy, I will."

"I'll give Lana a call this evening and see what she has in mind," he said to Maggie as he attached his cell phone to his belt and picked up his cowboy hat. "See you in a few hours, ladies."

Chapter Three

Amber finished her magazine and glanced at the clock, noting she had to start dinner in ten minutes. "I guess I could preheat the oven," she said. Clancy cocked his head as if trying to figure out to whom she was talking.

"I know boy, it is pretty bad when I am talking to myself. As long as I don't answer myself I guess I'll be okay." Tossing the magazine to the side, she rose and headed down the hallway.

The dog wagged his stubby tail and followed Amber into the kitchen. Deciding that no food was coming his way, he plopped down onto his bed and gnawed eagerly on his well-worn rawhide.

Amber set the oven to 350 then took out the meatloaf she had mixed earlier. She set it on the counter, and then mentally went through her checklist.

Let's see, the meatloaf takes an hour, the mashed potatoes about forty minutes, the cans of peas and corn don't take any time at all. I guess I'll put the bread in at the halfway point. Jeff should be home in about ninety minutes. The drive usually wears him out so I'll have dinner ready and we can chill out on the couch and see what happens, she thought, smiling to herself. *Maybe it's a good thing Julie is sleeping over at Kelly's house tonight after all. This has the makings of a perfect night.*

Just maybe that will lead to a perfect weekend.

She sighed. She couldn't remember the last time anything having to do with her relationship was perfect. As she reached for the meatloaf, the telephone rang. She set the pan back on the counter and answered it on the second ring.

"Hello?"

"Hey, Am."

"Jeff? Is something wrong?" Amber's voice was full of concern.

"Nothing's wrong. I just wanted to let you know I can't make it in this weekend. That's all."

Amber's heart sank. "Why not?"

"This is the busy time with all the potholes. You know that." Jeff sighed heavily. "There's a lot of pressure to get them filled before someone gets killed."

"Surely you didn't just find out about this," Amber said, her voice cracking.

Jeff hesitated before continuing. "No, I guess not. I would've called earlier but I've been so busy I didn't get a chance."

"Are you going to be home next weekend?" Amber asked.

"It doesn't look like it. Actually, it might be a while before I can get away."

Amber fought hard to hold back the tears. She knew when she married Jeff that his highway construction job would keep them apart at times. Heck, they had spent more time apart than together over the years, but it was different lately. It seemed like it didn't bother him to be away any more. Amber couldn't believe he didn't sound even the least bit disappointed about not coming home.

"How about we come see you?" Amber couldn't hide the desperation in her voice. "We could spend the afternoon…"

Jeff cut her off mid-sentence. "No, that wouldn't

work. I don't get done 'til late. You'd be bored sitting around the motel all day. Besides, I usually go back to the motel, take a shower and fall into bed. It would be crazy to drive all the way down here just to watch me sleep."

There was a long pause on the line. Finally, Jeff broke the silence.

"I have some paperwork I need to get caught up on while I'm still awake enough to do it. I had better go. I'll give you a call when I can."

Amber took a deep breath. She had to be strong. If Jeff could stand being apart, then so could she. "Okay Jeff. Call me soon. I love you."

"I know," came his usual response just before he hung up.

Amber stood there staring into space, the receiver pressed to her ear. It wasn't until the busy signal came on that she remembered to hang up the phone. Tears streamed down her face as she returned the meatloaf to the fridge. *No use in fixing a big dinner for one.*

The sound of a knock and the opening of the front door sent Clancy in a wild barking frenzy. He sailed down the hall, his nails clicking and sliding the entire way.

"Clancy, it's just me, get down you mangy mutt." Robin's voice rang out from the hallway. "At least you don't have to worry about someone breaking in."

As she entered the kitchen, Clancy was next to her, still jumping up seeking attention. "Clancy, knock it off!"

Chastised, the dog returned to his bed, plopped down and resumed gnawing on the now soggy rawhide. Shrugging out of her coat, she produced a bottle of red wine she had managed to keep hidden. She looked at the label.

"I felt bad about lecturing you earlier about Jeff. I figured the least I could do was drop off some wine for dinner tonight. I hope it goes well with red. Speaking of dinner, how come I don't smell it cooking?" When Robin saw the tears, she set the wine on the table and walked over to Amber, wrapping her arms around her.

Amber collapsed into her best friends arms. Tears streamed down her face. She cried for a full minute then straightened and reached for a paper towel to blow her nose.

"What did he do this time?" Robin asked, color rising in her cheeks.

"It's nothing really," Amber said, angry with herself for losing control. "Jeff just called me to let me know he wasn't coming in this weekend. I was just having another pity party."

Robin's eyes narrowed. She bit at her lip before speaking. "Well, if you ask me you've earned it. What was his excuse this time?"

"He has to get the potholes fixed before someone gets killed." Amber blotted her eyes.

"And he just realized this?"

"No, but he's been too busy to call," Amber said defensively.

"Listen, I know it's none of my business, but if you ask me you should be getting a lot more than upset. You should be downright pissed. This is not the first time he has waited until the last minute to call you." Robin took a seat at the table.

"I know, but he works hard," Amber said, once again making excuses. She could see the flush which crossed Robin's face and knew her friend wanted nothing more than to shake some sense into her. She braced herself as Robin opened her mouth to speak.

"I wouldn't get so damned mad if he at least treated you with respect. You know as well as I do those potholes didn't just show up. He's known about this for a while and for him to let you do all the shopping, cleaning and look forward to his coming home, then to call you at the last minute? That's just him trying to mess with you. You can only be in denial so long, girlfriend. You have to wake up someday."

Amber sat down and stared into Robin's hazel eyes. She knew Robin's anger was simply out of concern for her. It was the second time today someone had told her she was in denial. Maybe they were right; after all, she had spent all day shopping and getting ready for the weekend. Amber picked up the wine bottle and reached in the drawer for the corkscrew.

"No sense in letting this go to waste," she sighed. "Want to join my pity party?"

Amber plunged the spike into the cork. After several turns and a hard tug, the cork gave way with a soft pop.

"Count me in. Jack's away and the kids are all out for the evening, so why the hell not?" Robin said, a smile playing across her lips.

Amber poured them each a glass and took a sip. "I envy your relationship with Jack. You're both made for each other."

"We're soul mates," Robin said.

As they sipped their wine and chatted, Amber noticed the way her friend's face glowed when she spoke about the man she had been married to for more than twenty years. Yes, that was the face of a woman in love.

"Soul mates," Amber said dreamily. "I wish I had found mine." She blushed realizing she had made the comment out loud.

Robin gave Amber's hand a squeeze.

"I think the wine is getting to me," Amber lied, ignoring the fact she had not yet finished even half of her glass. "I don't know where things went wrong. You know, we were happy once upon a time, but we were never soul mates. I don't know if I believe that everyone has a soul mate."

Robin reached for the wine. As she re-filled each of their glasses, she laughed. "You've got to be kidding me.

You, not believe in something? The same girl who can't start her morning without reading the horoscope to see how your day is going to be? Everyone has a soul mate; they just have to find him. Yours is out there. We just have to find him."

Amber took a long drink. "I have a husband, I don't need to go looking for another one."

Robin laughed again. "Who said anything about another husband? We'll just get you a lover on the side. You'll have the best of both worlds. A husband who pays the bills but is never here and a lover who is always here and treats you like a queen."

Amber finished the last of the wine and studied her empty glass.

"Now who's had too much wine? I'm not the unfaithful type. I can't believe we are even having this conversation. Some wife I am. My husband is in the city working his ass off to support his family and I'm here talking about him like he is some horrible evil creature." Her fingers traced the rim of the glass as fresh tears began to stream down her face.

Robin sighed and shook her head. She got up and took Amber's hand. "Okay, enough of this pity party, I'm starving. Let's get some food in us and soak up this wine."

Chapter Four

After Jeff tossed his cell on the bed, he walked into the bathroom to splash cool water onto his face and patted it dry with the hotel towel. He sprayed mousse into his palm then pulled his hair into short little spikes, making a mental note to schedule an appointment with that cute redhead to have the highlights retouched. He dabbed a bit of alcohol on his earlobe. It was still a bit tender but he was glad he decided to get the earring, it made him feel young and the chicks really seemed to love it – that and the eyelashes. When he was younger, it seemed a curse to have thick, girly eyelashes, but at this stage in life, he found the chicks really envied this quality. If there was one thing he enjoyed it was the attention of the opposite sex.

Not much longer, he thought, glancing at the wedding ring on the counter. *I am so tired of living a lie.*

He wasn't sure why he had let things go for as long as he had. He had cared for Amber, once, in the beginning. She had a great body and those tits!

He still felt her best quality were those eyes of hers, they were so dark, like a mirror, he could see himself and, God knows, he never got tired of that. When they found out Amber was pregnant, it was only natural that they would get married. Wasn't that the right thing to do?

He was sorry she hadn't given him a son. Maybe, just

maybe, things could have been different if Julie had been a boy. He would have known how to deal with a boy. He had never been around girls before other than to date them. Of course, he had dated his share and then some, but how was he supposed to bond with a daughter?

It was much easier to let Amber deal with her. He started staying away more and more, only coming home on the weekends at first then eventually he found any excuse to stay away even then. Soon he had not only managed to distance himself from Julie, but also from Amber. It seemed as though the more Amber tried to pull him in, the more he needed to stay away. He could get the affection he needed elsewhere. There were always girls coming by the work site, offering themselves to the workers. It was much easier to take a stranger back to the motel room and screw her brains out than go home and pretend to be in love.

Jeff could not begin to count the number of girls he had been with. He justified it by sending home a paycheck every week, making sure the bills were paid and food in the house. Besides, as much as he was away, how did he know that Amber had always been faithful? She could have been having fun of her own just as he had been. He would tell himself this, but deep down he knew the truth. He knew he had been the only man to share Amber's bed.

Jeff took out his wallet, found the business card he had been given and carefully dialed the number.

"Thank you for calling Rogers, Smith and Taylor. This is Madelyn, can I help you?" came a pleasant voice on the other end.

Jeff sat on the edge of the bed, took a deep breath and spoke, "Yes, does your office handle divorces?"

Chapter Five

Dalton was just finishing with the new fence when his cell phone rang. He took off his glove, wiped the sweat off his wind-burned face with his forearm and answered the phone.

"Hey Boss, we're back with the stallion," came Carl's familiar voice on the other end.

Dalton could hardly contain his excitement. "Don't put him away. I'll meet you at the corral in ten minutes!"

"Guess who came along for the ride?" Carl snickered.

"He didn't?" Dalton gasped. "You should have left him there."

"Boss, you know as well as I do that if I left that cat anywhere, you'd have sent me right back to get him," Carl teased.

"I don't know what you are talking about," Dalton stammered.

"Sure, keep telling yourself that. You're not fooling anyone but yourself, Boss," Carl said before hanging up the phone.

Dalton picked up his tools and hopped onto his four¬wheeler. He headed home, reflecting on how good things had been going lately. He had been back and forth with old man Patterson for months trying to settle on a price for that stallion and now – at long last – he was finally his. The stud fees alone would make him a very rich man. The stallion had a presence, a commanding 'you-must-take-notice-of-me' aura. Dalton had owned, sold and traded horses for many years but even to him this horse was one to behold. Yes, life was good. He reached for his cell phone and dialed his house number, which was answered on the second ring.

"Maggie, can you have Katie Mae get her jacket and shoes on?"

"Land sakes, Dalton. It's nearly dinnertime. Where are you taking that child?"

"I won't have her out long, I promise. The stallion is here and I want her to see him." Though he sounded like a teenager asking permission to stay out past his curfew, Dalton knew this approach was the best one. She was more like a grandmother to him than a lady he had hired to help keep his life in order. Yes, it was better to let her think she was in charge than to tell her what to do.

There was an audible sigh on the other end. "Okay, I'll have her get ready."

"Thanks Maggie, you're the greatest," Dalton said, clicking off the cell phone.

He guided the four-wheeler down the well-worn path of the west field. The long-dead grass was just beginning to give way to the first buds of new spring grass, which dotted the low rolling hills.

Soon the land would be wrapped in the lush, blue-green grass for which the region was known. Dalton glanced up just in time to see a large red-tailed hawk take flight out of a tall, red maple tree. The graceful bird swooped down, whisked a field mouse in its right talon and flew away to enjoy its evening meal. By the time he arrived at the front porch, Katie Mae was running out the door, trying unsuccessfully to pull her purple hat over her head.

"Did you get him, Daddy? Did you get the new horsey?" she asked, running down the stairs.

"Yes we did, Little Bit." Dalton grinned, scooping her up in his arms and pushing her bangs out of her eyes.

"Can I ride him?" The little girl asked, taking his face in both her hands, grimacing at the feel of his afternoon stubble.

"No Darlin', this one isn't for riding," he said, sitting her in front of him on the ATV and adjusting her crooked hat.

"Then what's he for, Daddy?" she asked with wonder.

At a loss for words, Dalton quickly changed the subject. "Carl said Lucky went for a ride in the trailer again today. He said he almost left him there."

The little girl turned her head around as far as she could, her eyes wide with fear. "He didn't leave him, did he Daddy?"

"No, Little Bit. He brought him back," Dalton reassured her.

They pulled up to the corral where Carl and Jake were standing next to one of the most magnificent thoroughbreds any of them had ever seen. He was a rich, deep brown with white stockings and a white lightning bolt shape running the length of his nose.

Dalton was ecstatic. He got off the ATV and helped Katie Mae down. Holding hands, they walked up to the horse. Carl held the reins as they approached. The horse tossed his head back, snorted and made a soft whinny.

"Ladies and gentlemen, I present to you, Crazy Legs," Carl said, nodding to each in turn and patting the stallion on the neck.

"Oh Daddy," Katie Mae said, her voice almost a whisper. "He's so beautiful and so big!"

Dalton was delighted that Katie Mae could appreciate his splendor even at her young age. "Yes he is, Darlin'. He's one of a kind."

Carl looked over at Katie Mae with a grin. Winking

at Jake, he said to Katie Mae, "You know, when Jasper grows up, he'll be this big."

The child looked across the corral at her small cream Shetland pony. Her eyes widened. "Really?" she asked fearfully.

The men laughed.

Dalton lifted her in his arms, and gave her a reassuring hug. "No, Little Bit. Uncle Carl is just teasing you," he said, shooting a warning glance at his head foreman.

"Good." The child was visibly relieved. She looked up at the big horse towering in front of her. "Daddy, can I go see Jasper?"

Dalton set her down. "Sure you can, Darlin', but only for a minute. I promised Miss Maggie I'd have you back in time for dinner."

"Okay," she said, running toward the north corral.

"Hey!" Dalton called out to her as she trotted off. "How about after dinner, we come back and you can ride Jasper?"

Katie Mae whirled around, her eyes bright. "Goodie," she said clapping her hands. "I'll tell Jasper!" She raced toward the pony.

"That child is growing up so darn quick," Carl said watching after her.

"She sure is," Dalton said with a note of sadness. He saw so much of her mother in her. "Her mother would be so proud of her."

Awkward silence followed. A large orange cat appeared from out of nowhere, ran between the men and the horse, breaking the somber mood. The stallion reared up, nearly pulling the reins out of Carl's hands, sending the cat running for the safety of the barn. The horse's nostrils flared, the whites of his eyes showing his alarm. The horse began a dance-like step, lifting his legs up high then nearly crossing them together while backing up sideways. The men, having never seen anything like it, all roared with laughter.

"Well I guess we know how he got his name," Jake said, wiping tears from his eyes. He took the reins from Carl and soothed the frightened animal. Crazy Legs immediately settled down. "Shall I take him to his new digs, Boss?"

"Ah shoot, Maggie's going to be fit to be tied," he said, looking at his watch. He headed for the four-wheeler. "Yeah, Jake. Settle him in and then saddle up Jasper for me, will you?"

"Sure thing, Boss," Jake said, leading the big horse to the stables. "Come on boy, I'll introduce you to the ladies."

Dalton looked over to Carl. "Do you want to come in for dinner? Maggie's cooking up her famous fried chicken."

Carl lit a rolled cigarette, took a draw and tossed the match to the ground. "Shit, I'd love to, but I promised Thelma Jo I'd take her out tonight. They got karaoke down at South Sides."

Dalton laughed. "When are you going to make an honest woman out of her?"

Carl's face turned crimson. "Shit, Dalton. You know me. I ain't never going to get hitched. Besides, she likes things just the way they are."

Just as Dalton started to reply, his cell phone rang. Looking at the caller ID, he frowned. Without giving the person on the other end a chance to speak he said, "I'm sorry Maggie we'll be right in," then turned the phone off, looking like a little boy that had just been scolded.

Carl's eyes twinkled. "That right there's why I refuse to get married. I refuse to be henpecked. Hell, with the way Miss Maggie treats you, one would think the two of you are married."

Dalton started up the four-wheeler. "I can't complain.

She keeps me in line and that ain't such an easy thing to do." He waved goodbye to Carl and rode off to get Katie Mae. "Come on, Little Bit. Miss Maggie is going to eat without us."

"Bye Jasper. I'll see you later," Katie Mae said, waving at her pony as they rode toward the house. "Daddy, I'm glad Jasper's not going to get bigger. He's big enough already."

"Yes he is, Darlin'," Dalton said, pulling up to the front of the house. They walked in; the smell of fried chicken filled the air.

"Lordy, Maggie, it sure smells good in here," Dalton called from the foyer. He took off his boots and jacket, then helped Katie Mae finish taking off her shoes.

"You two hurry and wash up. Dinner has been on the table nearly five minutes. I don't know about you guys, but I don't care to eat cold biscuits," Maggie scolded from the kitchen.

"I think we're in trouble, Daddy," the little girl whispered.

Dalton took her hand and led her to the bathroom to wash their hands. "It's okay, Little Bit. Just tell her how good dinner is and she won't be mad anymore."

Katie Mae snickered. "Okay, Daddy. I will."

As they walked into the kitchen, Dalton pulled out a chair for Katie Mae and sat beside her. Maggie was already sitting at her usual spot across from Dalton.

"I'm glad to see you two could find time to join me," she snipped.

Katie Mae sat up straight in her chair, smiled her biggest smile and looked up. "This dinner is so good Miss Maggie."

The old woman arched an eyebrow, looking at Katie Mae's empty plate. "Now how would you know that?"

Katie Mae looked up; her doe eyes the epitome of innocence. "It didn't work, Daddy. I think she's still mad."

Dalton tried hard not to laugh.

"So this is a conspiracy," the large woman said, reaching for the potatoes. "Well, if you two want to get on my good side, maybe you should try to be on time for dinner for a change." She heaved a heaping spoon of velvety potatoes onto the plate in front of her.

Dalton loaded his plate with extra helpings to appease Maggie. He knew she wasn't really angry, this was just her way of maintaining control in the house. She was the one who held his family, as small as it may be, together. He would have to do something special for Maggie to show her how much he and Katie Mae loved and appreciated her.

Katie Mae broke the silence. "Miss Maggie, you just gotta see the new horse. He's so beautiful, and so big. Bigger than all the other horses." She wrinkled her nose. "What's his name, Daddy? I can't remember."

Dalton grinned excitedly. He felt like a little boy who had just found the best prize in the Cracker Jack box.

"His name is Crazy Legs and it fits too. Lucky scared the tar out of him. He did this crazy little dance." He raised his arms in demonstration. "It was the funniest thing any of us had ever seen. I thought poor Jake was going to pee his pants."

His enthusiasm was contagious, and lowered the elderly woman's defenses. "A dancing horse? Land sakes, maybe we could sell tickets to see that," she chuckled.

Dalton finished his dinner, leaving a mound of chicken bones on his plate. "Maggie, now that I ate way too much I can say with all honesty, that was the best darn chicken I've ever eaten."

Katie Mae finished the last of her chicken. She wiped her hands on her napkin and jumped out of her chair. "Now can I go ride Jasper, Daddy? Now?"

"Not so fast, Little Bit. I have to make a quick call to

Aunt Lana, and then we can go. You help Miss Maggie clear the table and I'll be ready when you're done."

Reaching for the cordless phone, he took a deep breath and dialed his sister's number.

"Hello," came a cheerful voice on the other end.

"Hey Sis, this is Dalton. You called?" he asked, keeping up his guard.

"Hey little brother! How are you?"

"Doing well. You?" he asked casually.

"Good here too. Just tired, been working all day. You know how that is."

"Do I ever." So far so good. He relaxed a bit.

"Hey, I know it's a few months away, but I wanted your help with a present for Kelly's birthday in June."

"I'll do anything I can, Sis. What did you have in mind?"

"She's always wanted a horse and she'll be thirteen, so I think she's responsible enough to care for one. What do you think?"

Dalton bit his tongue. Lana knew good and well that Katie Mae had been riding ever since she was big enough to sit in the saddle. Was this her way of starting another fight about the way he was raising his daughter? He took a deep breath. No, he would not get into it with her, not today. Today had been too good to end on a sour note.

"So what do you think?" Lana repeated, interrupting his thoughts. "Do you think she is old enough?"

"Sure she is. A few riding lessons and she will be fine."

"Great! Now how do I pick one? I saw some listed on the internet, but I have no clue what questions to ask or what to look for. That's why I decided to call you. Got any horse tips little brother?"

Dalton was ecstatic. This was the most pleasant conversation he could remember having with his sister in years. "Let me get the horse for you. I know a lot of people and can get a good deal. I know what to look for and can get one that's perfect for her."

His sister started to protest but Dalton cut her off. "I haven't been much of an uncle to Kelly lately. Let me make it up to her. I'll find a gentle horse for her and even bring it to her myself. How does that sound?"

"This is more than I could have hoped for! Will you be bringing Katie Mae with you when you come?" she asked hopefully.

"I'm not sure yet," he said curtly. "I still have to work out all the details. I'll let you know." Dalton knew as soon as the words came out that he had sounded defensive and for that, he was sorry. Before he could say anything more, Lana cut back in.

"No problem, I understand." She sounded hurt. "I just thought it would give us all a chance to visit. We haven't seen you two in so long. Just let me know what you decide okay?"

"I will, Sis." Dalton's tone softened. "I'll talk with you soon."

"See you, Dalton."

He clicked the off button, and then headed to find Katie Mae. All in all that had been a civil conversation. For that, he was grateful. As he rounded the corner, Katie Mae ran right into him. The force sent her stumbling backwards, landing on her backside.

"Hey, Little Bit, slow down," Dalton said, bending to help her up. "Are you okay?"

She rubbed her bottom. "Yep Daddy. I'm okay, I landed on my butt."

"Do you still want to go ride Jasper or did you hurt your bottom?" he asked, helping her up.

Katie Mae started jumping up and down. "I want to ride! I want to ride!"

"Okay, Darlin', let's go put your shoes and jacket on." He reached down to give Katie Mae a hug, welcoming the tiny arms that reached around his neck in return.

"I get to ride Jasper, Daddy. Are you so happy?"

"Yes baby, Daddy is very happy," he said, helping her with her shoes and jacket. They raced to the north corral. He let her win, as always.

"I beat you again, Daddy," Katie Mae said, obviously proud of the fact that she could run faster than him.

"You sure did, Little Bit," he said, helping her up onto her pony. He walked down the path, staying close to the child and the feisty pony. He went over the day's events in his mind. It was surely a good day. The best day in a very long while, but still there was the nagging feeling, one he had been having a great deal lately, the feeling that something was missing. Or was that someone?

Chapter Six

Clancy jumped up and bolted down the short hallway, barking madly, but settled down after hearing Robin's familiar voice.

"I'm in the kitchen!" Amber called out to her friend.

Amber had met Robin totally by accident, shortly after she moved to town ten years ago. Amber was in the baking aisle at the local grocery store buying some things to make homemade bread. She picked up a bag of flour and as she did so, Julie, who had just turned three, attempted to climb out of the shopping cart. Amber reached for her daughter, lost her grip on the five-pound bag of flour, which landed on the floor with a loud smack. She caught Julie, heard a startled squeal, and turned to find Robin totally coated in white flour. Amber was mortified, but all Robin did was burst out laughing. Introductions were made and they had been inseparable ever since.

Robin came in batting her hand at Clancy, who was jumping up in a relentless effort to be greeted properly.

"That's enough, you rotten dog," she said, scratching him behind both ears.

"Want something to drink?" Amber asked, refilling her own coffee cup.

"You have any of your delectable sweet tea?" Robin asked, making yet another motion for Clancy to get down.

Clancy protested for a second, and then realizing the attention was over, settled back onto his bed.

"You're in luck, I just made a fresh batch," Amber said, getting a glass out of the oak cupboard.

As Robin sat at the round table, she picked up the newspaper and turned to the horoscope section. "So how does our day look tomorrow?"

"Well, you need to take care of your health and take comfort in friends and family."

"Okay. You're the horoscope expert. What the hell does that mean?"

"I don't know. I don't understand them, I just read them." She laughed then her expression turned serious. "Look at mine for tomorrow. I have no clue what the hell it's supposed to mean either."

Amber placed a tall glass of iced tea on the table, took a seat and crossed her tanned legs.

Robin read Amber's horoscope aloud. "A change in lifestyle is needed. Tragedy is a blessing in disguise." She raised an eyebrow at her friend, "Hmm. I don't know what you think it means, but I think it says for you to stay in bed tomorrow."

Amber felt a chill run through her body and rubbed the goose bumps that sprang up on her arms. "But it did say it was a blessing in disguise," she said, trying to sound as nonchalant as possible.

"Hey, is the highway man coming home tomorrow?" Robin asked, taking a drink of her tea, and then chasing an ice cube around the glass with a slender finger.

Amber's brow creased into a frown. "I didn't think so, but I got a call from my insurance agent right before you came in. She said she was confirming Jeff's appointment for this Saturday. I asked her when he had made the appointment and she said last week."

"Did she say what it was for?" Robin asked, chomping on the ice cube she had finally managed to wrangle from the glass.

"I asked her. She hadn't spoken with him; her secretary had made the appointment. The note said that he wanted to update his insurance information. I told her I thought that it was weird because we updated it about six months ago. She said that was why she was calling; to make sure there wasn't a problem and even asked if I wanted her to keep the appointment."

Amber took another sip of her coffee and placed the mug on the table. "I told her to go ahead unless she heard back from either of us."

Robin drained the last drop of her tea and set her glass on the table. She raised her eyebrows and shot a pointed look at Amber. "So, it's safe to assume you haven't heard from Jeff?"

"No, not really," she said, shaking her head. "Not in nearly two weeks. He did leave a message on the machine the other morning. Nothing big, just saying he was checking in. Actually that was weird too, because he knew I wouldn't be home. I always run with Clancy at that time. I have tried to call his cell phone but it keeps saying his mailbox is full."

Robin bit her lip, stretched her neck and rolled her shoulders before she spoke. "Well, I guess you'll find out soon enough. If he made the appointment he must be planning on coming home tomorrow. Maybe you should tell him you need an emergency number instead of relying on his cell phone."

Amber looked up, eyes wide with shock. "Okay. Who are you and what have you done with my friend?"

"What?" Robin asked, blinking her eyes, feigning innocence.

"The Robin I know would take this chance to let me know how evil, deplorable, and hideous my husband is."

"Nope, not this time," Robin said, holding up her hand and shaking her head. "I've decided to back off. I've been trying to get you to leave his evil, deplorable, hideous, sorry ass for years and that hasn't worked. I figure if you love him that's your business."

She stopped and gathered her thoughts before continuing. Robin traced her finger around the brim of her empty glass, smiled and looked directly at Amber. "I promise you this: if you ever do decide to leave the son-of-a-bitch, have no doubt, girlfriend, I'll bring the moving truck and help you pack."

Amber let out a deep sigh of relief. "Thanks, Chickie, you really are the best." Suddenly her smile was replaced with a frown.

"What's wrong?" Robin asked.

"I was just wondering. If you're going to be nice to Jeff what will we have to talk about?"

"I didn't say I was going to be nice to him. I said I wasn't going to talk bad about him. Big difference," she said, smiling sweetly, and with that, they both burst into laughter. Robin got a mischievous look on her face. "Hmmm, should I be ready with another bottle of wine just in case he doesn't show up tomorrow night?"

"Don't you dare! I think I'm still hung over from the last bottle," Amber said, rolling her eyes.

Robin shook her head. "Yeah, you were pretty messed up. Look, I know I said I wasn't going to say anything, but do me one favor?"

"Yes?"

"Don't go crazy cooking a big dinner for the man if he hasn't even bothered to tell you he was coming home."

Amber looked over at her friend. She knew she was right, why should she be the only one making an effort in this relationship?

"Ok, I promise, if he comes home unannounced he can fix himself a hotdog."

Robin laughed. "That's the spirit, girlfriend." She got up, put her empty glass in the sink and turned toward the door. "I hate to run, but Jack is coming home Saturday night, so I have some things to get done."

Jack, Robin's husband, had been in the Navy Reserves for years along with working a civilian job. After the civilian company went bankrupt Jack started relying on the Navy more and more. It paid the bills and there was never a shortage of extra work if he didn't mind being gone.

"I forgot he was coming home this weekend. When will he be in?"

"Well, his plane doesn't even get into Flint until after nine, by the time he gets his sea bag and drives home, I don't expect to see him until around midnight."

"How long does he get to stay?"

"He'll be home two weeks for sure. He put in for orders to go to Mississippi, but he won't find out if they're approved until he gets back home and checks with the base."

Amber watched the way Robin glowed when she talked about Jack. She wondered for the umpteenth time what it would feel like to be that happy, that in love, that wanted. Her friend's voice interrupted her thoughts.

"So anyway, if he gets these orders he'll be off again soon."

"I bet you'll hate that."

"Yeah, we don't like being apart, but with jobs the way they are, we have to do something. Besides, Jack loves the Navy. It gets his testosterone going. And God knows I love that." Robin grinned from ear to ear.

"You are bad." Amber blushed.

"No girlfriend, I am good, I'm very good," she said, flipping her shoulder-length hair.

"I think when they were giving out sex drive, you got back in line! You have more than anyone I know."

"And the problem is?"

"No problem. I just think you got more than your

share."

"I'm not complaining and neither is Jack, so that's all that matters. Anyway, I'm going to go. Call if you need anything," Robin said, heading toward the front door.

"I will. Tell Jack hi for me," Amber said as she blocked Clancy, who had followed and was eyeing the open door eagerly. "Not this time buddy."

"I will. See ya." As Robin headed down the front walk she waved in the direction of the house next door, where the curtains were open just a peek, giving the ever-meddlesome Karen a view of what was going on in the neighborhood.

Chapter Seven

Jeff merged his burgundy double cab pickup into traffic. East bound I-94 was always packed this time of evening. The skies had been dark all day and were growing more ominous by the minute, deepening to a rich deep purple with low black clouds, which threatened to open at any minute. The weather channel had called for a chance of freezing rain. He hoped he would make it home before the storm hit.

He hadn't told Amber he was coming home. He hadn't even spoken with her in weeks. He thought about calling before he left but was afraid she would hassle him about not calling sooner. No, he figured he would just wait and face the music when he got home.

Home. Well, I guess this will be the last time I call it that, he thought as he changed lanes to pass a slow moving white Pontiac.

He was grateful that things were moving quickly. When he'd called the attorney, he thought it might take a while for the paperwork to be filed. Now, if everything went as planned, Amber would be getting a wakeup call on Monday morning. He was glad he would be gone by Sunday night, leaving her to think it was just a trial separation.

He laughed out loud at the thought. How could they get more separated than they already were? It wasn't that he was intentionally not telling her. Okay, maybe he was, but it would be so much easier to talk to her via phone so he would not have to look into those trusting black eyes.

Jeff was so deep in thought he nearly missed his Richmond exit. He got to the bottom of the exit ramp just as the light was turning red.

God, this drive takes forever, still about 40 minutes to go, he thought. He drummed his fingers on the steering wheel as he waited for the light to complete its cycle. His only consolation was that if things went as planned, this would be the last time he would have to make the trip north.

Traveling down the state highway, he went over everything he needed to take care of this weekend.

Let's see, I have the meeting with the insurance agent to switch over the life insurance tomorrow. I need to get to the bank to close the savings account. Pick up the trailer from U-Haul. I'll be there and gone before she knows what hit her, he thought with a smirk.

He slowed down as he entered the next town. There was usually a cop waiting for some unsuspecting speeder at the bottom of the hill, and sure enough, there was. He almost waved but thought better of it.

He wondered what Amber would say when he told her. Would she beg him to stay? Would she be shocked or would she agree that their marriage had been over for a long time? Oh well, he would get the answer soon enough. He glanced at his reflection in the rear view mirror.

I had better add a haircut to my list of things to do. My hair is beginning to touch my ears. Maybe I should just shave this thing off, he thought, scratching at the beard he was trying to grow. *You're a handsome man, why hide the face?*

"Damn!" Jeff cursed as freezing rain started hitting the windshield. Ice was already beginning to hang from the trees and glistened on the fields of snow that were the last holdout of winter.

Well, I was making good time, he thought. *Just as well. This is a homecoming I'm not looking forward to anyway.* He felt his truck slipping a bit.

Good ol' Michigan weather, he thought. *An ice storm in April.*

His thoughts turned back to the weekend ahead. *You know old boy, the weekend doesn't have to be a total loss; Amber doesn't know what's going on. A smile crossed his lips. Yeah, I could come home like nothing's wrong, butter her up, make some lame-ass excuse for not calling and get myself some much needed stress relief.*

On cue, he felt his manhood twitch with anticipation. Hell, just because he didn't love her didn't mean he couldn't screw her.

She has a great body, anyone can see that. A great ass and those tits! Yes, she's been looking extra good lately.

The thought of having one last piece of ass was getting him more excited than he would have ever imagined. It had been a long time since he had gotten this excited thinking about his own wife. His now rigid member was straining against his pants making it very uncomfortable to drive.

Jeff looked down at the bulge in his jeans. He shifted his weight in the seat, pulling at his jeans to give himself more room. He had taken his eyes off the road for only a second. He didn't see the car pull out in front of him, nor did he realize he was on black ice.

Not until it was too late.

Chapter Eight

Amber was lying on the couch, mindlessly watching an old black and white episode of Laurel and Hardy, commonly referred to as the fat guy and skinny guy, when the doorbell rang. Clancy jumped up from where he had been resting, took off barking and beat her to the door.

"Oh Clancy," Amber laughed, "my ferocious protector."

Grasping the dog's collar, she opened the door and was startled to see two police officers standing on the doorstep. She leaned down, pretending to take a better hold of Clancy's collar in order to suppress a smile at their extreme height difference, one being fairly tall and thin and the other being at least two feet shorter and rather pudgy. With the exception of the uniforms, Laurel and Hardy now stood on her front door step.

"Mrs. Wilson?" the shorter officer inquired.

"Yes, that's me. Can I help you?" Amber asked, tightening the grip on the collar.

"Do you have a place we could sit down?" he asked, nervously eying the dog.

Amber's heart raced. Had something happened to Julie?

"Yes of course, in here," she said, motioning them through the front entryway and into the living room.

"Um, do you think you could put your dog in another

room for a bit?" the second officer asked, motioning to Clancy who, deciding he did not like the new arrivals, was desperately trying to escape Amber's grip.

Now Amber was even more confused. Did this have something to do with Clancy? He had run off again this morning, but she had found him before he had been gone too long. Had someone complained about him running loose through the street? She pictured Karen, her nosy neighbor, doing just that.

Amber put Clancy in the spare room and then returned to the living room. She switched off the television and sat on the couch, motioning for the officers to do the same.

"Mrs. Wilson," began the shorter officer, "I am very sorry to have to be the one to tell you this. Your husband Jeff has been in an accident. I'm afraid he didn't make it."

Amber trembled as tears started streaming down her face. She felt as though she would throw up.

"Jeff's dead? Oh my God! No!" she cried. "How? When?"

The stocky man shifted in his seat, clearly uncomfortable delivering such tragic news. He took a deep breath and continued. "We got the call from the state police at 18:15. Sorry, I mean 6:15pm. Apparently, he hit some black ice. He rolled his truck several times before hitting a tree. No other vehicles were involved."

Amber started hyperventilating. The taller officer sat beside her and rubbed her back.

"I'm sorry, Ma'am. Is there anyone we can call for you? Family… a friend?" the short officer asked, narrowing his eyes in disapproval at his partner.

Amber tried to think, but she could only picture poor Jeff lying in a pool of blood, his body freezing.

"Ma'am please, tell us who you would like us to call for you?" the short officer insisted a bit more firmly.

Amber was in a fog. "Um Robin, call my friend

Robin."

"Robin. What's her number?"

Amber knew Robin's number as well as she knew her own name, but her head was pounding and she was having a hard time catching her breath. "It's on the board by the phone."

The tall officer left the room and went to make the call. Amber could hear him repeating what they had told her about the accident. Her stomach churned, her mouth started watering. She raced to the bathroom and had just reached the toilet when she began heaving. She stayed in that spot until there was nothing left in her stomach, but still she continued to heave. She thought her stomach would never stop contracting.

Finally, the heaves subsided. She grabbed some Kleenex, blew her nose and then scooped some water in her hand to rinse the acid from her mouth. As she opened the bathroom door, she looked into the faces of the two officers with their faces so full of concern. Or, was that pity?

"Are you okay, Ma'am?" the short fellow asked. "Can I get you anything?"

Amber was numb. Was she okay? Of course she wasn't okay. How could she be okay? Her world had just fallen apart. She would never be okay again. She felt so alone, just her and Julie.

"Julie!" she blurted out as a new sense of panic engulfed her. "Oh my God! How am I going to tell Julie?"

It was all too much. The room started spinning, she saw hands reach for her just as everything went dark.

Chapter Nine

When Amber came to, she was lying on the couch. The tall officer was kneeling over her calling her name. The short one was coming from the kitchen carrying a glass of water.

Again the tall officer spoke. "Are you okay, Ma'am? You gave us quite a scare. You passed out. My partner there caught you. You didn't seem to hit anything. Would you like us to take you to the hospital?" The look of concern on their faces reminded her why they were there.

"No… No, I don't want to go anywhere," Amber said, shaking her head. Once again, the tears were flowing.

The men showed obvious relief when Robin burst through the door. She shut the door and kicked off her shoes in one quick motion, then hurried over to the couch and gathered Amber in her arms.

"Oh honey, I'm so sorry," she said, her eyes welling with tears.

The police officers moved away, giving them some space.

"What… am I …going to… do Robin? What… a… am I going... to do?" She sobbed hysterically.

Robin looked up at the men who were still standing there shifting uncomfortably on their feet. A frown creased her brow. "It's okay Amber. It's going to be okay."

The short officer approached them with his brow furrowed. "Mrs. Wilson, I just wanted to let you know, the medical examiner has the body. When you decide which funeral home you'll be using, they can call and make the arrangements for getting it released."

Amber tensed and looked up with red-rimmed owl eyes. "Which funeral home? I don't know. We," she swallowed hard, "we never talked about it."

"How about the one around the corner?" Robin asked, pointing. "What's the name?"

"I pass it all the time, but I can't think of the name," Amber said, blowing her nose.

"You don't need to make the decision this instant," the taller officer interjected. "I guess that's all we need for right now." He turned toward the door and beckoned Robin to follow.

"I'll show them out and be right back," Robin said, squeezing Amber's hand.

When the officers got to the door, they paused. The shorter man looked at Amber. "She threw up in the bathroom quite a few times and then passed out. She was out for several minutes. I tried to get her to go to the hospital but she refused. Does she have any family?"

"None to speak of really. Her mom is dead and her father is never around. She has a daughter," Robin's stomach tightened, it was the first time she had thought of Julie, "Oh, poor Julie!"

"Will you be able to stay with her? I don't think she should be alone."

"Don't worry, I'll take care of her," Robin assured him. "Thank you both for everything."

"No problem, Ma'am. Just have her contact someone from the funeral home in the morning to make the arrangements."

"Will do, thanks again," Robin said, shutting the

door. She walked back to the living room, taking a seat beside her friend. "Amber? Where is Julie?"

"She's at Kelly's house. They're having a slumber party! Oh God, Robin, how am I going to tell her? What will I say?" Amber cried uncontrollably. Spasms racked her body. She ran to the bathroom and once again was met with dry heaves.

Robin stood next to her friend, holding her hair back, silently waiting until the spasms subsided. She handed Amber a wet washcloth to wipe her face.

"Listen girlfriend," Robin said quietly, "you are in no shape to talk to anyone tonight. Let Julie spend the night and have her fun. It might be the last she has for a while. You can tell her tomorrow. It will give you time to figure out what to say."

"Are you sure it will be okay? What if she hears it from someone else? I would never forgive myself!"

"Don't worry about that, I'll call Lana and tell her what happened. She'll keep her away from the television and radio. It will be all right, I promise."

Amber touched Robin's arm. "Thanks. I appreciate all of this, I mean that." She sank onto the couch, she was tired, so very tired, so alone and wasn't so sure her legs could hold her up anymore.

"Okay, I am going to call Lana now. Do you need me to make any more phone calls for you while I am at it? Is there anyone else you need to tell?"

"I guess you should call Jeff's parents." Her heart sank knowing they, too, would be devastated. "I guess for what it's worth you can try to call Dad. He's probably at the bar."

Kind of fitting, Amber thought, *that's where he was the night Mom died, too*.

Amber's mom had passed away when Amber was fourteen, after being diagnosed with an inoperable tumor in her brain. Her dad had been great until her mom had become sick, but after that, he started drinking to dull the pain. First, it was just a few beers. Then he was at the bar more than he was home, including the night she finally lost the battle with the dreaded disease. Sometimes Amber felt she lost both her parents that summer, and now she lost Jeff too. How could life be so cruel? Now her baby girl would have to go through what she went through.

"You don't need this right now. You are not your father," Robin said as if reading her mind. "Julie will be fine. She's a strong girl and you, my friend, are a great person. You'll be there for her, Amber. You always have been."

Amber relaxed, Robin was right. Now was not the time to dwell on the past. "I am just so tired. I need to lie down. I just need to lie down."

Robin helped her to her feet. "I think you'll be more comfortable in the spare bedroom."

As they opened the door, Clancy bolted out, jumping up, and nearly knocking them down.

"Oh Clancy, I completely forgot about you," Amber said, scratching behind his ear. "I had to put him up when the police came. I think the tall cop was scared of him. Do you mind letting him out? He's been in for quite a while. Oh, and don't forget his leash, he's been running off a lot."

"No problem. You get in bed. If you need anything just let me know." Robin reached for the phone and turned the ringer off then headed for the door. "Come on Clancy, let's go outside."

Amber tried to go to sleep but it eluded her. She thought about getting up, but her arms and legs felt heavy. It was as though she were encased in mud and try as she might she couldn't move. Her stomach was in knots, her heart was pounding and all she could think of was Jeff.

Why hadn't she tried harder to contact him? Why hadn't he called to let her know he was coming home?

Was he trying to surprise her? If only he had called, she could have spoken to him one last time. She was overwhelmed with guilt for not going to see him. Why did he have to be the one to make the drive? She could have visited him. But then, he had told her not to. He knew she would have been bored while he was at work. He was always thinking of her that way. He might not have been the most romantic husband, but he was a good husband. Tears streamed down her face. Sobbing uncontrollably, she clutched her pillow.

"Jeff, oh Jeff, what am I going to do without you?"

Chapter Ten

Amber awoke to the sound of birds chirping outside her window. She wasn't sure when sleep had come, but nightmares had invaded her dreams. She had fallen asleep in her clothes. She felt drained. She would cry, if only she had any tears left. As she opened the door from the bedroom the aroma of coffee greeted her, making her stomach turn and growl at the same time, reminding her that she had not eaten anything since lunch the day before.

Robin met her in the hallway looking as if she hadn't slept at all. "Did you get any sleep?"

"Yeah. A little. I think." She turned toward the smell of the coffee.

Robin placed a hand on her elbow. "Before you go in there, I need to tell you something."

Amber saw the apprehension on her friend's face. She took a deep breath. "Okay, shoot." She wondered if she was actually ready for what her friend clearly didn't want to tell her.

"Jeff's parents are in the kitchen. They got here about an hour ago."

Amber's face paled. "I can't go in there. Not now!"

"It's okay, Amber," Robin assured her. "I'll be right here."

Amber's voice was barely audible. "Okay, but don't leave me alone with them".

"I won't," Robin promised, taking her hand. Together they entered the kitchen.

Walt, Jeff's father, a short, small-framed man with thinning brown hair, rose to greet her.

"Amber," he said, holding out his arms. "I'm so sorry."

Amber hugged the man briefly then turned to face Jeff's mother. Her hair was perfect, as always, frosted highlights graced the edges of her spiked, short brown hair. Her nose turned up slightly at the end, adding to the snobbish look that was reinforced fully by her behavior. Connie looked up at Amber, but did not offer any condolences. Her grief-stricken green eyes were swollen and red.

"Thanks for coming, Connie. Thanks Walt," Amber said sincerely. She had never been close to Jeff's parents. They had been against the marriage and always blamed her for getting pregnant and taking their only son from them. Still, somehow their being there now was comforting. They all sat at the table not quite knowing what to say.

The back door opened. Clancy trotted in followed by Jeff's sister Dianna, who was the same age as Amber and they got along fairly well. Dianna always told Amber that Jeff wasn't good enough for her and that he didn't treat her right. Funny, she hadn't noticed how much Dianna resembled Jeff until now. She had Jeff's small frame and brown hair, the same green eyes and even his crooked smile. Amber got up to give her sister-in-law a hug.

"How are you holding up?" Dianna asked, holding her tight.

"As well as can be expected I guess," Amber said, returning to her seat. She still felt shaky and did not want to risk passing out again.

Robin brought Amber a cup of coffee and a slice of toast.

Amber's stomach churned at the sight of it. She pushed it away.

Robin sat it back in front of her. "You have to get something in your system. Lana told me to make sure you keep your strength up, and I know you haven't had anything to eat or drink since I've been here."

"Lana?" Jeff's mother asked in her strained, condescending tone.

Robin took a deep breath. "She's the Physician's Assistant that works in our office. Julie and her daughter are best buddies. Julie stayed at their house last night. Julie should be home anytime now." She looked up at the clock then into Amber's troubled eyes.

Amber looked around at all of the faces now focusing on her own. To her amazement, tears once again trickled down her cheeks.

Dianna handed her a tissue. "It's okay, honey, we'll be here when you tell her if you want us to."

"Of course we are going to be here," Connie interjected rolling her eyes. "Why on earth would we not?"

Before Amber could answer, Clancy took off running down the hallway. Seconds later came the sound of the front door being opened.

"Mom, I'm home!" Julie yelled from the living room and slammed the door. "Hey, was that Grandpa Walt and Grandma Connie's car out front?"

Everyone sat frozen at the table, exchanging worried glances.

Julie came running into the kitchen. "Grandma Connie! Grandpa Walt!" She gave them both a reserved hug.

Connie patted Julie's back once, then stepped back. She frowned as she smoothed her clothes.

"Dianna!" Julie squealed, giving her aunt a more affectionate squeeze. "Mom, why didn't you tell me they were coming for a visit? Mom? What is it? Why are you crying? Are you okay?"

"Come here baby, I have something to tell you." Amber said, holding her arms out.

Hugging her daughter tightly, she told her the news of her father's death.

Chapter Eleven

Amber sat on the queen-sized bed, pulling on her sheer stockings. She had taken to staying in the spare bedroom since the news of Jeff's death, not being able to sleep by herself in the room she was so accustomed to being alone in. Though she had slept alone in that bed more than she had shared it with Jeff, it was still their bedroom.

The last few days were a blur. Julie had taken the news of her father's death fairly well. Jeff's being away so much had actually severed what little father-daughter relationship they'd had, and any feelings Julie had for her father was simply because he was her father, nothing more. After an initial breakdown of uncontrollable sobs, she seemed nearly back to her bubbly self, especially since Dianna was doing such a great job of keeping her niece occupied.

They had all somehow managed to get through Sunday's visitation. Jeff didn't have many friends in town and what few friends he had on the job were making the drive today for the actual funeral. She was glad Jeff's parents had decided to stay at the motel. Amber knew his mother hated her too much to have considered spending the night in the house. Amber was, however, grateful that Dianna had chosen to stay with her. It helped having someone near. Robin had stayed the first night, but at

Amber's insistence had gone home to spend some time with Jack, who had returned the night after the accident.

Amber went to the closet and took out a black dress, a dress that she had never had the chance to wear. She shuddered at the sight of it. Tears welled in her already red-rimmed eyes. When she bought the dress months ago, she had pictured herself wearing it to a nice cozy dinner with Jeff, not to his funeral. She took it off the hanger, lowered the zipper and sighed as she slipped it over her head. There was a knock on her bedroom door.

"Come in," she said, still struggling with the zipper.

"Hey. Are you ready?" Robin asked softly as she entered the room.

Amber's arms were twisted behind her back, her shaky fingers fumbling with the black metal tab.

"I would be if I could get this damn zipper up." She dropped her arms with an exaggerated sigh and turned her back to her friend. "When did you get here?"

Robin smoothly slid the tab up and tucked it into place. "Just a minute ago. Dianna and Julie just left. They're going to do lunch before heading over the funeral home. Jack and the kids are going to meet us there. Jack said to tell you hi, and to let him know if you need anything. How are you holding up?"

Amber took one last look in the mirror. Her face looked drawn and pale. Her eyes, normally her best trait, had bags with dark circles and were red from days of crying. She looked as though she had aged ten years in the last few days. She grimly applied more powder. "There ought to be a law against going out in public looking like this."

Robin placed a hand on Amber's shoulder. "Hey, under the circumstances you look great."

Amber turned to face her friend, they embraced, each gaining comfort and strength in the other's friendship. The sound of the doorbell interrupted them.

"I'll get it." Robin said, heading for the door. "Go lay down." Robin gestured to Clancy, who was already at the door barking. He backed off a bit, but stayed close and continued to growl. When Robin opened the door, she stared at the face of a short, balding, heavyset man, suffering from a very bad comb over.

"Mrs. Wilson?"

"No, she's busy, can I help you?" Robin said, eyeing the man suspiciously.

"No," he said curtly. "I need to see Mrs. Wilson."

"I'm sorry, that will not be possible, her husband was just killed in an auto accident and she is not seeing anyone," Robin said firmly.

The strange little man looked as though he had been slapped. He looked wide-eyed at Robin then down at the large envelope he was holding in his hand. "But I… I was supposed to give her this."

"Would you like me to give it to her?" Robin asked curtly.

"No, no. I need to give it to her myself. I think. This is quite unprecedented." He looked confused. "I don't know if I need to now…"

"Listen," Robin snapped, "I don't know what you're selling, but we are not in the buying mood." She attempted to close the door.

The man put out his arm to stop her. For such a small man, he had amazing strength.

"Hey!" Robin yelled. As she struggled with the wretched little man, Clancy joined in, baring his teeth and growling a profound warning. Robin was barely able to grab the dog's collar as he lunged at the man.

"What on earth is going on in here?" Amber asked, running down the hall towards them. She helped hold Clancy, who had decided he was not willing to tolerate this man's intrusion any longer.

"Mrs. Wilson?" the man asked, gripping the door.

Amber thought it was as much to keep it open so he could see her, as it was to keep it from opening any further, thus leaving him at the mercy of the crazy drooling dog, which appeared to want to have him for lunch. She had never seen Clancy in such a state, and if he did not trust this man, she knew she would do well to keep her distance from him.

"Yes?" she asked warily.

"My name is Stanley Davis. I was supposed to give you this today, but under the circumstances, I am not sure whether I should or not," he said hesitantly. "Give it to you, that is."

"What is it?" Amber asked, gazing at the envelope he held in his free hand.

"Like I said, under the circumstances, I'm not sure if I should…"

"That's enough," she said to Clancy, who was still struggling to get at the man who continued to grip the door.

"Listen Stanley," Robin warned, "I don't know how much longer we can hold this dog, so either you give her the damn thing or not, but either way be done with it and get the hell out of here!" She narrowed her eyes at the vexing little man.

A determined look swept across his face. He ran his hand through the wisps of hair that straddled his balding scalp, and then he delivered his well-practiced speech.

"Mrs. Wilson, my name is Stanley Davis. Your husband," he paused clearing his throat, "has filed for divorce, consider yourself served."

He handed a stunned Amber the manila envelope, spun on his heel and sprinted to his car, his wayward strands of hair blowing in the wind.

Amber and Robin watched him flee down the walk. They were speechless. Shutting the door, they both walked without a word to the kitchen while Clancy sniffed at the door, fur raised down the length of his back, a throaty rumble still low in his chest. Amber set the envelope on the table. They sat staring at it in stunned silence. Amber was in shock; her eyes were dry and emotionless.

"Amber honey, talk to me," Robin pleaded.

Finally, tears welled in Amber's eyes; they streamed down her face and dropped onto the envelope.

"He didn't love me," she said in a barely audible whisper. "He wanted a divorce. Why didn't he tell me?"

"I don't know honey, maybe that's why he was coming home."

"What did I do wrong?" Amber sobbed.

Robin stared back at her in stunned silence.

Amber picked up the envelope. Wiping off the tears, she opened the flap, and with shaky hands eased the papers from within. Stanley hadn't lied. Jeff – her Jeff – had indeed filed for divorce.

Chapter Twelve

Amber sat dutifully in the front row. The preacher, a stocky, gray haired man with bifocals, read from the bible, quoting verses on love and marriage. He spoke of Jeff as though he knew him. Amber felt like screaming.

How could he think he knew him when she hadn't even known him? She, who had been married to him for the past thirteen and a half years, she who until two hours ago had thought he loved her too. She was angry with Jeff for leaving, even angrier that he had left with so many unanswered questions. She wanted to know why he had filed for divorce without discussing it with her, wanted to know what she had done wrong. Most of all she wanted to know when he had stopped loving her. She could have changed if he had asked her to.

Once again, the preacher spoke of Jeff as a loving father and husband. Amber felt the urge to jump up; wanted to tell him that Jeff didn't love her and that he had filed for divorce. Robin had convinced her to hide the papers, telling her that no one needed to know right now. The preacher looked at her like so many had in the last several days, with pity. Amber's skin was crawling; she wanted to escape.

Feeling a hand clasp hers, she looked down into Julie's tear-filled eyes. She had to be strong. Julie needed her; she would not let her daughter down. Amber looked past the preacher at the urn standing on the podium for all to see. She was glad they had cremated him. She could not have stood to look at him, not after all she had just been through.

The preacher said a final prayer and people started coming up to say their condolences. It was all a blur, everyone crying, hugging and saying they were sorry. So many people, she wondered if it would ever end. She glimpsed Robin and Jack out of the corner of her eye, standing and waiting for the line to end.

Jack's head was freshly shaved and he was in his formal Navy uniform, his arm protectively encircled around Robin's waist. A young, blonde woman with red-rimmed eyes stood in front of her. She did not reach out her hand. She merely stood and stared at Amber with troubled eyes. Amber thought the woman was about to speak when someone else moved in front of her. It was one of Jeff's co-workers, offering his condolences.

"I'm sorry, Amber," he said as he extended a rough, cigarette-stained hand to her. His dark hair was pulled back into a ponytail. His shirt was in desperate need of ironing.

Amber shook his hand. "Thank you, Randy," she said, wondering if the attractive blonde was with him.

"I spoke with the motel; they'll be sending Jeff's things to you." He glanced towards the young blonde then back to Amber. He passed Amber a card. "If you need anything let me know. Here's my number."

"Thanks," Amber said, placing it in her side pocket.

Randy reached around and gripped the blonde's arm as if to lead her away. Amber couldn't help notice the young lady tense at his touch. The line continued until everyone had stopped to express his or her regrets, then Robin and Jack stood by her side.

"Mom, I'm going to go with Dianna to find Grandpa and Grandma, okay?"

"Sure honey, I'll be out in a minute," Amber said, hugging her daughter. Amber looked at Robin then at Jack. When they were finally alone, she looked back at Jack. "Did she tell you?"

"Yes, she did."

"And?"

"What an asshole," Jack said, raising his voice a bit more than he intended. "You know I've never had a high opinion of Jeff. I've never cared for the way he has treated you. You could do much better."

Talking to Jack always made Amber feel better. He was like a brother and his opinion meant a great deal to her. The three of them walked out of the parlor together.

"Where are the kids?" Amber asked, scanning the halls.

"They left as soon as it was over. They had the jitters. I can't say as I blame them," Jack said, looking around. "I've always hated funeral homes. But I have to admit, it was a nice service."

"Yes it was," Amber agreed. "Some of his words got to me though. It was so very hard."

She walked in the middle leaning on the two of them for support. Though most of the visitors had left, some still lingered in the parking lot.

"Can I get a ride home? The kids took my car," Jack asked.

"Don't you want to come to the house? There's a lot of food that needs to be eaten," Amber offered.

"Maybe in a bit. I think I'd like to get out of this uniform first," Jack said, straightening his shirt.

"I meant to tell you how handsome you look. This is the first time I have seen you in your new officer's uniform." "Whoa! Who are you calling an officer?" Jack laughed, pretending to be offended.

"I thought Robin said you were an officer," Amber countered, looking confused.

"No, I said he was a Chief Petty Officer," Robin laughed.

"There's a big difference."

"Oh well, you look good whatever you're called," Amber said. She was too tired to try and sort it all out.

"We're parked over here, honey," Robin said, pointing to her black Durango. As they approached it, a small red car pulled up, effectively blocking them in. Amber recognized the driver as the blonde woman from inside.

"Who is that?" Robin asked, watching the pretty, young woman get out of her car.

"I don't know," Amber whispered. "I saw her inside but she didn't say anything."

The woman, obviously distraught, was crying as she approached them. She stood in front of Amber and looked her up and down with hate-filled eyes. When at last she spoke, her voice was full of venom.

"You owe me!" she spat.

Amber glanced at her friends, then back at the weeping lady standing before her.

"Excuse me? I don't even know you."

"Don't you?" she scoffed through gritted teeth.

"No, I'm afraid I don't."

"Well, I know who you are, BITCH!" the crazed woman screamed.

Jack positioned himself between the blonde and Amber, obviously ready to intervene if necessary.

"Jeff didn't love you, he loved me!" The young woman continued her rant, undaunted. She was close to hysterics, her eyes wide and tears streaming down her face. By now, the remaining visitors had wandered over to see what was going on. Everyone was watching this public display; including Jeff's parents.

"Jeff had it all planned out," she continued. "He was coming home this weekend to take care of everything.

That's why you owe me! The life insurance was supposed to be mine! He was going to change it over at his appointment on Saturday, but he got killed first, so you see, it's mine. It was supposed to be mine…" her voice trailed off, full of desperation.

Mascara ran down the woman's face on the trail of salty tears. She batted at the tears with the back of a trembling hand.

Amber froze as realization set in. That was why he had made the appointment. He had this planned all along. That was the reason he didn't tell her he was coming home. The woman standing before her was the reason he had filed for divorce. She was also the reason Jeff didn't love her anymore. Fighting back nausea, Amber raised a hand in dismissal.

"I don't want to hear any more," she said, turning away.

"WAIT!" The young woman hollered. "I'm not finished. This is why he loved me."

She flung open her coat. For the first time, Amber, along with everyone else, saw why the woman was so upset. Not only had she lost her lover, she had also lost the father of her unborn child.

Astonished gasps escaped from the bystanders. Amber's knees buckled, Jack and Robin kept her from falling. Dianna held Julie back, who had witnessed the whole scene and was desperately trying to run to her mother.

Connie and Walt approached the young woman. Walt spoke up, almost too calmly. "You need to leave."

"No, I'm not done," the woman wailed.

"You need to leave now, Heather!" he said more firmly.

Amber was stunned. He had called her by name. They knew her! How long had they known? How much did they know? She looked around at all the faces gaping at her. Faces so full of shock and disbelief, and of something else; something she had seen far too often over the last several days. They all showed pity – all but one. The face of the pregnant stranger; it only showed hate.

Chapter Thirteen

Jack and Robin helped Amber into the SUV. Jack then told Heather to move her car before he called the police. Reluctantly, the blonde returned to her car and drove off, still sobbing uncontrollably.

"I'll drive," Jack said, taking the keys from Robin. "Let's stop by the house so I can change, then we'll go to Amber's house."

"I thought you wanted to go home for a bit?" Robin questioned.

Jack glanced in the mirror at Amber, who was staring out the window, tears streaming down her face. "Do you honestly believe I am going to leave you two alone with that psychotic woman in town?"

Amber couldn't get the image of the pregnant woman out of her head. Jack was right. The girl had seemed desperate. There was no telling what she would do. Amber did not say a word; she was tired, so very tired. She had been through hell the last few days and wondered how much more she could endure. What else had Jeff been hiding?

Amber and Robin stayed in the SUV while Jack ran in to change his clothes. Neither spoke, each preferring to remain silent rather than discuss the events that had just taken place. Jack returned, and then drove them the short distance to Amber's house. Several cars were parked in the driveway. Once again, Amber started crying.

"Why can't this be over?" she sobbed. "I can't take anymore, I need to lie down. I just want to sleep."

Jack opened her door. "Don't worry Amber. You don't have to see anyone. I'll make your excuses, you can go lie down."

"That's right, honey," Robin said, helping her out of the SUV.

As Amber was getting out, she caught a glimpse of Jeff's parents silver Cadillac. She stopped. How could they dare show their faces here?

"You okay?" Jack asked, his face full of concern.

"I can't believe they had the nerve to come here," she sobbed. "They knew Jeff was cheating, knew and didn't tell me."

"It's going to be okay Amber, either Jack or I will be with you at all times," Robin promised her.

The front door opened. Julie came running out. "Mom, are you okay? I was worried! That lady scared me." She wrapped her arms around her mother. The girl looked up, her face full of worry. "Mom? Was she really Dad's girlfriend?"

Amber was at a loss for words. She had never lied to Julie. She looked down at her young daughter. Seeing the concern etched in Julie's face tore at her heartstrings. Amber wanted nothing more than to wrap herself up into a cocoon and stay there, but she knew she had to be strong for her daughter. She took a deep breath and gathered strength she did not know she had.

"I'm not sure, honey. I think so, but there are so many things I need to find out. Right now don't worry about things; too much has happened in the last few days, there will be plenty of time to figure it all out later." Amber kept her arm around Julie, each drawing comfort from the other. She turned to Jack and Robin. "What do you think?"

"Sounds good to me," Robin agreed.

"You want to know what I think?" Jack asked.

"Yes."

"I think someone needs to take her own advice," he said with a wink.

"Are you ready?" Robin asked.

"As I'll ever be," Amber said, wiping her eyes.

Together they all walked the circular driveway toward the big brick house. The house was full of people. No one said a word as they came in; once again, Amber saw the piteous looks she had become accustomed to seeing. Amber and Robin kicked off their shoes and headed up the stairs toward the master bedroom without saying a word, leaving Jack to make their excuses. Entering the sanctity of her bedroom, Amber breathed an audible sigh of relief.

"God, I am so tired," she said, lying on the bed. "I wish I could sleep. I tried last night, but my head was pounding. Funny, for the last couple of days I didn't even want to come in this room, but now – I want Jeff out. At least his things anyway."

She thought about going to the closet and ripping things out right at that moment, but exhaustion kept her planted firmly on the bed.

"You've been through a lot," Robin began. "Why don't I call Lana and ask her if she can call you in something to help you relax?"

"I don't know," Amber hesitated, "I don't like to take medicine."

"I know, but at least let her call something in while the pharmacy is open. That way if you need it later you'll have it," Robin insisted.

"Okay, I guess, but I'll only take it if I think I need it."

"Agreed," Robin said, pushing the buttons on the phone.

"Hey this is Robin, is Lana with a patient? Great." Robin placed her hand over the receiver and whispered, "She's getting her."

"Yeah," Robin said into the phone. "Can you call something in to the pharmacy for Amber? ... She's having a tough time. … Really? ... Are you freaking kidding? ... It figures. … Okay, let me check."

Once again she covered the phone. "Lana wants to know if Julie can sleep over. She said Kelly could play hooky tomorrow and keep her company."

Amber paused for a moment. She knew it was too soon for Julie to go back to school. "Sure, I think that would be great."

"Lana? Amber said that would be fine ... Sure ... I'm sure Jack will pick it up ... I will ... Ok thanks, Lana." She hung up the phone.

"What was that all about?"

"She said she would pick up Julie on her way home from work. She's also going to call you in a script for a low dose of Xanax," Robin said as she sat on the bed next to her friend.

"There's something else," Robin said apprehensively.

"I gathered as much. What now?"

"The reason she wanted the girls to stay home tomorrow. The rumor mill has already started."

Amber rolled her eyes. "Tell me."

"Lana left the funeral home before the fiasco. She has already had two patients fill her in. Seems like your neighbor, nosy Karen, was there and heard everything. She's made it her duty to make sure everyone knows."

"Jesus Christ! What the hell business is it of hers anyway? Remind me when I get my strength back to kick her ass!"

"There you go, get mad! If you ask me, I think you should be mad as hell about everything that's happened. You did nothing wrong." She paused before continuing.

"Well… you did marry an asshole!"

They both laughed. It was the first time either of them had laughed in days and it was interrupted by a knock on the door. Jack stuck his head in, an uncertain smile played across his lips.

"Yes?" both asked at once.

"Sorry to interrupt, but I cleared the house," he said, sounding proud of himself.

"Is everyone gone?" Amber asked, relieved.

Jack hesitated. "Almost. Dianna and Julie went for a walk, but Walt and Connie are refusing to leave until they talk to you. I think they'll leave afterwards though, because they had Dianna put her things in the car."

"Why would I want to talk to them?" she asked bitterly.

Jack threw his hands up in defense. "Hey, don't shoot the messenger."

"I know, I'm sorry," Amber said.

Robin got up and went to Jack and gave him a kiss. "It's okay, baby, I love you," she teased. "Will you do me a favor? Could you go to the pharmacy to pick up a script for Amber?"

"Sure. Which one?"

"The one on Elk Street, Lana is calling it in."

"Are you two going to be okay while I'm gone?" Jack asked.

"Sure. Take your time."

"All right, but lock the door. Okay?"

"Okay, worry wart, we will," Robin said, giving him another kiss.

They followed him down the stairs to the front door, locked it behind him, and then proceeded down the hall toward the kitchen. Jeff's parents were sitting at the table. Walt stood up as they entered the room.

"Can we have a few minutes alone?" he asked, looking at Robin.

Robin stood her ground waiting for Amber's response.

"She stays," Amber said firmly.

Defeated, Walt returned to his seat with a heavy sigh.

Amber looked at him as he sat, seemingly searching for words. He was a small man. Not skinny, just small in stature. He was a nice looking man. Jeff had clearly been blessed with his father's good looks. Her glance moved to Connie, who sat surprisingly quiet.

This all must be killing her, Amber thought, *not being able to gloat; to tell me she told me so.* She looked at the woman she had feared for so long. Her hair was perfect, as always.

Oh my, Amber thought looking at Connie's hands. *She's broken a nail. It must be driving her crazy. She's not perfect after all.*

"Amber?" Walt said interrupting her thoughts. "I am sure you figured it out by now. We knew. Jeff called us a few weeks ago and told us he was filing for divorce. He said he met someone and that she was pregnant with his son. He said he hadn't told you yet." He paused and looked at his still quiet wife. "Connie begged him to reconsider. He had already married you because you got yourself pregnant. We didn't want him to make the same mistake twice."

Amber exchanged a knowing look with Robin. Feeling a knot ball up in the pit of her stomach, she closed her eyes and took a deep breath to steady herself. Even though she had been a good wife, she had never been good enough. She had been the faithful one and yet "she" had been the mistake. Amber swallowed hard in an attempt to keep from losing control.

"Wow, I didn't realize Julie was a product of Immaculate Conception. It does take two, you know, and for your information, Jeff is the one who insisted we get married."

Neither Walt nor Connie uttered a word. Amber took a deep breath. Needing to lash out and feeling empowered by their silence, she continued.

"You know it seems like me and Heather - is that what you called her? It seems like we have something in common. We both had the misfortune of falling in love with your cheating son. I know Jeff is dead, but I think by now it's pretty clear he was not the saint you made him out to be.

Walt was speechless. Amber had never raised her voice to either of them. Connie's face turned crimson, Amber almost expected to see steam coming from her ears, but she was on a roll, mustering strength she didn't know she had.

"Listen, you may not approve of me, but I was a good wife to your son. I loved him, and was always faithful to him, which is a lot more than I can say for your precious Jeff," she spat.

"Well, looks like someone grew a backbone," Connie sneered. "So much for the grieving widow."

"Grieving widow," Amber said, seething. She loathed Connie, the woman that had treated her like a second-class citizen for the last thirteen and a half years, never calling to check on her, or even Julie for that matter, never acknowledging their existence at all, unless Jeff called them on it. With her high and mighty attitude, she was nothing more than a five-dollar millionaire. "How dare you judge me? How dare you tell me how to act! In the last three days, I have lost my husband, been handed divorce papers, found out that my dead husband has left me with a psycho, pregnant girlfriend and been humiliated in front of half the town. So don't tell me how I should be feeling."

Robin looked ready to start applauding and Amber quickly curtailed that with a shake of her head. Her friend settled for a subtle thumbs-up sign and remained quiet.

"Come Connie, I think it is time to go." Walt got up and picked up his hat, helping his wife to her feet. They walked to the front door without saying a word. As they got there, Dianna and Julie were returning from their walk with Clancy.

"Leaving already?" Dianna questioned.

"Yes. It's time to head back," Connie replied.

"Oh Dianna, don't go," Julie begged.

"It's okay Julie," Amber said. "They have a long drive back. Besides, Lana will be here soon, she wants you to spend the night with Kelly. You need to pack so you'll be ready when she gets here."

"On a school night? Sweet!" Julie exclaimed. She gave everybody a goodbye hug and headed up the stairs with Clancy on her heels.

Walt guided Connie to the door and gave her arm a squeeze. "You head on out, dear. I'll be right there."

They all watched as Connie headed for the car without saying a word. Walt shot Dianna a glance then motioned toward the car with his eyes. Dianna gave Amber a hug, leaning close to whisper in her ear.

"I don't know what I missed, but I am sure I will hear all about it on the way home." She released her embrace, stood and clasped her hand. "I'll call you. You be strong Amber."

"I will, I promise."

As soon as Dianna was out of earshot, Walt looked at Amber. For the first time, he had tears in his eyes.

"You need to remember one thing, Missy." His voice crackled as he spoke. "You are not the only one that lost someone. He was our son you know."

"Yes Walt, I know he was your son." Amber fought hard not to lose control again. "But that is the irony of the situation. He will always be your son, but never again will he be my husband."

Chapter Fourteen

Amber went through the house, opening the windows. It was still a bit chilly, but she had to get some fresh air. Today marked the one-month anniversary of Jeff's death and would have been their 14th wedding anniversary. Their home, even though large, felt as though it would close in on her.

Funny, she thought, *all the years I spent alone here; I've never felt as alone as I do now*. Amber picked up the doormat and went on the front porch to shake it out.

"Hey, girlfriend."

Amber looked up to see Robin riding up the driveway on her red bike. "Hey Chickie, why aren't you at work?"

"I had a sick day coming so I took it." She grinned, putting down the kickstand.

"Hmm, you don't look sick to me," Amber teased.

"Sure I am. I'm sick of work." Robin laughed.

Amber laid the rug across the porch railing. She walked down the steps to where her friend was standing. "You didn't have to stay home because of me."

"I told you I was sick, remember?"

"Sure. So sick that you rode your bike over here? Besides we both know what day it is don't we? " she said, looking her friend in the eye.

Robin shrugged, "I just thought you could use some company."

They walked through the yard, picking up twigs that had fallen during the winter months. The back yard was immense and lined on all sides by huge pine trees. Behind the trees in the back was a fence and beyond that several acres of farm land. Big maple trees provided shade throughout the yard. It was the branches from these trees that littered parts of the otherwise perfectly manicured lawn.

"I've always loved your house," Robin said, bending to pick up a stick. "I love the way it sits on the hill and I've always wanted a walk-out basement."

Amber sighed, "Yes, Jeff did a great job designing it. He may not have known how to be a decent husband, but no one could deny he was a wonderful provider."

"How are you doing?" Robin asked.

"I'm okay," Amber lied.

"Come on, girlfriend, this is me remember?"

"I'm good I guess. It's just that now it all seems weird."

"What does?"

"Being in the house alone. I mean, Julie's here and all, but she's at school most of the time and with Kelly the rest of the time. When I'm alone, I'm really alone. Before, I was always waiting and planning for Jeff to come home, now there is nothing to wait for."

"Maybe you should get a job."

"Oh sure. I'm sure there are lots of openings for a housewife. You know I've never worked. Hell, not even as a kid. I married Jeff right after high school and God forbid a wife of his should have to work. That wouldn't have looked good on him now would it?"

"How about going back to school?"

"I don't know. I'm just not sure what I want to do."

"You could volunteer. There are always people looking for help. I could get you some names. You don't need any training."

"That might be nice," Amber said, putting her pile of branches and twigs in the garbage can.

As they walked over and sat on the back deck, Julie came out the sliding glass door with Clancy. Clancy jumped up on Amber, licking her face, and then ran over to Robin.

"Just what I need, dog breath," Robin said, pushing him down. He managed to sneak in one last kiss before heading off to retrace their path in the yard.

"You did remember to make your bed, didn't you?" Amber asked Julie.

"Yes, Mom." Julie said, rolling her eyes.

"How's your spring break going?" Robin questioned.

"Anytime I don't go to school is good," Julie snapped.

Amber followed Robin's gaze as she looked up at the usually bubbly teen. Her long brown hair was stringy and in need of a good wash. Her eyes were narrowed and lifeless.

Robin's brow furrowed as she glanced back at Amber in alarm. Amber looked over at Robin and gave a little nod as if to ask her not to push the issue.

Without saying a word, Julie went back inside.

Robin looked worried. "My God, Amber, I didn't realize Julie was taking Jeff's death so badly."

Amber glanced toward the house and lowered her voice. "It's not Jeff's death. I thought so too, so I took her to a counselor on Monday."

"And?" Robin asked, clearly surprised.

"Apparently, as sad as it may seem, she could care less that Jeff is gone."

"You're kidding," Robin gasped.

"Let's face it Robin, as bad of a husband as Jeff was, he was an even worse father."

Robin did a double take. "Did you just say that Jeff was a bad husband?"

Amber laughed. "Yes, I said Jeff was a bad husband."

"And you only went to this counselor once? God, she's good. What's her name?"

"Actually his name is Brent and we've been going to him for a few weeks now," Amber confessed.

Robin gasped, her mouth dropped open. "Do we not talk every day? You didn't tell me? I'm hurt."

"I didn't want you to think I was weak. I'm so tired of everyone feeling sorry for me. I needed help from someone who wasn't personally involved."

"So it took him only a couple of weeks to convince you of what I have been telling you for how many years?" Robin pouted.

"Don't you see?" Amber pleaded. "He didn't tell me anything. I was the one who did all the talking. I've been going through life with blinders on. When Mom died, all I had left was Dad, only he was never around. He made sure I had food and clothes, but he was never there. Hell, he didn't even come to Jeff's funeral." Amber hesitated, her face showing her disappointment.

"Anyway, Jeff came along and showed me some attention and that was it, I was in love." She searched her friend's face for understanding. "After we were married he was gone most of the time, but even still what little bit of attention I got was more than I ever had growing up. So I took that as love."

Robin bit at her lower lip, tears welling up in her eyes.

"Hey!" Amber warned. "If you start crying you have to leave! There has been enough crying around here."

"Sorry," Robin said, wiping her eyes. "But if Julie isn't angry because of her father, then why?"

"The kids at school. You know how cruel kids can be. They have all heard what happened at the funeral and have been teasing her nonstop."

"Even Kelly?" Robin asked, stunned.

"No. She's been great, but from what Julie says, Kelly has been having it just as tough because they are friends. Both of their grades have dropped and it's all I can do to get Julie to go to school."

"That's terrible. What are you going to do?"

"I don't know, I have seriously thought about moving out west."

"What's out west?"

"Oh, I don't know, but it would be a fresh start and God knows we could use that. I just have to tie up some loose ends here first," Amber said, petting Clancy who had come to sit at her feet.

"Anything I can help with?"

"No, not this time," she said, her voice barely audible.

"What loose ends?"

"Remember Randy from the funeral home?"

"Who, the guy from Jeff's work? The one with the ponytail and wrinkled shirt?" Robin asked, wrinkling her nose in disgust.

"That's the one"

"What about him?"

"Well, he gave me his card and said if I needed anything to call, so I did. We're having lunch next week."

Robin gave a shudder and stomped her feet. "Ewww! You can do better than him!"

Amber gave her friend a playful swat.

"Very funny, and no, I am not that desperate." Her face turned serious. She looked directly at Robin, her dark eyes pleading with her to understand. "I need answers. There are too many questions unanswered. If I'm going to let this go, I need to know the truth."

"Are you sure you don't want me to come along?"

"I know you mean well, but I need to do this." She saw the worried expression on her friend's face. "Would you chill out? I will be just fine."

"I know."

"Then why the long face?"

Robin let out a long sigh. "I'm just afraid," she paused, choosing her words carefully. "I'm afraid that you don't need me anymore."

Amber erupted into genuine laughter. Her face turned serious as she gathered her thoughts. As she spoke, she held Robin's hands.

"I wouldn't have gotten this far without you. Don't you know that? You are the one person that has never tried to bullshit me. You have been my rock even when I didn't know I needed one." Tears threatened as she hugged the friend she held so dear. "I promise you Chickie, you will always be my best friend."

Chapter Fifteen

Amber pulled open the heavy glass door to the police station. Although she had lived in this town for many years, she had never had a reason to come here. Her hands felt clammy, her heart raced.

God, what am I doing here, she thought. She spun around and reached for the door through which she had just entered.

"Can I help you?" called a voice from behind her.

Damn, she thought, turning back around.

"Uh …y…yes," she stammered, "I was wondering if I could find out how to get a copy of a police report." Crossing the distance, she smiled tentatively at the grey-haired officer sitting behind the desk.

"Sure, what was the date of the incident?"

"April 28th," she said, relaxing a bit.

The officer reached for his reading glasses. "Can't read worth a damn without them," he said, turning toward the computer. "Don't ever get old, little lady. Name of the person involved?"

"Jeff Wilson."

He banged on the keyboard with heavy hands, eyes concentrating on the screen in front of him.

"That's strange. I'm not coming up with anything." He looked up at Amber. "Where did the incident happen?"

"I think it was just this side of Richmond, but I'm not sure of the exact location. That's why I wanted the police report."

"Well, that would explain it; it wasn't even in our county." He said, taking off his glasses. "We wouldn't have a record of it."

"I see," Amber said, her face feeling flushed, "I just thought because the cops came to my house, you would have a record of it."

"Ah, someone came to your house? Do you remember their names?"

Amber shifted her feet. Her hands felt clammy and her mouth was very dry. She wanted to leave.

The officer looked at her expectantly. "Well?"

As Amber tried to remember that night, a dull pain started in her temples. "No, actually I don't," Amber said. The only thing that popped into her head was Laurel and Hardy. "I just remember that one of them was tall and the other was a lot shorter."

"Okay," the officer said patiently. "What's your name? There should be something on record."

"Amber Mae Wilson."

He returned his glasses to his face and punched her name into the computer.

"Here it is." He pointed at the screen. "That was officer Murphy. He was the tall one, and officer Blome the shorter one. They can give you what information they have." He removed his glasses once again and pushed back away from the computer screen.

Amber breathed a sigh of relief. "Do you know where I can reach them?"

"Well, young lady, you're in luck. Their shift is ending and they should be here any minute. Why don't you have a seat and wait for a bit," he said, motioning toward the blue chairs that lined the sides of the small, well-lit room.

"That would be great," she flashed a smile and settled in a chair. She did not like being here and hoped her wait would not be a long one.

As if on cue, the door opened, making way for the two officers she recognized from that awful night. This time they did not conjure up visions of Laurel and Hardy, but did tighten the knot in her stomach.

"Hey Chet," the tall man called to the man behind the desk.

"Hi guys. There is a Mrs. Wilson here to see you," he said, pointing toward Amber.

The taller man grabbed the other officer by the arm wrangling his way around him. "I'll go," he said, walking over to her.

Amber stood up and reached to shake his hand.

"Mrs. Wilson." Officer Murphy said, shaking her hand just a second too long. He motioned her back toward the chair. "Please sit down. How can I help you?"

He waited for her to sit before taking the seat beside her. He looked into her eyes and held her with his gaze.

Amber felt her face flush and tore her eyes away. "I wanted to get a copy of my husb…"she paused. "Excuse me, my late husband's police report. I checked with the guy at the desk. He said it wasn't here."

The tall man was quiet for a moment then his face brightened. "That's right. If I remember right, the accident happened in Macomb County. The state boys handled it." He stared into her eyes, once again holding her gaze.

Amber shifted under the intensity of his gaze. Then, shaking her head, she broke free of his stare and sighed in obvious disappointment. "I guess I'll have to call there. Do I just call the Macomb Police department?"

"Yes… No. Hang on a minute," he said, getting up. "Let me try something."

He walked over to his partner, who was still talking to the officer at the front desk. They exchanged words then he returned to his seat beside Amber. "Do you have a couple of minutes?"

"Yes I guess so. Why?" The question was almost funny, like she had anything better to do than going home to an empty house.

"Rodger, that's my partner, has a friend over at the state police post in Richmond. He's going to call over there and have her fax him a copy of the report." He looked quite pleased with himself.

Amber breathed a sigh of relief. The last thing she wanted to do was to go into another police station.

"That would be wonderful," she said, returning his smile.

Once again, Officer Murphy stared intently into Amber's eyes.

Oh my God, he's flirting with me, she thought. She felt heat rise to her cheeks. Her first instinct was to turn away, but she could not, his gaze held her. She studied his features. *He's not a bad looking man, not by any means. He is tall, rather skinny for my taste, but a few home cooked meals would take care of that. He has nice green eyes, no, brown. I think they are called hazel. He does look good in that uniform.*

Amber felt her panties dampen. It caught her by surprise. She stood, breaking the hold his gaze had on her. Amber was surprised at her sudden attraction. It was not like she was interested in him, really. It had just been a long time, too long in fact, since anyone had paid her that much attention.

"Do you think that fax has come through yet?" she asked, slightly breathless.

"Let me check," he said, getting up and walking toward the desk.

Amber watched as the tall, uniformed man walked to the desk. She couldn't help but notice the scowl on his partner's face. A frown creased her brow. Was he not happy that he had been asked to get the report?

The men exchanged words but Amber was too far away to hear what was said. The tall man glanced her way then turned and said something to the shorter police officer. Again, she strained to hear what was being said and wondered if she was the cause of the disagreement.

She watched as the tall officer, Murphy, snatched a paper from his partner's hand, then turned and walked in her direction. His face was flushed when he approached her.

"Here is the report," he said, his voice tight.

She reached for the report then hesitated. "I am sorry if I caused any trouble between the two of you."

The man's face flushed even more. "Listen Mrs. Wilson, I'm sorry about that. Rodger, my partner, he had no reason saying what he did. He..."

Amber shook her head cutting him off in mid sentence. "No, I didn't actually hear the conversation; I was just worried that I had caused the argument. Your partner didn't look too happy."

Officer Murphy's color returned. He waved his hand in dismissal. "It's nothing, we just don't always see eye to eye." He handed her the paper and cast a glance back over his shoulder.

Amber folded the report and slipped it into her purse.

"Please tell your partner thanks for me. I really appreciate it, Officer Murphy."

"It's Marty."

"Excuse me?"

"My name, it's Martin, but my friends call me Marty," he said smiling.

"Thanks again, Marty. I really am grateful."

His eyebrows arched. He reached into his pocket and produced a business card.

"Here is my card, if you need anything," he stared at her intensely, "anything at all, Mrs. Wilson, please give me a call."

"I will." She took the card and slipped it into her purse. "Oh, and please call me Amber." She could feel his eyes on her as she walked away. Casually she glanced back. She returned his smile then headed out the door.

Chapter Sixteen

Amber locked the door on her blue Intrepid and headed toward the tavern entrance. It was a small, green-sided building with bright white awnings. A sign with a shamrock displaying the name "O'Malley's Place" hung over the front door. She felt a little queasy. Although the meeting with Randy was her idea, she wasn't sure if she was ready to hear what he had to say. Opening the door, she was caught off guard by the cheerful ambiance of the place.

I should have known it would be lively, she thought to herself. Amber waited for her eyes to adjust to the dim lighting then searched the crowd for Randy. Seeing him with his ever-present ponytail, she walked over to the high, round table where he was sitting.

"You made it," he said, not bothering to get up. "Did you have any trouble finding the place?"

"No, I just followed the Irish music," Amber said, settling into a chair that was just as uncomfortable as she was already.

Randy looked around. "I'm sorry, I didn't know it bothered you. Do you want to go someplace else?"

"No that's okay. I'll just try not to break out into a jig," Amber teased.

"I see you still have your sense of humor, Amber," Randy said, laughing as he caught the attention of the waitress two tables away.

Amber's smile faded. "It's funny, Randy. Lately I haven't found much to laugh about. I guess that's why I'm here. I want… no, I need some closure. I have so many questions I need answered." Amber looked deep into Randy's blue eyes.

Randy squirmed in his seat. He ran a hand through his hair, stopping at the band that held the ponytail in place. "I'll tell you what I know, but you might not like the answers."

"I only ask that you tell me the truth, Randy. Don't try to sugar coat anything."

The green and white clad waitress approached the table. Her top was cut so dramatically Amber half-expected breasts to topple out at any second. As the girl reached over to place a water glass on the table, Amber was even more surprised when they remained securely inside the thin material. Amber looked around and saw several more waitresses dressed the same way, leaving no doubt why Randy frequented this place.

"I see your friend made it," she said, sitting another beer in front of Randy. "Are you two ready to order now?"

"I'll have a cheeseburger with everything and fries," Randy said, taking a sip of his beer.

The waitress shifted her gaze to Amber. "And for you?"

She quickly scanned the menu before making a decision. "I'll have a BLT with fries and a sprite with no ice."

"Sure thing, I'll have it out in a jiff," the waitress said, sliding the pen behind her ear. As she turned to go, Amber could see there was just as much to see from the back of the uniform as there had been from the front.

Amber watched Randy's eyes follow the waitress as she walked away. Once a perv, always a perv.

"Randy?" she said, drawing his attention back to her. "How long had Jeff and Heather been together?"

Randy coughed on the gulp of beer he was in the process of swallowing. "I… I didn't realize you knew about her, much less her name," he stammered.

"Yes. I know."

He shifted in his seat. "How… How did you find out?"

"You did a pretty good job in the funeral home keeping her away but, unfortunately for all of us, she found her way back." Amber paused, remembering the scene in the parking lot. "She found me as I was leaving. She made sure that my daughter, the whole town and I knew she was pregnant with Jeff's child."

He looked highly embarrassed. "Amber, I'm sorry. I thought she left when I did."

"How long, Randy?"

"About two years now." He took another gulp of his beer, his eyes on the approaching waitress.

"Here you go," the waitress interrupted. She set a sprite in front of Amber. "Your lunch will be out shortly."

"Thank you," Amber said, taking a sip of her drink. She waited for the waitress to leave then returned to her questions. "Did he love her?"

"Yes Amber, this one he loved," Randy assured her, nodding his head.

Amber's heart pounded, this was not the answer she was expecting. This one? What did he mean, this one? She searched his face for some meaning.

Once again, Randy shifted uncomfortably in his seat. "I… I just assumed you knew that Heather was not the only girl Jeff had been with. Hell, he was always with one girl or another. He usually had a different girl every night. Until he met Heather that is, since then he has been a one woman man."

His face turned crimson, an uneasy smile played

across his face. "Umm with the exception of you, I mean."

Amber was livid; the color rose up her face. There had been others? How many others? Had he used protection? Of course he hadn't. If he had, Heather wouldn't be pregnant now, would she? How could he do that to her? She took a deep breath. "How long Randy? How long had he been cheating on me?"

Randy looked like a cornered rat, and heaved a huge sigh of relief when the waitress interrupted with their meals.

"Here you go," she said, bending over more than was needed to set the plates down. "Can I get you guys anything else?"

"No, we're fine," Amber said snidely, narrowing her eyes. As the waitress walked away, Amber felt a pang of guilt for taking her anger out on the girl who was merely trying to increase her tip. "Randy? You said you would be honest with me. Please tell me how long Jeff had been cheating on me."

Randy took another drink of his beer. "Amber, I'm sorry, but I've known Jeff for ten years, and to be honest with you, he has never in all that time acted like he was married. I'm sorry Amber. I really am."

Amber wiped her tears with her napkin. She was angry that she lost control. She had promised herself that she would never again allow Jeff to hurt her.

"Do you have a number or address for Heather?"

Randy nearly choked on the bite of sandwich he was chewing. "I can't give you that."

"I'm not going to do anything stupid, I just want it in case I need to contact her."

"I don't know an address. For the most part, she stayed at the hotel with Jeff. I have a phone number to her parent's house though," Randy said, searching his wallet.

"Her parents? How friggin old is she?" Amber

seethed, feeling the knot in her stomach tighten.

"She's twenty-two." Randy said, handing Amber the number.

"Shit, she's just a baby!"

"They all were, Amber. Jeff was never with anyone over twenty-five. The guys all called him a cradle robber."

Amber pushed her fries around with her fork while Randy wolfed down his food. Finally, the waitress interrupted the awkward silence, sliding the tab onto the table.

"Can I get either of you anything else?"

"No," they both said at once.

"Was there something wrong with yours?" she asked, looking at Amber's untouched plate.

"No. I lost my appetite." Amber said.

"Would you like me to wrap it for you?"

"No, that's okay," she said, somehow managing a weak smile. She reached for her purse.

"I'll get this Amber, it's the least I can do," he said, handing the waitress the money along with a generous tip.

"Thanks for meeting with me, Randy." Amber stood. "And thanks for answering my questions."

"No problem, Amber. If you need anything..." He slowly looked her up and down. "Anything at all, you've got my number."

Yeah, I've got your number all right.

"Thanks," she managed as she hurried toward the door. Amber felt sick to her stomach. She didn't want anything to do with Randy. He was just as bad as Jeff. He had known all about Jeff's womanizing all these years and had never told her.

The tears started again. Her hands shook as she unlocked the car door. She got in, locked the doors, pounded the steering wheel with her fists and wept. Several minutes later, she pulled herself together, put the car in gear and headed down the highway. Tears streamed down her face as she drove. All those years he was unfaithful. All those years she was there waiting for him to come home. Waiting for him to love her!

She wanted to get as far away from Randy as possible. She hated the way he had looked at her. She knew Jeff had looked at his young dates the same way. She drove for what seemed like ages, all the while never-ending tears stung her eyes. Finally seeing what she had been looking for, Amber turned her car in to a nearly deserted gas station.

This is it, she thought, pulling the car into the nearly empty lot. She parked in the front near the road and exited the car, clutching the police report in her hands. She waited for the traffic to clear then crossed the road.

Walking along the side of the road, she looked for a clue of what had happened here a little over a month ago. Her heart skipped a beat when she saw the marks at the side of the road; they were subtle but still visible if one knew where to look. Carefully she headed down the hill, making her way down the steep incline. She could see ruts in the hill where the tires had left their imprint in the then freshly thawed Michigan ground. She saw where the tracks stopped and were replaced by a huge chunk of torn sod.

That must be where the truck rolled, Amber thought.

Small fragments of glass were still apparent in several places. She knew from reading the police report that Jeff's truck had rolled several times before coming to an abrupt stop against the massive tree. Reaching the bottom, she rubbed the marred tree with her hand.

This was it. This was the place Jeff had died. Amber leaned against the tree for support.

Funny, she thought. *The same tree that had taken Jeff's life is now helping me*.

Amber slumped to the ground, numb to the cold

dampness of Michigan's nearly thawed ground. She drew her knees to her chest and screamed, sobbing helplessly. She cried because she was hurting, she cried because she felt so alone, but most of all she cried because after all those years, she truly hated Jeff.

Chapter Seventeen

As Dalton drove the truck up the long driveway, he was struck by the fact that the yard was in dire need of being cut. Although once a showplace, the barn was now in desperate need of fresh paint.

"Is this it, Daddy? Are we here?" Katie Mae asked impatiently.

"Yes, Little Bit, we're here," Dalton said, pulling up next to the barn. He got out of the truck and went to the passenger side. A large brown German shepherd with a black mask was barking. The dog's ears pointed forward and tensed and his tail curved upwards. The hair running the length of his back was raised. Dalton looked to make sure he was on a chain before helping Katie Mae down. As they walked toward the barn, they were greeted by a white-haired man who leaned heavily on a cane.

"Settle down, Bosco." The old man called to the dog. It stopped barking, but continued to keep a watchful eye on the new arrivals. The man offered a trembling hand. "Howdy Dalton."

"Hello Mr. Meyers." Dalton said, firmly grasping the weathered hand.

The man bent to shake Katie's hand.

"And you must be Katie Mae. Your Daddy said he needed you to help him pick out a horse," he said, winking at Dalton.

"Yes, it's for my cousin, Kelly." Katie Mae was smiling from ear to ear, happy to be included in such an important decision.

"Well then, follow me, Missy. I'll show you where the horses are." They followed as the man hobbled toward the barn. Several horses sticking their heads out of their stalls greeted them.

"All of them are for sale except this one," he said, pointing to an appaloosa. "She belongs to my granddaughter. They have to finish their barn before they can take her."

"Getting out of the horse business, Mr. Meyers?" Dalton asked, petting the spotted horse.

"I have to, Dalton." The old man sighed heavily and extended his hand to showcase grotesquely bent fingers. "This ol' rheumatoid is getting so bad I can't hardly get around anymore. You of all people know how much work the horses are."

"That I do, Sir." Dalton reassured him.

"Daddy! Look at this one!" Katie Mae called out.

Dalton walked over to the stall where she was standing. A big palomino mare was nuzzling her hand.

"He likes me, Daddy." Katie Mae giggled as the soft fuzz muzzle tickled her outstretched hand.

Mr. Meyers limped over and joined them.

"This here's a fine choice, little missy. Molly here is as gentle as a lamb. She's done trail rides and loves kids. My granddaughter loves to braid her mane and tail and that mare will stand there the whole time and let her do it. Now don't get me wrong – she has spirit, but loves attention."

The child climbed up on the gate to get a better view of the big yellow mare. "Daddy, I think Kelly would love Molly."

"She's not scared of the horses at all, is she, son?" the old man asked, scratching his head.

"Only one," Dalton said, looking into the palomino's mouth. "I've just gotten a new stallion. He's the most magnificent horse I've ever seen. He takes your breath away just to look at him. To tell you the truth, he even intimidates me. I got him from Mr. Patterson."

The old man looked up and cocked his right eyebrow. "You mean the one he called Crazy Legs?"

"Yes Sir, you know him?"

"Hell son, everyone that knows anything about horses has heard of that horse. You got yourself a prize stallion. Hell, I heard tell that right after Patterson sold him some big wig from Texas offered him ten thousand more than he sold him for and Patterson cried like a baby. I can probably get the buyer's name if you'd like."

Dalton beamed, feeling justified. He knew Crazy Legs was a good investment, but this proved it.

"Nah, that's okay. I think I'll hang onto him, but I can tell you that the asking price for his donations just went up. His colts will be Derby winners," Dalton said proudly.

"With everything I've heard about that horse, I don't doubt it one bit, son," the elderly man said, patting Dalton on the back. "What say we take ol' Molly here out and give her a whirl? She's no Derby winner, but she'll be a great friend."

Mr. Meyers opened the gate and led the large mare to the indoor arena. True to his word, Molly stood there placidly next to Katie Mae.

"Little missy, walk over to that gate over there," the old man said, pointing to the gate on the other side of the arena.

Katie Mae did as she was told. She walked over to the gate and was followed by the big mare.

"Okay, now run back." The old man motioned. Katie started running, closely followed by the big yellow mare. Halfway across the arena, Katie Mae lost her balance and fell. Dalton started to run toward his daughter, but the old man blocked him with his cane.

"Wait son," he said quietly.

Dalton watched with amazement as the big yellow mare stopped right beside Katie Mae. She lowered her head and gently nuzzled the girl's arm. Unscathed, Katie Mae got up and continued toward the men, followed by the large gentle horse.

"The horse ran with me, Daddy!" she said, breathing hard.

"I saw that, Little Bit," Dalton said, still staring in disbelief. He finished checking the mare out and then jumped on her back.

Mr. Meyers slipped a harness over her head, slid the bit into her mouth and passed the reins to Dalton. Dalton patted the horse's blonde mane then pulled backwards on the reins to back her up. He looked down at the child who was standing next to the old man.

"Wait here for a minute, Little Bit."

"Okay, Daddy," she said, watching him ride the docile animal around the ring.

Dalton put her through some paces, feeling for any problems. Coming back, he tightened the reins.

"Whoa, Molly." He slid off the horse and checked her mouth one last time.

"Well? What do you think, son?" the old man asked knowingly.

"I think, Sir, that the horse world is losing an incredible horse trainer."

"Can I ride, Daddy?"

Dalton looked down at Katie Mae. "I don't know, Little Bit. She doesn't have a saddle on her," he said, looking at the man standing beside him to back him up.

"Can she ride, son?"

"Better than most," Dalton assured the man.

The old man's eyes twinkled. "I would've been

disappointed if you would've answered any other way. She'll be fine, son."

"Are you sure?" Dalton asked, looking at the big mare.

"I'd stake my life on it, son."

Reluctantly, Dalton helped Katie Mae onto the big horse. He handed her the reins.

"Okay Darlin', but don't let her run. She doesn't have a saddle on."

"Okay, Daddy. We'll just walk. I promise," she said, lightly kicking her legs against the mare and turning the reins.

Dalton watched in amazement as Katie Mae trotted the big horse around the arena. After a few minutes, he turned toward the older man.

"Mr. Meyers?" he asked sheepishly. "Now can we find a horse for my niece?"

Chapter Eighteen

Amber finished tying her shoes, and then reached for Clancy's leash. Clancy was too excited to stay still.

"Easy boy," she said, trying to clip the hook onto his collar. She just managed to fasten it securely when the door opened.

"Holy shit!" Robin exclaimed, trying to get out of the way before the dog knocked her down.

"Hello to you too." Amber laughed, holding the leash tightly.

"I was going to ask if you were ready for our walk," Robin laughed, "but it looks like I should have brought my running shoes."

"He'll settle down in a minute. Clancy, heal!" Amber said, firmly correcting the rambunctious dog as she pulled the door open and they headed out. "It's my fault. I haven't taken him running in weeks."

Robin tilted her head and glanced at her friend. "You know, girlfriend, you can't shut down like this. It's not good for you."

"I know. I just haven't felt like getting out, but it does feel good to stretch my legs again, even if it is just walking."

"How is everything else?" Robin asked.

"All right I guess. Sometimes I feel like I'm in a fog or a dream." Amber shook her head. "Oh, who am I kidding? It's more like a friggin nightmare."

"How do you mean?"

Amber thought for a moment. "For as long as I can remember I was Jeff's wife or Julie's mom. So now, I'm ready for me to be happy. Don't get me wrong – I love being Julie's mom. I wouldn't trade that for anything in the world. My being happy will have to include her being happy. I'll never again put her in a situation where she's ignored."

"You never ignored her, Amber."

"Not me. Jeff. I didn't realize it until all of this happened. I was so caught up in finding my own happiness that I didn't realize that Julie was being neglected by him more than I was. When the time comes for me to find someone new to share our life with, he will have to love her as much as he loves me. I won't settle for anything else."

"What kind of man are you looking for?" Robin asked.

"I haven't given it much thought. Not with everything Jeff has put me through. When I was married to him I used to pray that one day he would change. He'd come in and tell me he was tired of us being apart all the time and he was quitting his job to stay home with me and Julie. I guess that's the kind of man I would like. One who wants to be near me, spend time with both of us. While I'm at it, I want the whole fairy tale. A soul mate, someone who worships the ground I walk on. I want what you have. You know – with Jack. Is that too much to wish for? Does that sound selfish to you?"

"No, girlfriend, not at all. In all the years I've known you, you've never been truly happy. It seems as though you had convinced yourself you were happy, but all the while, you were wishing for more. Now that we know what you want, we have to get to work on making it happen."

Amber turned her head sharply, staring wide eyed at her friend. "What do you mean?"

"We have to find your soul mate," Robin said simply.

"Oh, you make it sound so easy," Amber said, pulling on Clancy's leash to slow him down. "Clancy, heal!"

"Easy? No. But he's out there. We just have to find him."

"Well, if mine is out there, he's lost and too stubborn to ask for directions." Amber laughed.

Robin chuckled. "Well, one thing is for sure, you won't find him if you're sitting around the house all day. You need to get out. Start enjoying life. Meet new people."

"Are you talking about dating?" Amber asked, shocked.

"Sure. Why not?"

"Good God, Robin. Jeff has only been dead a few months."

Robin looked at Amber, obviously perplexed. "Are you forgetting the fact that Jeff dated the whole time you two were married?"

"I couldn't date. What would people say?"

"Who the hell cares what people say?" Robin stopped in her tracks. "The whole damn town has nothing better to do than gossip anyway. Sorry to say this, girlfriend, but what do you think they're saying now?"

Amber started walking again. She knew what they were saying. Poor Julie came home everyday telling her what they were saying. She knew most of it was just 'kids being kids', but she also knew that they had to hear it somewhere. Robin was right; if they were going to gossip anyway, why not give them something to gossip about? Still, how would she be able to start dating again after all these years? Who would she date?

Robin interrupted her thoughts. "You got awful quiet,

girlfriend. I didn't mean to upset you."

"You didn't," Amber assured her.

"Okay then. A penny for your thoughts."

"I was just wondering who there is to date in this small town."

Robin brightened. "Well, all right then! Being willing to date is half the battle. We'll find someone. Didn't you say that cop… what was his name?"

"Who? Officer Murphy?"

"That's the one. Didn't you say he was making eyes at you?"

"Yeah." Amber blushed. "I mean, I think so."

"Well? You can call him."

"Whoa! Slow down girlfriend! I'm not calling anyone."

"No problem. I'll call him for you."

Amber's heart raced. "Oh no you don't. I said I would consider it. I didn't say I was desperate."

"I know you're not desperate. As soon as word gets out you're ready to date, you'll be fighting them off with a stick."

Amber could see the wheels turning in her friend's head. She was her best friend, but once she set her mind to something there was no stopping her. She knew Robin meant well, but she couldn't help thinking she would need a very big stick. She held tightly to Clancy's leash.

No, she thought to herself. *I'll need the whole damn tree*.

Chapter Nineteen

Dalton pulled up to the corral, stopped the truck and helped Katie Mae down from the cab. He waved at Carl and Jake who were striding toward them.

"Have any luck finding your niece a horse, Boss?" Jake asked as they walked to the back of the horse trailer.

"Sure did." Dalton grinned.

Jake opened the back gate and was met by not one, but two swishing tails. Jake looked puzzled. "You bought your niece two horses, Boss?"

"No," Katie Mae said, tugging on Jake's pant leg. "Molly is mine!"

Carl suppressed a snicker; Dalton shot him a dirty look. Jake boarded the trailer to retrieve the horses. The first horse out was a nice quarter horse gelding, black with a white blaze down the front of his nose. Jake led him over to the corral and tied him to a post. Next, he led out a large palomino, with a pink blanket draped across her back.

Katie Mae reached for the reins. "I want to take her to show Miss Maggie."

Seeing Jake's hesitation, Dalton nodded toward him reassuringly. "It's okay, Jake."

Reluctantly, Jake surrendered the reins. Katie Mae ran toward the house, followed by the big yellow mare. Halfway across the yard, Katie Mae tripped. Carl and Jake both started running toward the child, fearing she was sure to be trampled by the big mare. They stopped in their tracks as the big mare stopped short, nuzzled Katie Mae to her feet, and continued following her to the house. Both men turned and gaped at Dalton who hadn't moved from his original spot. They walked back shaking their head.

"Holy shit!" Jake exclaimed. "That was the coolest thing I have ever seen."

"I would never have believed it if I hadn't seen it with my own eyes," Carl said, lighting a cigarette.

"The same thing happened in Meyers' arena. I like Jasper, but that pony is a bit temperamental. I'd never let her ride him alone," he smiled, watching Katie Mae with the horse. "But that horse, hell, she'll probably be sleeping with her before long."

"You'd think she was a dog the way she follows her around," Jake said, laughing. As they all walked toward the black horse, Jake asked, "How about this one?"

"This here is a nice horse too, he needs his hooves trimmed a bit and some new shoes, but he's gentle enough," Dalton said, petting the animal. "Jake, will you call the farrier and have him come out and give him a going over?"

"Sure thing, Boss," the boy said, untying the horse.

"Oh yeah, I almost forgot. If either of you know anyone in need of some good horses, Meyers is looking to sell all his trail horses."

"Is he getting out of the business?" Carl asked with surprise.

"Yeah, he was in pretty bad shape today. He said his rheumatoid is really acting up. He has some nice horses though; he had a gorgeous paint, but it was a little more spirited than I was looking for."

"Daddy!" Katie Mae hollered, running up followed by the big horse.

"Yes, Darlin'?" Dalton asked, scooping her up.

"Miss Maggie said to tell you aunt Lana called. She's supposed to call back in five minutes," she announced, holding up five fingers.

"Okay, Little Bit. I'll be right there. What do you say we let Jake put Molly in the barn and give her something to eat?"

"Okay, Daddy," Katie Mae said, handing Jake the reins. "Don't forget to feed Jasper too."

"I won't," Jake promised, taking the reins from her.

Dalton clasped the child's hand and walked to the house.

The portly lady came out onto the porch as they approached. Her tight curls were plastered against her head.

"Perfect timing," she said as they neared. She handed Dalton the phone, then took Katie Mae's hand. "Come on, love, you can help me get the sheets off the line."

"Looking good Maggie," Dalton said, taking the phone from her. He sat on the porch swing and pressed the phone to his ear. "Hello?"

"Hey, little brother," came a cheerful voice on the other end.

"You must have ESP. I was planning on calling you tonight."

"I'm not trying to be a pain, but I hadn't heard from you and wanted to see if you had found anything yet."

"I told you I would find Kelly a horse and I did, as a matter of fact I just picked him up a few minutes ago," Dalton said defensively.

"Oh Dalton, I wasn't calling to check up on you, I was merely worried about Kelly. She's been having trouble in school and I wanted to make sure this was going okay."

Now it was Dalton's turn to feel bad. Of course his sister would be checking on things if she were concerned for Kelly. His voiced softened. "What kind of trouble is she having?"

"It's a long story. Some kids are picking on her and a friend of hers. I just thought the horse would be a good distraction."

"I'm sure it will be," he agreed. "Does she know about it yet?"

"No, she doesn't. I think she might have been suspicious, but with everything that's taken place lately she hasn't caught on. We even had to do some work on the barn to get it ready for the horse."

"And she hasn't asked why?" Dalton asked, amazed.

"She did, but Tim has her convinced we're getting ready to raise a couple calves for beef."

Dalton smiled, picturing his sister's business suit wearing husband, Tim, raising cows. The man was not the farmer type!

"Boy, will she be surprised," he said, laughing. "Wait 'til she sees Blaze."

"Blaze?"

"Yeah, that's his name. He's a fine looking gelding. He's black with a white blaze that runs the whole length of his nose, and white on a couple of his legs."

"He sounds beautiful," Lana said, sounding relieved.

"He is, he needs his hooves trimmed a bit and new shoes, but we'll get that done before I bring him up."

"Oh Dalton, thank you so much. I don't know why you're being so nice to me after all that's happened."

"Just the kind of guy I am, I guess," Dalton teased. He was enjoying this renewed relationship with his sister; he only wished she didn't live so far away, "Hey Sis? One last thing."

"Yes?"

"If things don't settle down, you guys could always move back to Kentucky. There are plenty of hospitals around here."

"I know, little brother. Hopefully things will

improve. We really like it here. Living in a small town has its advantages you know."

"I understand, Sis. It was just a thought."

"I know. And Dalton? Thanks for everything."

"Anytime, Sis. We'll see you in a month."

"We?"

"Yeah, I've decided to bring Katie Mae. I think it would be nice to have some bonding time. We haven't all been together in way too long. I think a trip up north would be good for both of us."

Lana laughed. "Wouldn't it be funny if you are the one that decides to relocate?"

"I don't think we have to worry about that, Sis. I don't think there's anything in this world that could make me want to leave Kentucky."

"I know little brother, I was just kidding. Kentucky is in your blood. Besides, I don't see you ever leaving that mansion of yours," she teased.

"It's not a mansion," Dalton argued.

"Sure, keep telling yourself that," Lana said, laughing. "Anyway, I'm going to let you go for now. I'm looking forward to seeing you both."

"Okay Sis. See ya soon."

He switched off the phone and sat on the swing looking out at the horse farm he loved so much. Acres of gently rolling hills with past and present thoroughbred racehorses grazing in the pastures graced his view. The land far as he could see and beyond belonged to him. He had worked his fingers to the bone making this the place of his dreams. Anytime a neighbor decided to sell their land, Dalton was there to negotiate a fair price. To date, his property stretched to over seventeen hundred acres. His sister was right; Kentucky was in his blood. Nothing could make him leave all this. He only wished he had someone to share it with.

Chapter Twenty

Amber tucked her hair into a high ponytail as she walked across the fairgrounds lawn toward the horse barn. She was excited about getting out of the house for the day. A tall man standing just inside the door turned to greet her.

"Well hello," Officer Murphy said, reaching for her hand.

"Hello, Officer Murphy." Amber was caught off guard, and very surprised to see him. As she removed her hand from his, she caught a fleeting look of disappointment.

The tall man quickly recovered, and replaced the look with a smile. He was obviously pleased to see her. "It's Marty, remember? I was told we had a new helper coming today, but didn't know it was you. I'm glad you decided to join us."

"It wasn't really my idea. A friend talked me into it," she said, not disguising the reluctance in her voice.

Once again, disappointment crossed his face. "I get the distinct feeling you don't want to be here."

"It's not that, I just have the strangest feeling I've been set up," Amber said, looking around at the fairgrounds. The grass was freshly cut, but weeds grew unabashedly against the buildings and along the fence line.

"How do you mean?"

Amber couldn't believe Robin had set her up like this. She should have known by the way Robin had insisted she volunteer here, that her friend had something up her sleeve. She wasn't really upset; she just didn't like being caught off guard.

Amber laughed, letting the tension leave her shoulders. "It's nothing, really. My friend just thinks I need to get out more, that's all."

Marty's shoulders relaxed. "Well, maybe your friend is right. Sometimes our friends know us better than we know ourselves."

A genuine laugh escaped from her. "Yes, I think you're right. I do think it will be fun to get out for a while. So," she asked looking into his eyes. "What is it you want me to do?"

She was taken aback at the way he returned her look. Suddenly she was very afraid of his answer. His eyes said it all. There was no doubt in her mind what he wanted her to do, and that made Amber uneasy.

"Well?" she asked again in an effort to ignore his penetrating gaze and the thoughts she knew laid beneath the surface.

He blinked, and seemed for the first time to be aware that he was staring. "Well what?" "I asked what you wanted me to do for you."

His face turned crimson, confirming her suspicions.

"If you only knew," he said under his breath. Inhaling deeply he walked her into the huge red barn. "Have you ever worked with horses?"

"I have, but it's been years. My neighbor had some horses, and my mom used to take me riding. That was ages ago," Amber said, smiling at the fond memory.

"Well, that's something. At least you won't be afraid of them. We don't actually ride them, the kids do. Our job is to walk beside them to make sure they don't fall off."

"I can do that," Amber said confidently.

"The kids come from the Special-Ed class. Some of them have physical handicaps, but nothing too severe. The Sunshine Riders was developed to give the children confidence. It also helps with their motor skills. The kids really love it," Marty said enthusiastically.

"It sounds like a wonderful program," Amber agreed. "How long have you been doing it?"

"Four years."

Amber was impressed by his dedication. "Wow, you must love kids."

"They're okay," Marty said with a shrug. "But the main reason I do it is I get credit toward my retirement for volunteer work."

Amber was disappointed with his answer, but she didn't let it show.

"Are you ready to go to work?" Marty asked when a school bus, sporting the number 429, pulled up in front of the barn.

"Ready as I'll ever be," Amber said as she followed him.

"Hey Marty! Are you guys ready for us?" a lady asked as they approached the bus. Her soft, dark curls framed her friendly face.

"We sure are, Mary. We have a new helper today. This pretty lady here is Amber."

The lady finished helping a boy into his wheelchair then turned to face a blushing Amber.

"Hello, Amber. I'm Mary. Welcome aboard, this here is Jason." She shook Amber's hand, and then pointed to the boy.

Amber guessed he was around ten years old. He had sandy brown hair and thick black glasses that rested on a round, smiling face. His left hand was drawn up and Amber sensed it was not very useful, but did not see any other obvious reasons as to what was wrong with him.

"Hello, Jason," Amber said, smiling at the child.

The boy pushed up his glasses and smiled back at her, but refrained from speaking. Amber wondered if he could actually speak.

"Amber, if you're ready you can take Jason to his horse. He can tell you which one it is." Mary helped another child off the bus as she spoke.

"Okay," Amber said nervously.

"Don't worry, Amber," Marty assured her. "One of the helpers will put Jason on the horse for you."

"Oh, okay." Amber said, relieved. She began to push the boy toward the barn. "Okay Jason, here we go."

"I ride the brown one over there," Jason said, pointing.

Oh, so you can talk, she thought, suppressing a smile. "He looks like a very nice horse, Jason."

As they approached, the horse tossed its head.

"Easy boy," cooed the older, balding man holding the reins. "Hello Jason. Are you ready to ride?"

"Yes, I'm ready."

Jason unfastened his wheelchair belt with his good hand. The man handed Amber the reins to the horse, then lifted the boy out of the chair.

"Hey Jason, aren't you going to introduce me to your friend?" he asked, sitting Jason onto the now-steady horse.

"This is Amber, she's new," Jason said, struggling to get his feet into the stirrups.

"Hello Amber, I'm Shane Keller. Welcome to the program. I hope you like it," he said, extending a hand.

"So far so good," she said, reaching out the hand that was not holding the reins.

"Okay, I'm ready," Jason said impatiently.

"Yes Sir." Shane laughed. "Amber, I'll lead the horse and you just walk beside Jason in case he needs anything. Okay?"

"I can do that," Amber said as she handed the man

the reins and started to walk alongside the boy and the horse.

This isn't so bad, Amber thought, as they left the barn and headed toward a large fenced-in ring. She watched as other children on horseback entered the corral and noticed how each one was smiling. *Look how happy they all are. What a wonderful program.*

They started walking alongside another horse; Jason chatted with another child he obviously knew well. Amber's mind traveled back to her childhood, back before her mom died. She was so happy then. Her mom was a stay at home mom and always there when Amber needed her. The neighbors, Mr. and Mrs. Miller, had horses. They would charge people to go on trail rides, but they never charged Amber. Anytime she wanted to ride, her mom would take her over. Amber realized now that her mom had never actually ridden a horse herself, she had been content to walk alongside Amber while she did the riding. How she loved to ride that black and white horse.

It's funny, she thought. *I haven't thought about riding in ages. Maybe sometime I should find a place to ride. I'm sure Julie would love it. There has to be places around here that rent horses. That or we could go out west to a dude ranch. Mmm, cowboys! Hmmm I wonder if Robin would want to come. Who am I kidding; of course she'd want to come.*

Amber smiled, picturing Robin in cowboy boots and a hat.

The horse stopped, jolting her back to the present. Amber looked at her watch and was surprised to see they had been walking nearly forty-five minutes.

"Awww man!" Jason said, realizing the ride was over. "Just one more time?"

Mary approached with his wheelchair. "Sorry kid, it's time to head back." She looked at Amber. "How was your first day?"

"Wonderful," Amber replied and truly meant it.

"Great," Mary said. "So we'll see you back next week?"

"I'd love to." Amber smiled.

Mr. Keller helped Jason off the horse and sat him in his chair. Jason snapped his seat belt and looked up at Amber.

"Will you walk with me again next week?"

"Sure I will, if it is okay," she said, looking to Mr. Keller for conformation.

"Okay by me," the old man agreed.

"Then it's settled," Mary said, pushing Jason toward the bus.

"How did it go?" Marty asked as he helped a little girl off the horse he had been leading.

"Really good," Amber answered, petting the horse.

"I'll see you next week," Mr. Keller said, leading the horse toward the barn.

Amber turned and waved. "Okay, I'll be here. It was nice to meet you."

"Call me Shane, and it was nice to meet you too," the man called back over his shoulder.

"So that means you'll be back next week?" Marty asked hopefully.

"Yeah, I told Jason I'd walk with him," Amber said. She looked up, surprised to see the boy knocking on the window of the bus and waving to get her attention. She smiled at him and waved.

"Lucky boy," Marty said, looking at Amber.

Amber blushed and reached around to fix her ponytail that threatened to come loose. She pretended not to notice Marty's hungry eyes roaming over her body.

"Well, I guess I'd better be going," Amber said as she turned to leave.

"Amber," Marty said, touching her arm. "I hope this isn't out of line, but I was wondering if you'd like to have dinner with me tonight."

Amber felt the heat rise to her cheeks. Her first thought was to say no. She wasn't ready. She opened her mouth to decline and her words shocked her.

"Sure, Marty. I'd love to." As soon as she said it, she regretted it. She had to take those words back; she couldn't possibly go, but as she looked into his eyes and saw how overjoyed he was with her answer, she knew it was already too late.

"Great!" he said, grinning from ear to ear, "I'll pick you up at six. Or is that too late?"

"No six… is fine," she stammered.

"Great, then it's a date," he said smiling. "See you at six."

"See you then," Amber said walking away. Even though it was warm outside, chills ran through her as she walked towards the car. She was scared to death. What had she just agreed to do? For the first time in nearly fifteen years, she was going on a date with a man she barely knew.

Chill, girlie, she said to herself. *It's not the end of the world it's only a date. Only a date.*

Chapter Twenty-One

"Are you sure it's okay?" Amber asked her daughter for the umpteenth time.

"Mom, I told you. I think it's good you're getting out," Julie insisted.

Amber clasped Julie's hand. "Honey, I know you've been through a lot lately, I'm just worried that someone might see me out on a date and…"

Her daughter cut her off. "Mom, I'll be okay, I promise. Besides, you've been through more than I have and if you can handle it then so can I."

Amber put her arms around the girl. "I love you, baby."

"I love you too, Mom," Julie said, returning her hug.

"Look at you," Amber said, pushing back the dark hair that hid Julie's eyes. "You're growing up so fast. Why don't you and I have a girls' day this weekend? We'll make the trip to Port Huron, go to the mall, get our hair done and even get a manicure. How does that sound?"

"That sounds fun," Julie said, looking at her hands. "I've never had a manicure before. While we're there, can we get Kelly a birthday present? Her birthday is next Saturday."

Amber was pleased with her daughter's enthusiasm. "Sure we can. Do you have anything in mind?" Amber asked, overjoyed that Julie had agreed to go without her begging.

"Maybe, but I'll see if I can get any hints tonight while I'm at her house. Mom?" Julie asked, changing the subject. "What's this guy like? You know – the one you're going out with tonight?"

"Well, he's tall. Not bad looking. Kinda skinny though," Amber said, wrinkling her nose.

"How skinny?" Julie asked, laughing.

"Pretty skinny," Amber laughed.

"If he's so bad, why are you going out with him?" Julie asked, sounding confused.

"I never said he was bad," Amber countered, "I just said he was a little thin. He's actually a nice guy and it couldn't hurt to have a cop for a friend."

The girl's eyes opened wide with alarm. "A cop? You're going out with a cop? What's his name? I probably know him," Julie said, suddenly less enthused.

"Officer Murphy."

"Oh my God! You're going out with M&M!" The teen groaned, rolling hers eyes and acting as if Amber had made the worse mistake a parent could ever make.

Amber laughed, "M&M?"

"Yeah, Marty Murphy. Everyone calls him M&M. Oh, Mom, I can't believe you're going out with him!"

Amber laughed once more. "I guess it is a funny name if you think about it, but he really is a nice guy, honest."

Julie pouted and shook her head in disbelief. "To you maybe, but he doesn't like kids."

Amber frowned, suddenly regretting her decision. "What makes you say that?"

"He's always hassling the kids in town, even when they aren't doing anything. He won't even let them hang out in the parking lot."

Amber fought hard to settle the butterflies that were

suddenly taking flight in her stomach. "Well, I'm sure he's just doing his job, honey. Maybe he thinks if too many kids get together there will be a problem."

"Maybe, but I still think he hates kids," Julie insisted.

"I'll tell you what, tonight during dinner I'll ask him."

Julie threw her hands up. "Don't you dare! All I need is a cop not liking me."

Amber stood up and hugged Julie. "Don't worry, Julie. I was just teasing you."

Julie relaxed. "I know," she sighed.

A horn sounded outside.

Julie ran to the window. "Mom, Lana's here and a green jeep just pulled in beside her. It looks like M&M."

"Shit!" Amber said, rushing to check her makeup. "He's early."

Julie came up behind her. "Okay, Mom. I have to go. Don't worry, you look great, and remember – don't go too far on your first date."

"Julie!" Amber exclaimed in shock.

"What? I read Cosmo." Her daughter laughed.

"Not any more you don't, besides, it's only dinner."

"I hope so," Julie said, smiling mischievously. "He is driving a green jeep, you know."

"And?" Amber asked.

"That makes him a green M&M. And you know it's the green ones that make you horny," she said, scurrying out the door.

That child is incorrigible, Amber thought as she hurried to put her shoes on.

Clancy came trotting toward her.

"Don't even think about it young man! If you jump up and snag these pantyhose, I'll take you right to the pound."

Clancy whined, but didn't push his luck. The sound of the doorbell sent him off barking in the other direction.

"Clancy!" Amber scolded. "Go lay down!"

He backed off, but continued a low, disapproving growl as Amber opened the door.

"Hello, come in. I just have to get my jacket," Amber said, opening the door.

Marty entered, standing just inside the door under Clancy's watchful eye.

"Ready when you are," Amber said, slipping on her jacket.

"You look great." Marty reached for the door. He glanced down at Clancy who stood alert, emitting a low growl. "I see you still have your guard dog."

Amber had nearly forgotten that he had been here before and shivered. "Yes. I still have him. He's my fearless protector." She stepped out, making sure Clancy didn't follow them out the door.

Marty led her to the Jeep and opened the door for her. "I'm more of a cat man myself, never had much use for a dog in the house."

"Oh? I like having him around. He keeps me company when no one is around, and keeps me warm at night."

"Lucky dog," Marty said with a grin. His smile faded. "Hey, was that your kid that left a minute ago?"

"Julie? Yes, that was my daughter. Why?"

"Oh nothing, I just didn't realize you had a kid." He started up the Jeep and put it into gear. "I hope you're hungry, this place piles on the food."

"Actually I am," Amber said, trying to quell the uneasy feeling she was beginning to have in the pit of her stomach. She was out on a date, the first date in years, with a guy who didn't like kids or dogs. This evening was not starting out very promising.

"I thought we would drive out to the lake shore. There is a nice restaurant out there called the Light House. It's built over a marina and has great fish. Have you ever eaten there?"

"No, I haven't. I haven't been out much lately." She was grateful he had not chosen a restaurant in town; it was less likely she would see anyone she knew and less chance of adding to the rumor mill. Amber loved living in a small town; loved the safety, security, the fact that everywhere you went you were likely to run into a familiar face, but as with small towns across the nation, people liked to talk.

"Yeah, I guess you haven't had the opportunity to get out," he said.

Amber felt the awkward strain and decided to change the subject. "So, are you from around here?"

"I grew up in Chicago. I moved here to get away from all the crime. I figured if I was going to be a cop, I should at least do it where I wasn't likely to get shot." He smirked. "I had an uncle that used to live here. When I was a boy, I came to visit and liked the charm of the place. It was like stepping into Mayberry. It's grown since then, though. When I used to come here, there was only one traffic light. Now we have three! In Chicago, you couldn't walk the street at night without worrying about your safety. Being a cop was like having a target painted on my head. I figured here I'd have a pretty decent chance at staying alive. That's the thing with small towns – it's rare to get called out for anything big. I liked the idea of being a cop without all the drama of city life, so I sent in my résumé and here I am. How about you? Are you from around here?"

"I was born and raised in Lansing."

"That's a nice town. What brought you to Alliance?"

"Jeff, that was my husband, had settled here. When we got married I moved up here to be with him."

"How did you two meet?"

Amber shifted in her seat. She was not used to talking about her relationship with Jeff and certainly not with someone she had just met. “He was working construction. His company was putting an addition onto our school.”

“You were in school?” Marty asked, sounding surprised. “How old were you?”

“Seventeen.”

“How old was he?”

“Twenty-five.”

“Wow, that’s quite an age difference. Your parents didn’t mind?”

“My mom died of cancer when I was fourteen and my dad was never around,” she said, staring out the window at the freshly tilled fields.

“Sounds like a pretty lousy childhood and life’s not getting much better, huh?” Marty said.

“Well, I can always hope, can’t I?” Amber shifted her gaze to Marty. “What was the disagreement about?”

He glanced at her raised eyebrows then turned his attention back to the road. “Disagreement?”

“At the station that day. Your partner seemed pretty upset.”

Marty shifted in his seat, a frown creased his brow. “He accused me of flirting with you. He thought I was being uncouth and coming onto you. I told him he didn’t know what he was talking about. He can be a real jerk sometimes.”

Amber considered this for a moment. “But you were, weren’t you? Flirting?”

The color rose in his cheeks. “I suppose I was, but he made it sound so… wrong. Like I was planning on jumping your bones right there in the station.” A smirk played across his lips. Turning his head, he looked her up and down before returning his eyes to the road ahead. “I would like to think I am not that ill-mannered. I would at least have the decency to buy you dinner first.”

Amber studied him, trying to determine if he was serious. Her eyes darted toward the speedometer, sixty-eight, then to the door handle. For a second she wondered what her survival rate would be if she pulled the lever and attempted to jump to safety. Sighing, she leaned back into the seat and prayed he was teasing. After all, he was a police officer. To serve and protect, wasn't that their motto? Surely he would not do anything she didn't want him to do.

Both sat quietly for the remainder of the drive, Marty looking straight ahead and Amber watching out the window.

"We're here," Marty said, breaking the silence as he turned into the gravel parking lot.

The bottom of the modest building served as the village's only marina and the top had been converted to a restaurant, which overlooked Lake Huron.

"It's not fancy, but they have great food here." Setting the emergency brake, he got out and walked around the Jeep to open Amber's door.

"It looks just fine and I have heard good things about the food. I was hoping that Jeff and I could come here for our anniversary, but that never happened." As soon as the words came out, she regretted them. Not only had she mentioned her late husband, she made it sound as though she was melancholy about him not being here, something that couldn't have been further from the truth.

Amber looked into his eyes and didn't like what she saw. She knew that look all too well. She had seen it all too often lately. Pity.

"You look like someone who could use a hug," he said, and without warning, pulled her close. He held her tight, almost too tight. She struggled to catch her breath.

"Marty, I think we should go in now," she said, squirming away from him.

"Huh? Oh sure," he said, clasping her hand almost possessively.

They walked up the outer stairs to the restaurant in

silence. Once again, Amber wondered if she had made a mistake in accepting his dinner invitation. As they entered the restaurant Amber took a deep breath.

Good, it's not crowded, Amber thought as she surveyed the room, looking for any familiar faces. She was relieved when she didn't recognize anyone.

A middle-aged lady dressed in black dress slacks and a white blouse greeted them with a smile. "Hi. Two for dinner?"

"Yes," Marty replied.

"Right this way," the lady said, retrieving two menus and leading them to a far table. "Can I start you two with something to drink?"

Marty glanced at the menu. "I'll have a JD & Coke, how about you Amber?"

"I'll have a Zinfandel, please," Amber said, relaxing a bit.

"Great, your waitress will be right with you," she said, walking away.

"It all looks so good," Amber said, looking at the menu.

"It is good," Marty assured her. "I hear they have really good fish." He pointed to it on the menu.

The waitress approached and set their drinks on the table. She, too, was dressed in black pants, but unlike the hostess, she was wearing a black shirt. The black apron combined with the outfit and made her appear a lot thinner than she actually was. Her short, spiky red hair stood on end, reaching out in multiple directions.

"Hi, I'm Felicia. Are you two ready to order?" she asked, reaching for her pen.

"Ladies first," Marty gestured toward Amber.

"I'll have the perch with new potatoes and steamed vegetables."

"Would you like soup or salad?" the waitress asked, jotting on the form.

"Salad, with ranch on the side," Amber said, handing her the menu.

"And you, Sir?" the waitress asked, turning to Marty.

"I'll have the same thing she's having," he said, surrendering his menu.

"Okay, I'll be right back with some fresh bread for you." She smiled at each in turn then headed back toward the kitchen.

Marty took a sip of his drink. "Did I tell you that you look beautiful tonight?"

"Thank you," Amber said, feeling her face flush. She had not been told that in years. "You look rather nice yourself." She took a sip of her wine.

Marty clasped her hand. "Red is truly your color, Amber," he said, staring at her a bit too intensely.

Amber wasn't sure what to do. She hadn't been on a date in years, but she was sure Marty was moving way too fast. She was more than grateful when the waitress brought the salads and a basket of warm bread and deliberately ate slowly in order to keep her hands occupied. She figured if she had a fork in one hand, he wouldn't feel the need to hold the other one. The strategy worked. She had just finished her salad when the main course arrived.

"Wow, this looks incredible," Amber said as the waitress set the plates on the table.

The waitress cleared the salad plates. "Can I get either of you another drink?"

Before Amber could speak, Marty answered for her. "Bring the lady another glass of wine and I'll have water. I'm driving." He took a bite of his fish. "Mmm, this is good."

"Yes it is," Amber agreed.

Just then, a couple with two small children was seated next to them. Amber thought she saw a flash of anger cross Marty's face.

"Is something wrong?" she asked, feeling the butterflies return.

He lowered his voice. "I think people should leave their kids at home if they go to a nice place for dinner." He took another bite of his fish and let out a sigh.

Amber wasn't sure what to say. Was Julie right? Did Marty really hate kids? No, he couldn't, he volunteers with children, but then hadn't he told her that he was just doing that for the retirement?

You're being silly, she told herself. *He's a cop, how could he hate kids*?

"Marty? Have you ever been married?" she asked between bites.

"Who me? Nah, never have."

"Why not?" Amber pressed. If he hated kids she wanted to know – *had* to know.

"Never found the right woman I guess."

"Not even close?"

"Well, there was this one girl, we dated for a couple years, but we didn't see eye to eye on a few things."

Amber was more than intrigued; she had to know if what she suspected was true. "What kind of things?" she pushed.

"She wanted kids," he said, looking ruefully over at the next table.

"And you weren't ready at the time?" she asked quietly, trying to give him an out.

"It wasn't that. I have just never had any desire to have kids. They take up so much time and money. I like doing things, going places. I don't want to be stopped because I have to buy shoes or something," he said, searching her eyes.

"How is everything?" the waitress asked, setting down the glass and picking up the empty one.

"Wonderful," they both agreed.

As the waitress walked away, Marty looked at

Amber. "Did what I said shock you?"

"A little, but it explains why you were shocked about Julie."

He took a deep breath. "Growing up I had seven brothers and sisters. We could never afford to go anywhere or do anything and I decided a long time ago that I wasn't going to put any kids through that."

"I understand your point," Amber said softly, "but I also know that I would've been very lonely over the years if I hadn't had Julie around to keep me company."

They both finished their dinner without talking.

The waitress approached the table and cleared their plates. "Did either or you save room for dessert?"

"Oh no," Amber laughed. "I ate way too much as it is."

"Same here," Marty agreed.

Balancing the plates in one hand, she pulled a black folder out of her apron. "I'll take this up when you're ready," she said before walking away.

"I need to go to the ladies room," Amber said, excusing herself.

"Okay hurry back, Am," Marty said as she left.

Amber rushed to the bathroom. Why had he called her that? No one called her that! No one except Jeff! She cupped her hands and splashed cool water on her face. An elderly lady came out of one of the stalls.

"Are you okay, honey? You look as though you have seen a ghost."

"I'm fine," Amber said, grabbing a paper towel. "I think I just had a little too much wine."

"Yes, that will do it," the lady chuckled, washing her hands.

Amber went into the stall. The sound of the door assured her that the lady had left.

Well, this date was a bust, she thought as she finished up.

She washed her hands, checked her makeup, and returned to the table just as the waitress was collecting the money.

"All set?" Marty asked, getting out of his chair.

Am I ever! Amber thought. "Sure if you are," she said, reaching for her jacket.

Once again, Marty took Amber's hand as they walked down the stairs.

"Dinner was very good," she said, making small talk.

"Yes it was. We'll have to do it again sometime."

Amber was confused, hadn't he just told her they had no future together? As Marty unlocked the door, he reached in and kissed her. Amber's head swirled. The wine was affecting her judgment.

This is wrong, she thought, leaning into him. Her lips parted and his tongue found its way inside her moist mouth. She felt her body respond and pulled away.

"Wow, that was nice," he said, coming up for air.

Why the hell did you kiss him? Amber scolded herself. She hurried into the jeep and fastened her seatbelt.

"Would you like to go someplace else?" Marty asked, starting the jeep.

"I think I'd just like to go home," she said quietly.

He smiled. "Home it is." He shifted gears, pulling out of the parking lot.

They drove the whole way home without speaking. Amber's head was whirling.

Damn, why did I have to have that second glass of wine? I wanted to relax, but I didn't realize I would relax this much, she chastised herself.

Marty pulled the jeep into the driveway and shut off the engine. "Here we are, safe and sound."

Amber reached into her purse for the keys and got out of the jeep. "Thank you for dinner, Marty."

He came around and stood close to her. "No problem. Thank you for going with me." He leaned in for another kiss.

Once again, she felt herself losing control. She had been lonely too long and the wine wasn't helping. His tongue darted into her waiting mouth, finding hers in return. Marty's arms held her close to him; his hands explored her back then dipped lower, grasping her buttocks. He pulled her tightly into him. Amber felt his manhood press against her. She yearned for release. Marty relaxed his grip and Amber was surprised at Marty's boldness as his hands slowly moved down and found her heat. The warmth of his touch excited her.

"We should go inside," he whispered in her ear. His breath was hot against her neck. "I need you, Am."

Amber's blood went cold; she pushed herself away from him.

"No, I can't!" she cried out. "It's wrong."

He tried to touch her face tenderly. His voice was full of desire. "It's okay Amber, we both need it."

"Marty, no, I can't." She ducked, avoiding his touch. "Please, it's not you, it's me, and it's just too soon."

She tried to unlock the front door, but her hands were shaking. Inside, Clancy was jumping at the door and barking. Marty took the keys from her and unlocked the door.

Resigned, he handed her the key ring. "Are you okay?"

"I'll be fine, Marty, thank you for a wonderful dinner," Amber said, hurrying inside. Once inside Amber locked the door. Clancy jumped up, snagging her stockings.

"Oh Clancy," Amber bent down and hugged him. "What am I going to do?" She sunk to the floor and cried as she was greeted with slobbering kisses. "What am I going to do?"

Chapter Twenty-Two

Amber was just returning from her morning run with Clancy when the phone rang. "Hello?"

"Hey, girlfriend. You sound out of breath." "I guess I'm a little out of shape, Clancy and I just got back from our run," she said, unhooking Clancy's leash.

"Good for you! You're getting back into it," Robin encouraged.

"Yeah, I figured I'd better get him out running again before he destroys the house."

"Not Clancy!" Robin laughed.

"Are you at work?"

"Yeah, but I wanted to call and see how your date went."

"Don't ask," Amber groaned, wiping sweat from her brow.

"Why, what happened?"

"Oh nothing much, we had a nice dinner, he took me out to the Light House."

"I've heard that's a nice place. So, what went wrong?"

Amber put her foot on the stair to stretch her hamstring. "Hmmm, let me see. He doesn't like kids."

"Really?" Robin sounded surprised.

"Yeah, he freaked out when a family with kids sat next to us."

"Maybe he just wanted to have a quiet dinner," Robin offered.

Amber sat on the stair and began unlacing her shoes. "No Robin, seriously. He actually told me he doesn't like them."

There was a swift intake of air on the other end of the phone. "Holy shit!"

"Yeah, and he doesn't like dogs either. Clancy can tell! He freaks when he's here."

"Oh well, Clancy doesn't like a lot of people."

"True, but he even told me he didn't have any use for a dog in the house."

"Strike two," Robin laughed. "Anything else?"

"Well, there was the M&M thing."

"What are you talking about?" Robin asked, sounding confused.

"You know what the kids call him?"

"Not a clue!"

"M&M"

"Why?"

"His name is Marty Murphy."

"Oh, that's bad. But I've heard worse," Robin said sympathetically.

"It gets better!"

"Better than that? You're kidding!"

"He drives a green Jeep."

"Okay… now I'm really lost"

"Well, the green M&M's are supposed to make you horny."

"Shit, girlfriend! Did he make you horny?"

"Well, he didn't, but the wine did."

Robin gasped into the phone. "Oh my God, you had wine? You know what that does to you!"

"Yeah, two glasses."

"Holy shit! Did you two do it?"

"No, we didn't get that far, but it wasn't because he

didn't try and God knows my stupid body was responding."

"So, what happened?" Robin pressed.

"It was awful," Amber said, her voice cracking, "He was kissing me, and feeling me up big time. Then, out of nowhere he called me Am."

"Oh no he didn't!" Robin gasped.

"Yeah, it was the second time. He did it at the restaurant too."

"Okay then, strike three, he's out!" Robin said.

"The weird thing is, he wanted to see me again. What do I tell him if he calls?"

"Tell him the truth. Tell him you two have too many differences and it wouldn't work out."

"That's true," Amber sighed. "Better to be honest."

"That's right and if he pushes you further, tell him he reminds you too much of your dead asshole husband." Robin laughed.

"Yeah, I guess that would stop him cold," Amber said, laughing.

"I would hope so," Robin agreed. "Hey, I really want to hear more of the juicy details, but I need to get back to work."

"Wait. I wanted to ask you, does Lana or Dr. Langley have any openings today or tomorrow?"

"I can check," Robin said, sounding concerned. "Are you sick?"

"No, but I've been thinking, if Jeff was sleeping with everyone under the sun I should get checked out." Amber swallowed hard.

"Unfortunately, that probably wouldn't be a bad idea," Robin agreed. "Let me check."

"Okay."

"I have today at three or tomorrow at one."

"Today at three should work. I have a meeting with my attorney tomorrow at one."

"Your attorney?"

"Yeah, John Grether."

"Is everything okay?"

"Yeah, I just want to go over things and see where I stand. Jeff used to handle everything. It's kind of scary having to do it all."

"I understand that. If there's anything I can help with, I'm here you know."

"I know, Chickie, you always have been."

"Okay, but right now I had better get some work done. We have patients in all three rooms and a drug rep hoping to get in to see Lana before she leaves for lunch."

"No problem, see you after while."

"Okay, see you at three."

Amber hung up the phone and walked up the stairs to her bedroom. The thought of getting tested scared the hell out of her, but the fear of the unknown scared her even more. She looked in the mirror as she got undressed to take a shower. She did not look sick. She felt fine actually.

I'd know if I was sick, wouldn't I?

Chapter Twenty-Three

Amber pulled into the parking lot of the Alliance Medical Center. She was early, but figured she could chat with Robin while she was waiting for her dreaded appointment. Taking a deep breath, she entered the building.

"Please let everything go okay," she whispered to herself.

"Hi Amber," came a cheerful voice behind the opened glass window.

"Hey Regan, long time no see," Amber said, as she approached the front desk. Regan, Robin's daughter, was the spitting image of her mother, except she wore small plastic framed glasses and her hair was not quite as blonde.

"Yeah, I know, I've been so busy lately," the thin girl replied as she fastened up the papers in the chart she had been working on.

"Your mom told me you were working here. How do you like it?"

"Oh, it's great," the girl answered enthusiastically. "I love the hours and I don't have to work weekends."

"That's a plus," Amber agreed. "How are you and your boyfriend getting along?"

"Great! We should be moving into our house by the end of the month."

"Wow! What's your mom going to do without you?"

"A lot less laundry," Robin said, coming around the corner wearing white scrubs with little pink and blue cherubs on them.

Amber and Regan laughed.

"You'll miss me and you know it," Regan teased.

"You're only moving around the corner," Robin chided playfully.

"Two down and one to go," Amber said with a wink. "How is Connor doing?"

"He's doing great, he has a job he likes, bought himself a truck and even has a girlfriend."

"I'm glad to hear he's doing well."

"He's a little homesick, but that seems to be getting better, now that he has met this new girl."

"That's a plus. How does he like living at your parents' house?"

"I think that is a battle of wills. Dad made him get rid of the tongue ring, but now he has both ears pierced," Robin said, rolling her eyes.

"How does he like Kentucky? The weather has to be warmer than it is here."

"Oh, it is," Lana said, entering the conversation.

Amber looked up at the familiar voice. Lana was dressed in a white doctor's coat, which splayed open over a violet turtleneck sweater, which clung, accentuating her large breasts. "Baboombas" Robin had said she referred to them as. The rest of her was fairly dainty, which made their size seem all the bigger. A red stethoscope hung loosely around her neck and reading glasses peaked slightly out of her coat pocket.

"I talked to my mom this morning, it was near eighty," Lana said, running a hand through her short black hair.

"Wow, that would be nice. That's right; you're from Kentucky too, aren't you? I completely forgot. What is it with people from Kentucky moving to Michigan and Michiganders moving to Kentucky?" Amber questioned.

"I don't know, but you notice we all work in the same office," Robin laughed.

"That's why I hired her," Lana nodded, pointing to Robin. "I heard her accent and realized how homesick I was."

"Is all your family in Kentucky?" Amber asked, looking at Lana.

"Yeah, my mom and dad live there, so does my brother and my niece," Lana said as she handed the chart she had been working on to Regan.

"Wow," Amber replied, "so you two do have a lot in common. All your family is there too, right Robin?"

"Mine and Jack's," Robin said, nodding.

"Does your family know each other?"

"No, our family is from Louisville and Lana's family is from Lexington."

"Lexington? That's cool, we have a Lexington too."

"Yeah, but our Lexington has bluegrass and horse farms," Lana said, with a hint of melancholy.

"It sounds nice," Amber said sincerely.

"Do you want me to take Amber back to a room?" Regan asked, getting up.

"Oh, I just thought she was here to chat," Lana said, checking the schedule. "Since you're seeing me, I'll take you back."

Amber nodded and followed Lana as she picked up Amber's chart. She walked around and opened the door.

"Right through here," she said, motioning for Amber to follow her. "Hop up here on the scale for me."

"God, I hate this part," Amber groaned.

"Like you have anything to worry about, look at you." Lana chuckled, and then moved the weight over until it leveled out. "Seems like you've lost twenty-two pounds since you were last here. Are you eating?" Lana's voice was full of concern.

"I eat when I'm hungry," Amber answered truthfully.

Lana scribbled something on the chart. "Are you trying to lose?"

"I was. I was down where I was comfortable, but I guess I have lost a few more pounds since Jeff died."

"That's understandable," Lana said, taking Amber's blood pressure. "Okay your BP is good, your pulse is a little low, but that is probably just because you're a runner. You are still running, aren't you?"

"I quit for a while, but I've been back into it for about a week now."

"How have you been feeling?"

"Good, a little tired though."

"Is that why you're here?" the woman asked, still jotting on the chart in front of her.

"No," she said, clasping and unclasping her hands. Amber could feel the color rising in her cheeks as she looked up at Lana. "This is a little embarrassing, but well, with what I have found out about Jeff lately, I just thought maybe it would be wise to be tested for STDs."

Lana sat down in the chair beside her and placed her hand on Amber's arm. "I know this is hard for you, but I think you are doing a heck of a job with this whole mess and with Julie as well."

"Thanks," Amber said with tears in her eyes.

Once again, Lana looked at the open chart in front of her. "I show that after the funeral I called you in a script for Xanax. Did you take all of them?"

"No," Amber replied, shaking her head. "I only took one the first night, after that I didn't want to."

"That's great," Lana said, writing in the chart. "It can be easy to get hooked on things when you're in pain."

"I think I am better now. It was really tough at first. Losing Jeff was awful, but I have found out so much since then. You know that Jeff had a girlfriend and that the girlfriend is pregnant, well I found out he had been sleeping with other girls during our entire marriage." Amber made sure to put emphasis on the word girls.

"Oh Amber, I didn't know."

"Yeah, and on the day of the funeral, I got served divorce papers," Amber said coldly.

Lana was taken aback. "You're kidding!"

Amber shook her head. "I wish I was."

"I'm amazed you are still in one piece. So, where do you go from here?"

"I'm not sure. Robin convinced me to go on a date."

"And?"

Amber gave a little shudder. "He wasn't my type. I don't know, I guess I just have to take it one day at a time."

"That is a very good attitude."

"Yes, my therapist told me to take it slow."

"Oh, so you are seeing someone?"

"Not any more, I think I have a handle on it, really. I took Julie a couple times. She seems to be doing a little better."

A frown crossed Lana's face. "Maybe I should take Kelly."

"I'm sorry about all of this," Amber said. She genuinely regretted all the trouble Kelly had to go through.

"Don't you blame yourself, not for a minute. I mean that," Lana said firmly.

"Thanks, Lana."

"While I'm thinking about it, Kelly's birthday is Saturday. We're having a small party with a big surprise gift. Will you and Julie come?"

"Oh umm…"

"Don't try to make excuses, we would love to have you there," Lana insisted.

"Okay Lana, we'll be there," Amber assured her.

Lana's face turned serious. "Have you been having any discomfort? Any bumps, rashes, unpleasant odors, unusual discharge?

Amber shook her head. "No, nothing at all. I had a yearly exam in March and everything came back normal."

"That is wonderful news," Lana said, getting up. "Most likely if there was anything to worry about it would have been discovered at that appointment. What say we get that blood drawn, so we can put your mind at ease?" She took the chart and left the room.

Lana returned with a needle and glass tube. "Okay then. Which arm?"

Amber stuck out her left arm. Lana tied a long rubber band around her bicep and wiped the bend of her arm with alcohol.

"Just a little stick," she said, inserting the needle. "There, that wasn't so bad now, was it?"

"Easy for you to say," Amber laughed.

"I could have let Robin do it," Lana said, laughing. "I'm sure she would've taken great pleasure in sticking you with a needle."

Lana untied the tourniquet and finished filling the small glass tube with blood, took that tube out, then inserted another, repeating the process. Unhooking the tube, she set it on a rack on the counter, freed the needle and placed a cotton ball on Amber's arm.

"Here, bend your arm up and hold this," she ordered. She put the needle into a red plastic container, picked up a roll of tape and wrapped a small piece over the cotton ball on Amber's arm. "Now listen, the results will be in the first thing in the morning. I'll call you as soon as they're in, I promise. And Amber? Try not to worry, okay?"

Amber managed a slight smile. "Again, easy for you to say."

She followed Lana down the hall. She knew this would be a very long night.

Chapter Twenty-Four

Amber grabbed the phone on the first ring.

"Hello?" she answered, her voice cracking.

"Amber? Are you okay?"

"Oh, hi Robin," she replied, disappointed.

"Well, good morning to you too."

"Sorry, I thought you were Lana," Amber explained glancing at the clock.

"Oh shit, I forgot you were waiting on your test results. I didn't see anything on the printer when I came in this morning, but someone else could have gotten them already."

"Well, I guess I'll know soon enough." Amber sighed.

"I was calling to see if you want to do lunch today?" Robin asked hopefully.

"I'd love to, but I have the meeting with the attorney this afternoon."

"Oh, that's right, I forgot. How about tomorrow?"

"No can do. Julie and I are having a girls' day out; nails, hair, shopping. The works."

"Good for you two. How is she doing?"

"She seems to be doing a little better."

"Has the teasing stopped?"

"No, but she seems to be handling it a little better," Amber said, looking at the picture of Julie beside her on the small end table.

"That's good. Kids can be so cruel."

"I know. I just wish they would get over it. It's been almost four months; you'd think they'd find someone else to pick on," Amber said, exasperated.

"You know how kids are, once they find your buttons they keep pushing as long as they get a response. The best thing Julie could do would be to ignore them."

"I don't know if she can," Amber said with a sigh.

"Amber, I speak from experience. If she stops reacting to them, it won't be fun anymore, so they'll move on to someone else."

"That sounds like good advice; I'll try to talk to her tomorrow while we're out. If it works, then maybe for our next session we'll come see you." Amber laughed.

"I'm sure I would be cheaper," Robin teased. "Damn!"

"What's wrong?" Amber asked.

"The computer is down again. I wonder if it's going to be that kind of day, where everything goes wrong," Robin said, sounding frustrated.

"I sure hope not," Amber said.

"I'm sorry, girlfriend. I didn't mean anything by it. Besides, what did your horoscope say?"

"I don't know. I haven't been following it."

"Since when?" Robin asked, sounding surprised.

"Honestly, since Jeff died."

"Why on earth not?"

"You don't remember do you?"

"Remember what?"

"My horoscope the day Jeff was killed?" Amber said, twirling her fingers through her hair.

"No, I'm sorry. I don't."

"I'll never forget it," Amber said fearfully.

"Care to refresh my memory?"

"It said," Amber recanted slowly, "that a tragedy

would be a blessing in disguise."

"Holy shit! That's right, I remember. God, I have goose bumps, but you know it was."

"Was what?"

"A blessing in disguise," Robin said softly.

"How do you mean?"

"Well, I know you've had to deal with a lot, you're hurt and angry, but you do still have your house and all the insurance money. If Jeff had his way you would have been left with nothing, so in a way it actually was a blessing in disguise."

"I guess I never thought of it like that. I always thought of it as just a premonition of things to come. You're right though, it could have been much worse..." Amber mused, her voice trailing.

"So, you're going to start reading them again?"

"Maybe I will. I do miss them."

"So what's on your agenda today?" Robin asked.

"Well, I'm waiting for Lana to call, and then later I have the meeting with the attorney, Mr. Grether."

"Duh, I keep forgetting."

"I dropped off a bunch of paperwork right after Jeff died. Most of it was in those boxes they sent from his hotel. I asked him to go through it for me. I didn't have the strength to deal with it at the time. He has called several times to set up an appointment, but I haven't been ready. I guess it won't go away though, so I'll get it over with."

"I hope it goes all right for you," Robin said sincerely. "Amber. Wait a sec."

"Okay." Amber picked at her fingernails. It had been a long, sleepless night with her mind envisioning the worst. What was she going to do if the results were not good? What would she tell Julie?

"I'm back, Lana is here. She wants to talk to you."

Amber took a deep breath.

"Amber?" Lana asked.

"Yeah, I'm here."

"Great news, your test results are back. Your HIV is negative. The rest of your blood test was good except your iron is a little low. That would explain your fatigue. That can be fixed easily enough by taking a daily iron supplement. The bottom line is, you're going to be fine."

Amber breathed a sigh of relief. Tears started to well up in her eyes. "Thank you so much, Lana, I was so worried."

"I know you were, Amber. Here, I'll let you talk to Robin again."

"Congratulations, girlfriend," Robin said gleefully. "You just got a new lease on life."

"Yes I did. Now maybe the knots in my stomach will go away."

"It's smooth sailing from here," Robin assured her.

"Nothing would make me happier, I can assure you of that, but for now I better let you go so that you can get some work done."

"Gee thanks." Robin laughed. "You take care."

"You too, Chickie." Amber switched off the phone.

"Clancy!" she yelled, bringing the dog running down the hallway. Picking up the leash and let out a huge, freeing breath. "Come on boy, we're going for a run."

As she bent to hook his leash, Clancy snuck in a wet kiss. Amber grabbed both ears and hugged him tightly.

"It's going to be all right, boy." Salty tears trailed unrestrained down her face as she clarified her words. "I'm going to be just fine."

Chapter Twenty-Five

Mrs. Wilson, come in. I'm glad you finally made an appointment," the tall man said as he opened the door for her.

"I know," Amber said apologetically. "I realize I should have come in sooner, but I just couldn't." She looked around at the attorney's office fearfully, not knowing what to expect.

He motioned for her to sit down in an oversized brown leather chair.

"Well, you're here now, so let's get some things done." He gathered his notes and began. "I have a question for you. Did you go through any of the paperwork that you brought me?"

"Honestly? No, I didn't. The papers were in a box that came from the hotel where my husband stayed. I didn't know what to do with them, and I couldn't deal with them at the time, so I just brought them here. I'm sorry." She wrung her hands together nervously. "I guess I just figured you would take care of it."

"Well, it was a lot of paperwork but I'm glad you brought it to me. I had my assistant go through it and she found some pretty disturbing things in there," he said, looking directly at her.

Amber studied his face. He was a pleasant looking man, older, but distinguished. His black hair was just starting to gray at the temples, his mustache curled up dramatically at each end. Amber couldn't help but think she was looking at a man out of a western movie. His soft brown eyes looked at her with concern, but showed no pity.

He opened a folder on his desk and studied the contents. "We have a couple things that we need to sort out. Then we can put this whole mess to rest. Who handled the bills?"

"I guess, for the most part, I did. We really didn't have many. Most everything we had was paid for. Jeff didn't like to buy on credit. Anytime we bought anything he made sure it was paid off as soon as possible. His parents gave us the property as a wedding gift. We used that to get the money to build the house and we were able to pay that off as well. The car and the truck are paid for also, although the truck is totaled now."

As she spoke, he jotted down notes on a yellow pad. "Have you contacted the insurance company?"

"I've talked with the agent, but haven't been in to see her yet. After Jeff died, I got some of his life insurance right away, for the bills. There are some other policies that need to be settled."

"Okay, make sure you make an appointment to get all that settled, and make sure to remind them about the truck. You should get replacement cost on that also. Now, the life insurance you received, what did you do with that?"

"I put it into checking. I figured with the funeral and all I'd need it to pay the bills."

"I see," Mr. Grether said, once again writing on his notepad. "Have you been into your savings account lately?"

Amber's face creased with concern and knots began to form in her stomach. "No, I haven't. Jeff took care of the money and he would transfer it over to the checking account so I could pay the bills. Why?" She wasn't sure where the questions were heading, but she knew it wasn't good.

"Well, it seems as though Jeff had transferred over forty-six thousand dollars out of your savings account and into a private account."

Amber couldn't believe her ears, how could that be? Tears welled in her eyes.

In a practiced motion the man reached for a box and handed her a tissue. "Brace yourself, there's more. A week before he died he applied for a large mortgage on the house.

Amber's mouth gaped open; her eyes went wide. "How? Why?"

"So my hunch was right, you didn't know about it?"

She shook her head furiously, fresh tears trailing down her face. "Absolutely not! How could he do that without me?"

"I'm not sure, unless he forged your name. Either way I'll have a nice long talk with the financial institution."

"What can I do?" she asked, sobbing.

"It was a good thing you brought me all this paperwork or we could have had a real mess." He sat back, looking rather pleased with himself. "Here's the good news. When you didn't get back to me, I took the liberty as your attorney to cancel the mortgage. Your husband hadn't signed the final papers, so that is a non-issue. As for the house, even though Jeff had filed for divorce it wasn't final so you are still his wife. Plus, we have the will you both made, so the house will go to you. It's just a matter of a little paperwork.

"Now, as for the savings, as soon as I caught that, I put a freeze on the account. That will also revert back to you. There was an accidental death policy on Jeff from his company of one hundred thousand dollars. We need to get copies of Jeff's death certificate and then we can get the ball rolling on that. We can also apply for his social security and look into his pension fund." The man's face turned serious. He reached across his desk for his calculator. "Let me put this all in perspective for you, young lady. The insurance policy from work, the money from the truck… How much life insurance did Jeff have on him, do you know?"

"A hundred thousand, but the agent said it was doubled if it was an accident."

"That's another two hundred thousand," he said, returning to the calculator. "Then there's the house, any idea how much it is worth?"

"It was appraised last year at one hundred seventy five thousand." A price that made Jeff very happy as it was quite high for the community.

"Okay, we'll use that, but I'm sure it's more by now. The bottom line, Amber," he said, looking directly at her, "without counting Jeff's social security, pension plan or any stocks, your net worth is well over a half a million dollars, and it will easily go up when we get everything sorted out."

Mr. Grether smiled, turning the calculator around for her to see. He looked up into Amber's shocked eyes. She was speechless.

"I don't want to scare you, but I want you to realize how important it is for you to keep this information to yourself. Unfortunately, Mrs. Wilson, there are a lot of desperate people out there. They'll become your new best friends if they think they can get at your money and I can tell you there are guys that prey on widows for their money."

Amber repeated the word aloud, "Widow. Wow, I guess that's my title now. I had never thought of it before." She rubbed absently at the goose bumps that had suddenly appeared on her arms.

Her attorney's voice cut through her fog. "Amber, I know you've been through a lot, but in the long run it has worked out for the best."

"How do you mean?"

"Your husband planned to screw you over royally. You probably would have gotten the house, but you would have been left with a very large mortgage on it, not to mention the money he had stolen out of savings. I know you've been through some tough times and they probably aren't over yet, but I really think your husband's death was a blessing in disguise."

Once again, chills ran through Amber's body. She felt the blood drain from her face.

"Are you all right?" the man asked, sounding worried.

"Yes I'm fine," Amber assured him, "it's just that you're not the only one to have told me that lately."

"I'm sorry, I didn't mean to upset you."

"No you didn't. It has just been a long day."

"Well, we are done here," he said, getting up.

"Wait there's something else I'd like to take care of." She retrieved a piece of paper from her purse and handed it to him.

He sat back down and studied the paper. "What is this?"

"It is the number for Jeff's girlfriend."

"I don't understand," he said with a frown.

"I'd like to set something up for the child she is carrying, a monthly allowance and a trust fund. Can I do that?"

"Of course you can." He tilted his head in surprise and smiled. "You are truly a remarkable woman Amber."

"No I'm not," she said, shaking her head. "I just don't want an innocent child to suffer because of Jeff. This child will at least grow up thinking his daddy loved him enough to leave him something."

Amber thought of her own daughter, always longing for her daddy's love. She didn't want Julie's half-sibling to have to suffer the same fate.

She rose to leave, a grim smile on her lips. "It's the least I can do."

Chapter Twenty-Six

"A re you sure you don't want me to come along and help with Katie Mae?"

"Maggie, we've been through this a million times. We'll be fine. You need some time off. You work too hard as it is," Dalton said, smiling appreciatively.

"I don't know what I'll do with myself." She nervously fumbled with the contents of the already-packed suitcase. "You two are going to be gone for a week, the house will seem so empty, and what about the trip? What happens when Katie Mae has to go to the bathroom? She can't very well go in with you, can she? Don't tell me you intend on letting her go in alone. Lord knows what would happen to the poor child." Maggie wrung her hands.

"Maggie, you worry too much," Dalton assured her. "I'm telling you, I've got it covered."

To prove his point, he reached into a backpack that was lying across the bed. "Look!"

"What in the world?" the robust lady said, looking at the two devices he held in front of her.

A smile spread across his face. "Walkie-talkies; one for me and one for Katie Mae. When she goes into the bathroom, she can take it with her. If there's a problem, she can let me know. Besides, we'll be traveling at night so she'll probably be sleeping the whole way."

The elderly lady frowned then brightened. “All right, Mr. Smarty Pants. What about the toilet seat?”

His smile spread, as once again he reached into his bag, this time retrieving a thin white paper. “Butt gaskets!”

“But what?” Maggie said, laughing.

“You know, they go over the toilet seat to protect you when you sit down.”

The old woman’s face softened. A look of relief crossed over her.

“Well, I must say I’m impressed. I guess you don’t need me after all,” she said, pretending to be upset.

“Oh Maggie,” Dalton said, hugging the stout woman. “You know we could never survive without you.”

Letting her go, he reached into his pack and pulled out a small box, which was brightly wrapped with yellow tissue, and placed it in her hand.

“Maggie, this is for you.”

She held it up and admired the wrapping. “What in the world?”

He eyed her anxiously. “Open it and see.”

She pulled at the brightly colored tissue with trembling fingers. “Land sakes, Dalton, I don’t know what I’m going to do with you.”

Inside the box were two plane tickets to Branson, Missouri along with a large check made out in her name. Her eyes opened wide in surprise.

“Dalton, what is this?” she whispered.

Dalton was pleased with her reaction. “Maggie, you do so much for us, it’s time we do something for you in return. Katie Mae and I are going to be gone a full week. There’s no reason for you to stay here alone all that time.”

“But why two tickets?” she asked, still confused.

“Well you don’t think I’m going to let you go by yourself do you? Sally knows all about it. Heck, I think she’s been packed for a week. Carl is going to pick you both up on Wednesday morning to take you to the airport. There are tickets in there for some shows, the shuttles and enough money for shopping, dinners, and whatever else you two wild women want to indulge in." He placed his arm around Maggie.

Tears streamed down the woman's face. "Dalton, I don't know what to say."

"Say you and your sister will go and have a great time. You deserve it!"

"Oh my God!" she said, jumping up. "I have to pack! I have to call Sally and see what she is taking. That sister of mine has never kept a secret in her entire life and now she keeps this one! Can you believe it? I could've been done packing by now. Land sakes, how am I going to get it all done in time?" She hurried out of the room.

Smiling, Dalton picked up his cell phone and dialed his sister's number.

"Hello?" Lana answered.

"Hey Sis, are you ready for us?"

"Oh Dalton, I still can't believe you two are coming," Lana said, her voice trembling with excitement.

"Yes'm, we leave tomorrow night. That should put us there early Wednesday morning barring any trouble."

"Great, now the only thing is keeping the horse a secret until Saturday. I told Kelly I had a big surprise for her birthday. I plan on letting her think you and Katie Mae are that surprise. As for the horse and trailer, I made arrangements for you to keep them at the fairgrounds until Saturday."

"That'll work," Dalton agreed, "Do I ask for anyone in particular when I get there?"

"The groundskeeper's name is DJ. He should be there early. They have some kind of horse riding program on Wednesday mornings. Make sure you have my number at work with you, just in case there is a problem."

"Will do, Sis, and I'll have my cell phone with me if

you need me. Do you have the number?"

"Sure do, and I just want to say thanks again, little brother."

"No problem, Sis. I really am looking forward to our visit," he said sincerely.

"So am I, Dalton. See you in two days."

"See ya, Sis." He switched the phone to off and went to check on Katie Mae.

"Hey, Little Bit," he said, entering her room.

"I cleaned my room, Daddy," she said, putting the last of the toys in the toy box. "Will you read me my new "Little Sally Snippy Snot" book now?"

Without waiting for his answer, she got the book off the shelf.

"Did you brush your teeth?"

"Yes, see?" Opening her mouth, she displayed her small white teeth.

Dalton examined her teeth, smiling. When he was satisfied they were brushed properly, he gave her a nod and she jumped up onto the bed and patted the covers beside her.

"Sit here, Daddy." She handed him the book and looked up expectantly.

Dalton tucked the covers around her, relaxed and started reading the book.

"There once was a girl called Little Sally Snippy Snot…" he began. As he read the book, Katie Mae drifted off to sleep. He bent down to kiss her forehead.

"Sleep tight, little one," he said tenderly, "we have a big day ahead of us tomorrow."

Chapter Twenty-Seven

"Hey, Chickie. I won't keep you but a minute," Amber said into her cell phone.

"Hey, girlfriend. What's up?" Robin asked cheerfully.

"Nothing really," Amber said unconvincingly.

"Don't "nothing" me, I can hear it in your voice," Robin pushed.

"It's just that I'm at the fairgrounds and I'm scared to get out of my car."

"You can't avoid him forever," Robin said sympathetically.

"I know, but I haven't talked to him since our date. When I see his name on the caller ID, I just let the machine get it."

"You're going to have to face him sometime. This is a small town. You might as well get it over with while you're in a public setting."

"I know, but what do I say?"

Robin thought for a minute, and then she spoke into the phone. "Tell him the truth. Tell him he's a pig."

"Robin!" Amber gasped. "I can't tell a cop he's a pig! Be serious."

"Fine, don't start whining," Robin laughed. "Seriously, just let him know that he made it perfectly clear that he's not interested in kids. Remind him that you have a daughter and nothing will change that. Tell him that you two don't have anything in common. The important thing is not to let him pressure you into another date."

"Do you think he'll try?" Amber asked, sounding worried.

"Honestly? Yes I do. From what you've told me, you were pretty receptive to his advances."

"Wait, that's not fair. It was the wine," Amber said defensively.

"Hey girlfriend, I know that and you know that, but he's a guy. All he knows is that you two made out. If he thinks he has a chance of getting into your pants, then he'll try again."

"Maybe I should just go home," Amber said.

"And let him show up on your doorstep? Your best bet is to get it over with today," Robin assured her friend.

"I guess you're right," Amber said, pouting.

"You'll be fine. You're the new, strong Amber. Remember?"

"I am? Oh yes, I am." Amber laughed.

"That's better."

"Wow!" Amber said suddenly.

"What?"

"I guess they are bringing in more horses for the kids," Amber said, looking out the window. "A huge, black double cab pickup truck just pulled in with a matching horse trailer. It's all painted with the words 'Sunset Meadows' down the side of the trailer. The horse trailer has a breathtaking sunset painted all the way down the side of it. Boy is it nice."

"Sounds like your cue to get to work." Robin laughed.

"Okay, okay I'm going," Amber agreed.

"Good. I'll call you later to see how it goes."

"You'd better, Chickie! See ya." Amber clicked off

her cell phone and slowly walked toward the horse barns. As she approached, she once again saw the matching truck and trailer.

Nice setup, she thought. As she neared the truck, the driver side door opened and a man slid out of the seat.

"Hello, Ma'am," Dalton said with a deep southern drawl. "Can you tell me where I might find the groundskeeper?" He stretched, fully showing off a lean frame and well-muscled arms.

Amber let her eyes trace the contours of his arms then, pulling her eyes away, stared at the stubbled face of the handsome stranger. A low-slung black cowboy hat nearly hid his piercing blue eyes. She noted how his crisp, white t-shirt clung to his chest, lending contrast to his deeply tanned arms. Tight jeans and black cowboy boots completed the package. Amber couldn't help wondering if she was drooling.

"The groundskeeper? I'm not sure, but I think someone over there can help you," she said, finding her voice and pointing toward the barn.

"Great. Thank you much Ma'am," Dalton said and flashed a big smile. He took off his hat and ran his fingers through his thick black hair. He peered into the cab of the truck then looked back at Amber, smiling. "Just checking on the little one."

Deflated, she bit her bottom lip to keep from pouting as the realization hit her. *Shit, he's married. Of course he's married, look at him, he's a dream.*

"Are you bringing a horse for the Sunshine Riders?" Amber asked, in an attempt to cover her disappointment.

"Who, Blaze? Oh no, Ma'am, that's my niece's horse," he said motioning toward the trailer. "The Sunshine Riders, is that a riding club?"

"I guess you could call it that. This is only my second time volunteering, but what they do is let children from school come over and ride for the morning. Most of the children have special needs and it helps build their motor skills."

"That it would," Dalton said, shaking his head appreciatively. "I am sure the horses love the attention just as much as the young'uns."

Amber smiled as he spoke to her, enjoying the sound of his voice. Carefree and sexy, the southern accent rolled off his tongue, melting across her like butter. She snuck a glance, trying not to show the effect his voice had on her. She noticed the lines that creased the edges of his eyes and lent a boyish charm to his rugged good looks. As they walked, she caught his eye and he smiled at her. She bit her lip and stuffed her hands in her pockets in an attempt to hide her trembling hands.

Get a grip, she scolded herself. *He's married remember*. She was almost grateful when they reached the barn.

"Here we are," Amber said smiling.

Dalton stopped and turned toward her. His eyes met hers and just as he opened his mouth to speak, Amber saw Marty out of the corner of her eye. She cringed inwardly.

"Hello, sweetheart. Back again? Did you miss me?" Marty asked, putting his arm possessively around her.

Amber froze. What on earth was he doing? She managed to wriggle free from his grasp.

"Marty, this gentleman is looking for the groundskeeper. Do you know where he is?" she asked, flustered.

"Sure, right over there by that truck," he said, pointing in the direction from which they had just come.

"Thank you much, Sir. And thanks for your help also, Ma'am," Dalton said, tipping his hat.

"You're welcome," Amber said, flashing a smile.

Dalton turned and headed back toward his truck.

Amber was disappointed to see him go. It's probably for the best, she thought, remembering he was married.

Marty interrupted her thoughts and caught her completely by surprise when he reached out, full palm, and caressed her face.

"You know, Amber, I had a wonderful time the other night," he said, attempting to pull her in close to him.

"Marty," Amber said, pulling away from him. "I'm sorry if I gave you the wrong impression, but this is not going to happen."

"What's not?"

"Us, Marty."

"Why not? I had a great time." He reached for her hand.

"Marty that's enough," Amber said, avoiding his grasp. "We went on one date. You told me you don't like kids or dogs, both of which I have."

"Hell, Amber. I'm not looking to get married; I just want to have a little fun."

"I can't do that Marty. I don't want to get married, but I'm not going to enter into a relationship just to have fun. I have Julie to think of."

He looked puzzled. "Who?"

"Julie," she repeated, flustered. "You know, my daughter."

"Can we at least be friends?" Marty asked.

"Only if you can keep your hands to yourself," Amber said firmly.

"Not even a kiss every now and then?" he asked, puckering his lips.

Amber's eyes narrowed. "Not even a kiss, Marty."

"Okay Am, whatever you say," he reluctantly consented. "What say we go let those kids ride their horses?"

"That I will agree to," she said, walking into the barn.

Chapter Twenty-Eight

As Dalton walked away, he thought about how stunning that lady was. Her jet-black hair had been pulled back into a ponytail that playfully swished as she walked. A bright yellow tank top clung to her body, allowing him to fully appreciate her curves. A small mole rested just above her lips.

Stunning, he had thought, *just stunning*.

When their eyes had met, he smiled and she bit her lip and tucked her hands into her pockets. Dalton couldn't help notice how white her teeth were in contrast to her golden brown tan and those eyes, those dark entrancing eyes, a man could get lost in there.

Dalton walked a few paces, then realizing he hadn't gotten the raven-haired lady's name, turned around. He was disheartened to see her standing there with the tall man's hands caressing her face.

Damn, he thought, turning back toward his truck. *She is involved.*

Dalton saw a man in his mid-twenties admiring his truck and trailer. The man was clean-shaven with short brown hair.

He had tattered jeans and a loose fitting t-shirt with a 4-H logo on the pocket, which led Dalton to believe he had just found the man for whom he had been looking.

"This here your truck?" the young man asked

appreciatively as he approached.

"Yes it is," Dalton said, extending his hand and firmly shaking the younger man's hand. "Dalton Renfro."

"DJ. Nice to meet you. You must be the guy who wanted to board a horse for a few days. You can back the trailer over there," he said, pointing to a nearby field. He turned and nodded in the opposite direction. "This barn right here has plenty of empty stalls. The fair won't be coming for a few more weeks, so no one will bother it. I stay on sight, and can keep an eye on him for you."

"That'll be great," Dalton said, sounding relieved, "I would appreciate that very much."

"Will you need any hay for the horse?" the young man asked as he scratched his head and kicked at the hard ground with his boot.

"No, that's okay; I have some in the trailer. However, I would like to leave that here as well," Dalton said, gesturing toward his trailer.

"Not a problem. You can back it over there next to the barn. I'll check on you in a bit, I'm going to go over and make sure the school kids don't need anything."

"Thanks again," Dalton said, watching him walk away. He scanned the grounds, half hoping to get another glimpse of the raven-haired beauty he met earlier. Not seeing her, he turned, clicked the key and opened the front door to his pickup truck.

"Katie Mae," Dalton said tenderly. "Wake up, Darlin', we're here."

Opening her eyes, Katie Mae looked around. "Was I good, Daddy?" she asked, rubbing the sleep out of her eyes.

"Yes, Darlin', you were very good," Dalton said, hugging his daughter. "Do you want to help Daddy put the horse in the barn?"

"Okay, but I have to put my shoes on first." Katie Mae unbuckled the seat belt of her booster seat. She grabbed her shoes and hurried to put them on then stuck her feet up to Dalton. "Will you tie them for me, Daddy?"

Dalton tied the shoes then helped her out of the truck. They walked to the back of the trailer. As he opened the trailer door, they both got a surprise. There, looking quite pleased with himself, was none other than Lucky, the orange cat.

Katie Mae squealed with delight, "Lookie, Daddy! Lucky came too," she said, clapping her hands.

"I see that, Little Bit," he said, picking up the orange cat and scratching it behind the ears. "What on earth am I going to do with you? One of these days, you're going to get yourself trampled by one of those horses.

"Daddy, what's trampled?"

"Oh. Uh, stepped on," Dalton answered.

"They wouldn't trampled Lucky, they like him," she said, petting the large orange cat.

"Let me put him in the cab so he doesn't run off. Don't go into the trailer," Dalton warned.

"I'll stay right here, Daddy," Katie Mae promised.

"Hang on, baby. I have to make a quick phone call." Dalton put the cat in the truck and reached for his cell phone. He dialed the phone and hit send.

"Carl? ... Yeah we made it ok. … No, no trouble. I just wanted to let you know if you are missing anything, I found it. … Very funny Carl, I checked the trailer myself. … Not a clue. … Okay, see ya next week."

"What did Mr. Carl say that was so funny, Daddy?"

"He said Lucky must have wanted to go on vacation too."

"Yeah," Katie Mae laughed, "Lucky is on vacation too."

"One more call, honey," he said, pushing the keys on his cell phone.

"Hey Sis, I just wanted to let you know we made it… We're at the fairgrounds... Okay see you in a bit." Dalton hesitated, "Just so you know, we brought a guest with us.... Lucky, our cat... it's a long story; I'll tell you when I see you."

Chapter Twenty-Nine

"All right, I'm here. What was so big you couldn't tell me on the phone?" Robin asked excitedly as she entered Amber's house.

"Oh nothing," Amber teased.

Robin grasped Amber's shoulders with both hands and looked straight at her. "Listen, girlfriend. Don't "nothing" me. You call me up, tell me to come over the minute I get out of work and then say nothing is up! Spill it or else!"

"I just wanted to tell you about my day, that's all," Amber said nonchalantly.

"What was so big you couldn't tell me over the phone?"

Amber smiled a dreamy smile but remained silent.

Robin studied her friend. "Something is different. Your eyes twinkle. And that smile. Amber! You didn't have sex with Marty? Did you?" Robin asked, her mouth hanging open with shock.

Amber wrinkled her nose with disgust. "No, I didn't have sex with Marty! How could you think such a thing?"

"Then what?" Robin questioned. "Something happened.

Tell me!"

"I saw the most incredible man today," Amber said smiling. "A total heart stopper."

"Here in Alliance? You're kidding!" Robin said in mock disbelief.

"I know, but he wasn't from around here. He had the dreamiest southern accent."

"Really? What was his name? Where was he from?"

Amber groaned. "I don't know. I didn't get it. It doesn't matter though, he's married," Amber said, pouting.

"Amber! I'm shocked! Look at you. You, of all people, sitting here drooling over a married man," Robin said, sounding worried.

"I know it's bad, but ever since I saw him I've been having these vivid fantasies of him taking me in every room of the house," Amber purred.

"Honey, you need a man," Robin said flatly. "It's been way too long for you. We have to get you laid. I've never seen you like this."

"I know. Look at me, I'm sweating!" Amber said, fanning herself.

"That's because it's hot," Robin laughed.

"No, it's because I want to go find that guy, rip his clothes off and have my way with him over and over again." Amber was practically drooling.

"He must be fine if you're talking that way. I mean seriously, me I could understand, but you? This is not like you at all."

"Yeah, I know," Amber agreed, "but it really makes me want to move to Texas now."

"What? Why?" Robin asked confused.

"Well, this guy is southern and if that's what the guys look and sound like, then I'm going to go get me one!"

"Ah yes, the southern charm," Robin laughed. A renewed look of curiosity crossed Robin's face. "Now wait a minute. What happened to Marty?"

"Oh, him." Amber said, disappointed with the change of conversation. "After he stopped pawing me this morning, I told him it was over between us."

"Pawing you?"

"Yeah he was all over me this morning, arms around my waist, hands on my face, you name it," she said, shuddering.

"No way! What did you do?"

"I told him I would be his friend only if he promised to keep his hands to himself."

"And?"

"He agreed, but we'll see how long that lasts. Now, can we talk about my cowboy again?"

"Cowboy?"

"Oh yeah! The hat. The boots. The horse. The works!" Amber said, smiling at the memory.

"That explains it," Robin laughed. "You always did have a thing for cowboys."

Just then, the front door opened. In burst Julie followed by Kelly and Clancy.

"Hi Mom. Hi Robin," both girls said at once.

"Hey girls," Amber said, petting Clancy, who had run up to her.

"Hey Julie. Hi Kelly," Robin said, petting Clancy who tried to jump on her once he had finished with Amber. "Yuck, he smells like dog."

Amber motioned for him to get down. "Yes, he does. You need a bath young man."

"We can do it," Julie offered.

"Yeah, I can help," Kelly said eagerly.

"Okay by me," Amber said, "but only if you two promise to clean up the mess when you're done."

"You got your haircut, I really like it Julie," Robin said. "Where did you get it done?"

"Mom and I went to the mall in Port Huron Saturday, I got it done there. I also got a manicure," she said, showing off her painted nails.

"Very nice, I love the color," Robin said.

"Thanks," Julie said, then turned towards Amber. "Mom, which towels do I use?"

"They're in the utility closet, on the shelf. The two blue ones are his. The shampoo and his hair dryer are right there also."

"He lets you dry his hair?" Robin asked.

"Oh yes, he loves baths. The hardest part is getting the towel on him before he shakes and gets you soaking wet."

"Come on Kelly, let's go," Julie said, motioning for Clancy to follow.

"They get along so well," Robin said, watching the girls leave. "I see Kelly calls you "Mom" too."

"Yeah, they're inseparable and Julie calls Lana "Mom" too. We don't mind. I think those two are almost as close as you and I are," Amber said, smiling at her friend.

"Is Kelly spending the night tonight?" Robin questioned.

"No, she spent last night because Lana was doing something to get ready for her party on Saturday. Lana said something about a big surprise, but before she could tell me what it was the kids came into the room."

"Oh, I know," Robin said, clearly eager to share. She looked around and then lowered her voice to a whisper. "Apparently, Lana's brother is coming up from Kentucky to visit and he is bringing Kelly a horse for her birthday present. As a matter of fact, Lana left early today to meet him at the fairgrounds."

Amber's jaw dropped. Realization spread over Robin's face.

"Oh my God! Lana's brother…!"

"IS MY COWBOY!"

Chapter Thirty

Dalton waited patiently alongside the road for his sister's car. Glancing in the rearview mirror, he saw lights flash, letting him know of her approach. After she passed, he eased the truck onto the road and followed closely behind.

As Dalton followed Lana back to her place, he looked over at his daughter. "Now remember, Little Bit, we have to keep the horse a secret until Kelly's birthday party."

The child looked up and smiled. "I know, Daddy, and if I don't tell I get three dollars, right?"

"That's right, Darlin', one dollar for each day you don't tell," Dalton said with a wink.

"I won't tell, Daddy," she promised, petting the cat which was sleeping contently beside her.

Dalton followed as Lana turned onto the long driveway and headed toward a large farmhouse. It was exactly as he remembered it. It was made entirely of fieldstone, which was unearthed from the neighboring farmlands. Each stone had been carefully carried from the fields and painstakingly placed, forming the outside structure of the house. The stones were various shades of brown. Dalton reckoned the house was well over a hundred years old. Mauve shutters adorned the windows. Dalton knew this because he had mistakenly called them pink during his last visit, only to have Lana correct him. A matching barn sat at the rear of the property. Dalton was glad to see they had added a corral for the horse.

He pulled in behind his sister and shut off the truck. The passenger-side car door flew open, followed by Kelly running in his direction. He got out and greeted his niece.

"Uncle Dalton! I can't believe it! I haven't seen you in so long." She reached up, hugging him tightly.

"Hey sweetheart," he said, wrapping his arms around the teenage girl. He touched her wavy auburn hair and looked into her big blue eyes. "You get prettier every time I see you. You're the spitting image of your mother when she was your age. Hey, look who else is here." He pointed to the cab of the truck.

Kelly let out a gasp. "Wow, is that Katie Mae? She's getting so big!"

Dalton opened the driver's side of the large truck.

"Yes, she sure is. Come on down, Little Bit and say hello to your cousin, Kelly and your Aunt Lana." He reached up to help her down.

"Okay, Daddy, but don't let Lucky run away." Katie held Lucky tightly.

"He won't go far, Katie Mae," he assured her.

"I'm ready, Daddy," she said, reaching for him.

Dalton eased her to the ground. Katie let go of Lucky, who went off to explore his new surroundings.

"Wow, Katie Mae you sure have grown," Kelly said, reaching in to hug her little cousin.

"I'm bigger now. I'm four." She held up four fingers. "Ain't I, Daddy?"

"Yes you are, Little Bit."

Katie ran over and gave Lana a hug then got a strained look on her face.

"Daddy, I have to go to the potty!" she said, dancing from side to side, her voice urgent.

"Okay, Darlin', hang on."

Lana looked over at her daughter. "Kelly, will you take Katie Mae to the bathroom."

"Sure Mom." Kelly took the child's hand and they both hurried to the house.

"She's beautiful, Dalton," Lana said, watching the girls walk away. "And not the least bit shy."

"No, that she is not," Dalton agreed. "She's very independent, too."

"How was it traveling with her?"

"We did fine. I drove at night so she would sleep most of the way."

"Did it work?"

"For the most part it did, but after the bathroom stops she would be awake and ask a million questions."

"Bathroom breaks? That must have been difficult."

"No, actually they were quite comical," Dalton said, laughing.

Lana turned her head to look and her brother. "Comical?"

"Oh yeah, I got these walkie-talkies and gave her one. I told her if she had any trouble to let me know. The whole time she was in there she had it on and described everything in explicit detail, from her going poo poo in the potty to wiping her butt."

"Oh no," Lana laughed.

"Oh yes. Once she even told me somebody farted."

"Out of the mouths of babes," Lana said, laughing. "They tell it like it really is."

"Yes they do. Now if we can just keep her quiet about the horse until Saturday," he said, looking toward the house.

"Do you think she'll tell?"

"No," Dalton said with a yawn.

"How can you be so sure?"

"Easy." He grinned. "I bribed her, but just to make sure, we better check on them."

He put his arm around his sister as they walked toward the house.

Chapter Thirty-One

"Mom! Robin's here," Kelly sang out, as the black SUV pulled into the driveway. "It looks like Regan and Logan are following in Regan's car."

"Tim," Lana called, turning toward her husband. "Our guests are starting to arrive. How is the grill coming?"

"I'm starting it now. You worry about everything else and leave the cooking to me, love." Tim kissed her cheek and gave her a playful pat on the backside.

Dalton smiled, watching the exchange between his sister and her husband. He finished combing Katie Mae's hair and set the brush on the deck rail. "What can I do to help?"

Lana looked around. "Would you bring the coolers out of the house for me? The pop is in the fridge. If you need more ice, there is some in the big freezer in the basement." She started toward the front door.

"Pop? Sis, I'm afraid you've been gone too long. The Lana I know would never call a soda a pop." Dalton shook his head in dismay as he went to fetch the coolers. He picked up one of the coolers and headed for the back door. "Grab the door, would you, Little Bit?"

"Sure, Daddy," Katie Mae said, running toward the door.

He set down the cooler on the back deck and went

inside to retrieve another cooler. As he came back out the door, Lana was coming around to the back of the house, followed by several other people.

"Hey, little brother, I want to introduce you to some fellow Kentuckians," his sister said as they approached.

"Well if you don't mind, I would like to put this cooler full of SODAS down first." He gave her a stern look, and then smiled a mischievous grin.

"Dalton was just giving me a lecture about calling a soda a 'pop,'" Lana explained to her newly arrived guest.

"As well he should," Robin agreed, obviously admiring the bulging arms on the man standing in front of her.

Dalton set down the cooler, wiped his hands on his jeans and walked over to greet them.

"This is Robin. She works in our office," Lana said, pointing at the pretty blonde. "She and her husband are both from Kentucky. Her husband is in the military. He's away again, keeping us safe."

"Nice to meet you, Ma'am," Dalton said in a deep southern drawl.

"Nice to meet you also," Robin said.

"This is Robin's daughter, Regan." Lana said, placing her hand on the young, blonde girl's arm.

Exchanging grins with her mother, Regan reached out a hand and shook Dalton's. She blushed as she spoke. "Hello."

"And this handsome star football player is Robin's son, Logan." Lana turned to the boy and smiled. Logan was a good-looking boy. His hair was cut short and his face freshly shaven. He lacked any of the tattoos or jewelry that seemed to be more of the norm these days.

"Nice to meet you." Dalton took a step forward and clasped his hand, returning the boy's firm handshake. He glanced back at Robin. "I must say, you don't look nearly old enough to have kids this age."

"Thank you," Robin smiled. "I have a son that's even older than these two."

"Yeah, we were in Wal-Mart last month and the lady that checked us out thought she was my girlfriend," Logan said, rolling his eyes.

"Well, we are from Kentucky," Regan teased.

"Very funny, Sis," he said sarcastically.

"Okay you two, knock it off," Robin insisted.

"What part of Kentucky are you guys from?" Dalton questioned.

"Louisville," they all said at once.

"Oh, okay. I'm from Lexington."

"Ah, horse country," Robin added.

"That's a good thing too," Lana said, glancing around the yard. She lowered her voice and continued. "Dalton brought a horse up for Kelly's birthday present."

Dalton followed her glance and smiled, seeing Kelly and Katie Mae across the lawn petting Lucky.

"Sweet!" Logan said, looking around. "Where is it?"

"It's in the barn. Kelly doesn't know yet."

"How did you manage that?" Robin asked.

"Tim took Kelly with him this morning to pick up the cake and some party favors. Then Dalton went to pick up the horse from the fairgrounds. I called him when the coast was clear."

"That's great! She will be so excited," Robin smiled.

"Hey, are you guys going to stand over there all afternoon, or come have a seat in the shade?" Tim asked, motioning toward the back deck where he was standing. He had a kiss the cook apron and a matching chef's hat. In one hand was a bottle of barbeque sauce and in the other a beer.

"Hi, Mr. Storm," Regan said, waving over to him.

Tim lifted his beer in response.

"Okay, everyone into the shade, doctor's orders," Lana said, ushering them to the back deck.

"I wonder where Amber is," Lana said, glancing at her watch.

Dalton glanced up. "Who?"

"Amber, that's Julie's mom. Kelly and Julie are best friends. Kelly, be careful with her!" Lana hollered at the teen, who was swinging Katie Mae around by the arms.

"Hey Lana, when did you get a cat?" Regan asked.

"He's mine," Dalton said, looking over at Lucky.

"Do you always travel with a cat?" Robin asked.

Dalton smiled sheepishly. "Not usually. It's a long story. It was a surprise when we got here and realized the cat had come along for the ride."

Dalton followed Robin's gaze and wondered at the smile that played across her face. He was further perplexed by the mysterious grin that replaced it just before she turned and walked toward the driveway.

Chapter Thirty-Two

"Mom, everyone is already here," Julie complained.

"I'm sure Kelly hasn't opened the presents yet," Amber assured her daughter.

Julie scooped up Kelly's present and ran toward the back of the house.

"Wow, I scarcely got a "hello" out of her," Robin said as she approached Amber's car.

"She's not happy with me, she thinks we're late," Amber explained. "Is everyone here?" She casually glanced at the black truck parked in the driveway.

"If you mean is your stud here, yes, he is," Robin laughed.

"I was just wondering," Amber said defensively. Her voice softened. "Is his wife here?"

"Nope, near as I can tell he and his daughter are alone. Actually, he hasn't mentioned a wife at all," Robin said, smiling reassuringly.

Amber inhaled deeply and slowly let out her breath, then started toward the back of the house. "Hmm, there could be something to my horoscope after all."

"I thought you stopped reading it?" Robin questioned.

"I did, but I decided it couldn't hurt to start again."

"What did it say this time?"

"Something about finding common ground. It also

said luck would cross my path today. God knows I could use some of that," Amber sighed.

As they came around the back of the house, she caught sight of the man in the cowboy hat. His back was facing her yet she had no doubt that it was the same man she had seen at the fairgrounds. She ran her fingers through her jet-black hair.

"How do I look?" Amber asked in an anxious whisper.

"You look great as always," Robin whispered back.

"There you are," Lana said, drawing everyone's attention to the new arrival. "I was worried you weren't coming."

"I'm sorry we're late, Clancy took off again. We had to track him down before we could leave," Amber said as they came onto the deck.

"This is my brother, Dalton," Lana said, motioning toward Dalton. "Dalton, this is Amber."

"We've met," Dalton said, extending a hand to Amber. He shook Amber's hand, holding on longer than normal, a feat that was not lost on the onlookers.

"Oh?" Lana asked, surprised by his announcement.

"At the fairgrounds the first day I arrived. She helped me find the caretaker," Dalton said, finally releasing her hand.

"I don't know how much help I was," Amber said, blushing.

"Hey, we found him. Didn't we?" Dalton reminded her.

There was an obvious attraction between the two.

"Mom, can I open the presents now?" Kelly asked, coming onto the deck, followed by Katie Mae and Julie.

Katie Mae ran over to Dalton. "Daddy, can Kelly see our present now? I didn't tell her what it is. So I get to have three whole dollars, don't I Daddy?"

Dalton picked her up and looked her in the eyes.

"You sure do, Darlin'. You did a wonderful job at keeping our secret, but we have to wait just a little longer until Aunt Lana says it's time."

Amber watched as Dalton spoke with his daughter, noting the obvious love and affection they shared.

What a beautiful little girl, she thought to herself. *Those dimples are adorable, and those dark eyes.*

She realized at once that the features she was admiring did not come from the little girl's father. Except for the hair, maybe. It was just as dark as her father's was and nearly as dark as her own. Moving closer, she spoke to the child.

"What is your name?"

"Katie Mae Renfro," the little girl announced proudly.

Amber smiled broadly at the little girl. "Katie Mae? My name is Mae too. Only my name is Amber Mae."

"Daddy, her name is like me!" Katie Mae squealed, thrilled with the news.

"Yes it is, Darlin'," Dalton agreed, smiling at Amber.

"Okay everyone," Tim said, removing his apron and his chef's hat. "Before I work my magic on the grill, we all need to take a short walk."

"Where are we going, Dad?" Kelly asked, grinning.

"You'll see in a minute, keep your britches on."

Lana handed Tim a silk scarf.

"Okay, Kelly," her father said, rolling the scarf up. "Close your eyes."

Carefully he tied the scarf around the young girl's head, making sure her eyes were totally covered.

"All right everyone, we're ready."

Everyone followed as Tim led Kelly across the yard toward the barn. Even those who knew what the surprise was held their breath with anticipation. Upon entering the barn, Julie let out an excited gasp when she saw the horse.

"What is it?" Kelly asked anxiously, unable to

control her curiosity any longer.

"Well, Dumpling," Tim began, untying the blindfold as he spoke. "Your mother and I think it is time you get a grown up present."

Kelly opened her eyes, blinked twice and squealed with delight.

"OH MY GOD!" she screamed as she ran toward the horse. "Oh my God! Oh my God! When? Where? He's mine? Really?"

The horse laid his ears flat and backed toward the rear of the stall.

"Easy kid, you're scaring him," Lana said, trying to calm her daughter.

"Thank you so much, Mom," Kelly said, hugging her zealously, and then giving her father a peck on the cheek. "Thanks, Dad."

"You need to thank your Uncle Dalton," Lana said, turning toward her brother, who had moved close to reassure the jittery horse.

Kelly walked over to where Dalton was standing.

"Thank you Uncle Dalton, you're the greatest," she said, giving him a big hug. She reached up to pet the horse. "What's his name?"

"His name is Blaze," Dalton pointed toward the white stripe that ran from the horse's forehead to just under his nose.

"Blaze," Kelly repeated. "That's a perfect name." She carefully extended a hand to stroke the horse's nose.

"Would you like to ride him?" Dalton asked, knowing the answer.

"Oh my God! Would I? Yes!"

Amber watched as Dalton patiently put the saddle on the horse, making sure to let Kelly see how it was done. She watched the way he talked to the girl as an equal, answering all her questions in great detail. Julie was watching also. Amber could tell she was just as happy as

Kelly was about the horse, but she seemed a little quiet. Amber wondered if it was jealously over the animal, or if there might be more to it than that.

Robin moved up beside her. "A penny for your thoughts."

"I was just watching how caring he is. That's all," Amber said softly.

"So talk to him," Robin pushed.

"Oh sure," Amber laughed. "Hi, I know you're married, but you're the most gorgeous man I've ever seen in my life, so how about it?"

"Works for me," Robin said, eying the handsome man up and down. "Besides, I have it from a good source that he's not married."

Open mouthed, Amber turned to follow her friend. Catching her just outside the barn, she grabbed Robin's arm. "What do you mean he's not married?"

"Well, I just happened to bring it up in conversation to Tim, and he said Dalton's not married. His wife apparently died right after his little girl was born."

"Really?" Amber looked over her shoulder at the man leading Kelly out of the barn on the black horse.

"Hey, didn't you say your horoscope said something about common ground? Maybe that is what it meant," Robin said. "Both of you have lost a spouse, so you have something in common."

Amber looked up at her friend. She was just about to say something when a large orange cat ran out of the barn, running right in front of her. Reaching out, she grabbed hold of Robin to keep from falling.

"Are you okay?" Dalton asked. He was a few feet away, still holding onto the reins of the horse.

"I'm fine," Amber said, embarrassed. She tried to compose herself. "Lana? When did you get a cat?"

"He's not mine, he belongs to Dalton. His name is Lucky."

Robin and Amber exchanged glances.

"Are you thinking what I'm thinking?" Amber whispered to her friend.

"I'm thinking that luck just crossed your path," Robin said, rubbing the goose bumps that had just appeared on her arms.

"Yep, that is what I was thinking," Amber said softly.

Amber was nervous. The reason she had stopped reading her horoscope in the first place was because it had been so accurate, and now this. She shook her head. No, she wasn't going to let this scare her, it was just a cat and not even a black one. Besides, the horoscope implied it would be a good thing. Actually, the last time her horoscope had been just as accurate, it had said it would be a good thing also. Tragedy would be a blessing in disguise, it had read. The same night Jeff died.

Yes, she thought, knowing what Jeff had been planning, *it really was a blessing.*

"Earth to Amber," Robin said, bringing her back to the present. "You're missing it."

Amber looked up to see Dalton helping Julie onto the black horse. Julie waved at her mom. This was the first time she rode a horse, and she looked excited.

Dalton handed the reins to Kelly, suggesting she lead the horse for a few minutes to allow her friend to become accustomed to riding the big animal. As Amber watched Julie being led around on the black horse, once again she was reminded of her early childhood. She saw herself on a painted horse; her mother was at her side.

"You look a million miles away," Dalton said.

Amber looked up into the most magnificent blue eyes she had ever seen. She blushed, not having noticed him coming up beside her. "I guess I was day dreaming."

"A penny for your thoughts," he said, reaching into his pocket and retrieving a shiny penny.

Amber was tempted to take the penny. It was the

second time today she had been offered one.

"It was nothing, really," she said, looking over at Julie, sighing with a hint of melancholy. "Just a memory from my childhood."

"Now I'm really intrigued. Please tell me," he pressed, seeming genuinely interested.

Amber couldn't resist his sincere blue eyes, not to mention his boyish grin.

"Okay, you asked for it, but I can promise you it's very corny. When I was a little girl, I used to ride a neighbor's painted horse while my mom led it around the trails. Mom was scared to ride, so she would never get on a horse herself, even though the neighbors had lots of them, but every day she would take me over there and lead me around on that old painted horse. That was so long ago." Her eyes took on a faraway look, remembering things she had lost. "I haven't been on a horse since she died. I was about Julie's age when Mom passed away. I was just thinking of that and wishing she was still here, but that was just wishful thinking."

She inhaled deeply, fighting back tears that threatened.

Dalton stared at the woman standing beside him. Once again, her beauty enthralled him. Her raven hair, which had been pulled back when he had first seen her, was now draping across her shoulders. A red t-shirt hugged her body, clinging to her rounded breasts. The neck scooped down in a v, showing just a hint of cleavage.

He wasn't sure what to say. He could tell she was on the verge of tears. He regretted pushing her to talk about a memory that bothered her so much, he wanted to find a way to lighten the mood, but more than anything he wanted to put his arms around her to comfort her. He didn't know why, but he felt drawn to her and even though he was pretty sure she was involved with the man at the fairgrounds, he still couldn't take his eyes off her.

When he had seen her arrive alone with her daughter, he had been pleased. Once again, he found himself wondering what the relationship was between this beautiful lady and the tall, scrawny man at the horse barn. He promised himself he would ask his sister when he had the chance.

Dalton watched as her eyes followed Julie and Kelly taking turns on the horse. She was radiant as she relished in their joy. He was happy see the threat of tears had passed.

She turned to him and smiled, her eyes beaming. "I haven't seen them have this much fun in months."

"Lana said Kelly and one of her friends was having some trouble at school. Was that your daughter?" Dalton asked, frowning toward the girls.

"Yes, Julie and Kelly have had it pretty rough this last four and a half months," Amber said solemnly as her smile left her.

He debated asking, but he wanted to know why. "Do you mind if I ask why?"

She looked up at him, obviously weighing her answer, her eyes searching his. So much time passed, he wondered if she was even going to answer. Finally, a decisive look crossed her face and her shoulders relaxed. She took a deep breath then began with her story.

"Several months ago my husband, Jeff, was killed in an accident."

"I'm sorry to hear that," Dalton said sincerely. It sure wasn't the answer he had expected to hear.

"Don't be," Amber said. "The day of his funeral I was served with divorce papers."

"That must have been difficult," Dalton offered, secretly wondering what kind of fool would ever let go of such an exquisite raven-haired beauty.

"It gets better," she said with a fake laugh. "Unbeknownst to me, Jeff also had a girlfriend – a pregnant one at that. Right after the funeral in the parking lot, she decided to introduce herself to me and everyone else standing around. It was a grand scene. It's a small town, things get around, and that is why the girls are being teased so badly."

Dalton was stunned. How could anyone in his right mind cheat on such a lovely lady? She was hurting, he could tell, but he admired her strength. The fact that she could stand there without shedding a tear and tell a complete stranger the anguish and humiliation which she had so recently endured told him she was all cried out. The grieving period was over; he had been there before, yes, this he understood. He had loved his wife and mourned her, but for him, too, the grieving period was now over.

"I lost my wife, also. Mary Katherine died almost four years ago, right after Katie Mae was born." He wasn't sure why he felt the need to tell this woman that he had just met about Mary Katherine, he rarely spoke of her, but there was a need to connect with this woman on a deeper level than just casual friendship. He couldn't explain it, but he was afraid if he didn't bond with her now it might never happen.

"Did she die in childbirth?" Amber asked softly.

"No. She died four months after Katie Mae was born. We had been married for seven years before she got pregnant with Katie Mae. We had almost given up hope of having children, but then it happened. Everything was fine at first, except for the morning sickness – it never let up. Mary Katherine was very tired all the time and losing weight even though she was pregnant. During her fifth month we found out the reason." Dalton looked at Amber, his voice shaky, but he continued with his story.

"Mary Katherine was diagnosed with bone cancer.

She was too far along to terminate her pregnancy, not that she would have if given the choice. She wanted a child more than anything. She was willing to risk her life for that of our baby. I pleaded with her, I told her we could adopt, but she refused to listen. She refused chemotherapy until after she had Katie Mae and by then it was too late. Katie Mae never knew her mother, but someday I hope she'll realize just how much her mother loved her." Looking across the yard at his daughter playing with Robin and Lana, Dalton shuddered at the sudden realization that if his wife had chosen life he would not have Katie Mae.

He looked down at the woman he had only just met and wondered at their willingness to share such personal things. Things he had not spoken of in so many years. He saw the tears in her eyes and felt the strange connection they seemed to share.

He caught his breath as she enclosed his hand with her own. She held it firmly and he gripped hers tightly in return. In silence, he held onto the hand not wanting to let it go. He took a deep breath; not wanting to lose control. He hadn't talked to anyone this openly in years. Why now? Why with this beautiful stranger?

Chapter Thirty-Three

"You two sure looked cozy," Robin remarked, as Amber approached.

"We were only talking," Amber said innocently.

"Don't play coy with me, lady! I saw you two holding hands," Robin said, narrowing her eyes. Smiling, she changed her tactic. "Come on Amber, tell me."

"What? There's nothing to tell. We were just talking."

"Okay," Robin said, sounding flustered. "What did you two talk about?"

"I told him about Jeff," Amber said simply.

"You didn't!" Robin said. "Amber, I don't want to tell you how to start a relationship, but talking about your dead asshole husband during your first meeting doesn't actually sound like the right thing to say."

"Normally I would agree with you, Chickie, but for some reason I felt I had to tell him. Besides it wasn't really our first meeting, right?"

"What did he do when you told him?"

Amber looked over at Dalton, who was talking to Tim and Logan, catching his eye; she returned his smile then looked back at Robin.

"It's more what he didn't do, Robin."

"What do you mean?" Robin asked, confused.

"He didn't look at me with pity. He looked at me as if

he had been there, like he understood what I had been going through." Amber sighed. "After that, he told me about his wife and how she had died after his little girl was born."

"Wow, this is serious stuff," Robin said, wide-eyed. "Tim told me he doesn't talk about her. Not even to Lana."

"It was amazing Robin," Amber gushed. "When I was talking to him, I felt as though I've known him forever. Like I could tell him anything,"

"Well, girlfriend, I think you're going to get your chance," Robin said, elbowing her friend. "Here he comes. I think I'll go and see how the girls are getting along with the horse."

"I hope your friend didn't leave on my account," Dalton said as he approached.

Amber looked over her shoulder at her retreating friend. "I'm sure she did."

Dalton pretended to sniff his underarms, and then shrugged his shoulders. "I know it's hot, but I did use deodorant this morning."

Amber laughed. She enjoyed his boyish charm.

Katie Mae ran up onto the porch, holding herself.

"I got to go potty," she said, making a face.

"Ok, Little Bit, hurry up," Dalton said, opening the door for her.

"She is adorable," Amber said watching the child run inside. "Does she need any help?"

Dalton took a seat beside Amber. "Nah, she's fine."

"Was it difficult traveling up here with her?" Amber asked conversationally.

"No, not at all. We traveled at night, so she slept most of the way. She only had to stop for a couple bathroom breaks."

"I would have been afraid to let her go in alone."

"Oh, I had that worked out before I left. I bought

walkie¬talkies." He grinned. "She had one and I had one, she talked to me the whole time."

Amber smiled, envisioning the kinds of conversations they would have had. "The whole time?"

Dalton changed his voice to sound like Katie Mae. "I'm in the bathroom, Daddy. I'm putting the paper on the toilet, Daddy. I'm going poo poo, Daddy. Ewww somebody farted, Daddy." He rolled his eyes.

"Oh no," Amber bit at her lip, suppressing a smile. "What did you do?"

"What could I do?" Dalton shrugged. "I just told her to hurry."

Amber felt as though she had known this easygoing man all her life. She was happier right then at that moment than she could ever remember being.

Katie Mae came running out of the house holding her pants up with both hands. "Could you button my pants, Daddy?"

"Sure, Little Bit, did you go potty?" Dalton asked as he snapped shut her pants.

"Yeah, I pooped," she replied proudly.

Dalton and Amber exchanged smiles.

"Daddy, they won't let me ride Blaze," Katie Mae pouted.

"Well, its Kelly's horse, honey. She wants to ride him now," Dalton explained.

"Everybody else is riding him. Aunt Lana said I'm too little." Lucky ran onto the porch and Katie Mae ran off to pet the orange cat.

Amber couldn't help notice the change in Dalton's mood. The expression on his face was not the boyish one she found so charming. He seemed agitated.

"Amber, will you excuse me? I think Katie Mae needs to go ride a horse," he said, getting up.

"Is there a problem?" Amber asked, wondering what had caused his sudden mood change.

Dalton sat back down, looked at her and then toward where his sister was standing near the horse.

"Lana doesn't always agree with the way I'm raising Katie Mae. She tried to get me to give her Katie Mae after my wife died. She didn't think I was capable of raising her. She didn't seem to understand I needed her with me, she was all I had left."

The pain on his face drew Amber to him. She put her hand on his.

"That doesn't sound like the Lana I know. Maybe it wasn't that she didn't think you weren't capable, maybe she thought you were hurting too much to know what the baby needed," Amber said, trying to make sense of what he had told her. She smiled. "You know what I think? I think that if anyone ever had any doubts, all they would have to do is to watch you two together. Anyone can see that you adore each other. She's a wonderful, well-mannered child, Dalton. You're doing a wonderful job of raising her."

"Thank you, Amber. I appreciate you saying that," he said, kissing her on the hand. He stood up. "It's been nice talking to you."

"I've enjoyed it also," Amber said, getting up to leave. She was sorry that she had made plans to go out with Robin.

"Are you leaving?" Dalton asked, frowning. "We haven't even eaten yet."

Seeing the disappointment on his face almost made her change her mind. The regret was plain in her voice. "I know, but I made plans with Robin for later."

"Well, you two lovely ladies have fun and try not to get into too much trouble," he said with a wink and a flash of his boyish grin.

Amber almost melted at the sight.

Maybe I should cancel my plans with Robin and stay here, she thought. Just as she was about to suggest just that, Katie Mae interrupted.

"Daddy, can I ride now?" she asked impatiently.

"Sure you can, Darlin'," he said, heading toward her.

Why didn't you say something? she chided herself as she watched him go. *You just let the man of your dreams slip right through your fingers without even trying. Oh well, if he had been interested he would have asked me out, not waited for me to make the first move. But then, why would he, you already told him you had other plans?*

Amber longed to call after him, beg him to stay so they could get to know each other better, but she didn't, instead she just watched as he walked away.

Dalton stormed across the yard. How dare Lana not allow Katie Mae to ride the horse he just brought?

"Daddy, you're going too fast," a little voice cried from behind him.

Dalton turned to look at Katie Mae who was running to keep up. He reached down and scooped her up.

"I'm sorry, Sunshine," he said, kissing her on the forehead. "Come on, I'll give you a lift." He lifted her to his shoulders to carry her the rest of the way.

"Katie Mae would like a turn on the horse," he said without preamble as they got to the field where everyone was standing.

"Okay," Lana said.

Dalton stopped short. *Okay? She agreed?*

"What's wrong?" Lana asked.

"Oh… well it's just… well... Katie Mae told me that you said she was too little," Dalton stammered, feeling foolish.

"I only said that I thought she shouldn't ride by herself without you near," Lana said softly. "I don't know horses, Dalton. I wasn't about to put her up on it without you being around."

Dalton felt his face redden. "I'm sorry, I just

thought…"

"You thought I was trying to tell you how to raise your daughter again," she said, finishing his sentence. Lana touched his arm and smiled. "Do me a favor, little brother, put her on the horse, we can talk later."

Dalton was embarrassed. Without realizing it, he had been waiting for a chance to mince words with his sister. Ever since Katie Mae was born, she had been insisting he allow her to raise the child. He had thought for sure this was her way of staying in control.

As he led Katie Mae around the field, it dawned on him that the reason Lana had wanted to take the baby was not that she thought he wasn't capable of caring for her; it was because she thought it was in Katie Mae's best interest.

Dalton felt awful. All these years he had let the pain of losing Mary Katherine get in his way of seeing the truth. How could he have thought Lana was trying to hurt him when all she ever wanted was to help? Why hadn't he been able to see that before? Why only now? How had Amber seen it so clearly? Amber!

He turned to look for her, but she was gone. She was gone and he would be leaving tomorrow. He had planned to ask her out tonight since he would be leaving the next evening. But what chance did they have anyway? It was not as if he could stay. Still, he must admit he was pleased she was not leaving to meet the man from the barn.

If only we didn't live so far apart, he thought with a sigh. *Then, just maybe, there would be a chance.*

He looked again in the direction where he last saw her. If only.

Chapter Thirty-Four

Amber wiped the sweat from her face, slowed her pace and reined in the dog. "It's too hot to run this morning, Clancy."

Passing the bank, the readout put the temperature at ninety-two degrees. "Wow, 92 at nine a.m. that's not a good sign."

Clancy took her slowing down as a chance to explore and stopped to sniff a tree.

"I see you're not into the run either, huh boy?"

The dog looked up at the sound of her voice then continued his investigating.

"Let's take the short route." She turned toward the park and continued walking, grateful for the shade of the big trees that lined the city park. Her heart leapt when she caught a glimpse of a black truck.

That looks like Dalton's, she thought, scanning the park.

Sure enough, Dalton was pushing Katie Mae on the swings.

"Let's go through the park, boy," Amber said, heading in their direction.

God he has a great ass, she thought, looking at his tight jeans as she made her way towards the man and his child.

Katie Mae and Dalton seemed to be deep in

conversation, so Amber decided to wait to announce her arrival not wanting to interrupt them.

"I wish Miss Maggie was here, Daddy."

"I know, me too, Little Bit," Dalton said, pushing the swing.

"I miss her, Daddy."

"I miss her too, Darlin'."

"I love her, Daddy."

"I know Darlin', I love her too. Don't you worry; she'll be home when we get there."

Amber couldn't believe what she was hearing.

How could I have been so blind? Of course he has a girlfriend. Someone as great as Dalton would have to be gay not to have one, but what about at Lana's yesterday? Was it just my imagination? I thought we clicked. Was I just imagining it? Without realizing it, she had loosened her grip on Clancy's leash. Seeing a squirrel, he was off.

"Clancy!" Amber yelled after him.

Dalton turned around to see what all the commotion was about. Seeing Amber, his face lit up.

"Why hello," he said in his sexy southern drawl.

"Hi," Amber said, unsure of what to say. "I saw your truck and thought I'd stop by and say hi."

"I'm glad you did," Dalton said reassuringly.

Katie Mae jumped off her swing and ran toward Amber.

"Hi Katie Mae," she said smiling.

Amber was confused for a moment, and then realized what she meant. "No, you're Katie Mae, I'm Amber Mae."

"Amber Mae," Dalton repeated smoothly. "I sure like the sound of that."

Clancy, apparently realizing he was never going to climb the tree to get the squirrel, came running back to see what was going on. He immediately started licking Katie Mae's face.

She squealed with delight. "A puppy!"

"He's not a puppy," Amber said, grabbing hold of his leash. "He's just Clancy."

"Hiya, boy," Dalton said, kneeling to pet the rambunctious dog.

"Be careful. He doesn't really take to men." She watched as Clancy seemed to smile from all the attention. "That's strange; he's usually standoffish when it comes to strange men."

"It must be the clothes. He probably smells the horses and the cat," Dalton suggested.

"I guess you're right," Amber agreed.

"Can I walk him?" Katie Mae asked hopefully.

"You have to hold on real tight," Amber said, handing her the leash. She watched in amazement as Clancy stayed right by the child's side as they walked away. "I would never have believed it if I hadn't seen it for myself."

"She has a way with animals," Dalton agreed. He beamed with pride. "You ought to see her with her horse. It's as gentle as a lamb with her."

They walked over and sat on top of the picnic table, enjoying the comfort of the shade.

"You run?" He asked, eyeing the sweat rings on her shirt.

"Every morning." It was the first time she became aware of her appearance and how awful she must smell.

"I do too. I haven't since I've been up here though, I didn't want to burden anyone with Katie Mae while I was out running. I was going to go this morning, but she was awake early and I didn't want her to wake everyone else, so we came here instead. It's a good thing too, or we wouldn't have gotten to see you again," he said with a wink.

It must be fate, she thought, wishing she had read her horoscope this morning. "When are you heading back home?"

A look of disappointment crossed his face. "We're leaving this afternoon."

"I guess you'll be glad to get home." Amber's heart sank. She wanted to ask him about this Maggie person, but didn't dare. What business was it of hers? She had no claim on him.

"I'll be glad to get back home, but I also found a reason for wanting to stay," he said, staring pointedly at her.

Amber felt herself leaning in toward him, unable to resist. His eyes were the kindest, bluest eyes she had ever seen. So trusting, she could almost lose herself in them.

Dalton leaned in and kissed Amber fully. He parted his lips slightly, sending his tongue into her waiting mouth. Their tongues circled each other in a snake-like dance. Dalton's arms encircled her, pulling her into him. Amber reached for him in return. Her hands ran through his hair. Her body melted under his touch, dampness escaped from within her. Their breathing was heavy, their need tremendous.

"Eeewww!" came a high pitch squeal.

Dalton released his grip on Amber and looked down into the wrinkled face of Katie Mae.

Amber felt her face flush. She wondered how long the little girl had been watching them.

"What's so eeww?" Dalton asked, composing himself.

"You two were kissing," she said, handing Clancy's leash to Amber.

"So?" Dalton asked.

"So, I'm going to tell Miss Maggie!" Katie Mae said, and started running.

"You better not!" Dalton cried out and chased after her.

Amber was floored. Not only was there a Maggie, but

he didn't want her to know about her. She held onto Clancy, who was trying to join in on the chasing game.

"Come on Clancy," she said, pulling him toward her as she started walking away from the man with the trusting blue eyes. How could she have let herself be taken in like that? He was a player, just like Jeff. He had a woman back home and he wanted to have some fun here, too. Well, she would never allow herself to be used like that again. She cringed as she heard Dalton call out her name. She forced herself to keep walking. She had fallen for a loser once, she would not, no, she could not allow herself to be used like that again.

Tears streamed down her face as she hurried down the street away from the only happiness she had known in a very long time. Once again, Amber felt betrayed.

Chapter Thirty-Five

"I don't know what happened," Dalton insisted. "I turned around and she was nearly running to get away. I called her name and she didn't even turn around. No goodbye or anything!" He paced the floor in obvious distress.

"I've known Amber for years. It doesn't sound like her. What was going on before she left?"

Dalton shifted uncomfortably in his chair, staring at his hands. "I um… well, I kissed her."

Her eyes widened. "Did she kiss you back?"

"She didn't pull away if that is what you're asking," Dalton said defensively.

"Well, I didn't think she would be repulsed," Lana said, smiling at her brother. "You're good looking; it runs in the family you know." She patted at her hair.

Dalton let down his defensiveness. "So why did she run off like that?"

"Why is it bothering you so much? You're leaving tonight anyway."

"I don't know Lana. I can't explain it. For some reason I feel drawn to her. I don't know her, but I want to know her. I need to know her," Dalton said. "Do you believe in love at first sight? I have been lonely for so long, but with her, it's as if I've known her forever. I want to be with her, to hold her, to protect her…"

His voice trailed off as he pictured Amber sitting on the picnic table just before he had kissed her. She was breathtaking. He even found the beads of sweat on her upper lip sexy, and those eyes, so dark, so inviting. He wanted her. He wanted her more than he had ever wanted anyone, even Mary Katherine.

How could that be? Why did he need her so? Maybe it was because they had both lost someone they had loved. They seemed to have so much in common.

Lana took both his hands in hers, interrupting his thoughts. "Dalton, give her some time. She's been through a lot these past few months."

"I know. She told me her husband was killed."

Lana got up and poured them both a fresh cup of coffee. "Did she tell you anything else?"

"She said she got served with divorce papers and that he had a pregnant girlfriend on the side."

"Did she tell you she got served with the divorce papers as she was leaving for his funeral? Or that the pregnant girlfriend decided to make herself known in the parking lot right after the funeral? The poor thing never knew what hit her."

"I can see why she would want to be cautious," Dalton said, taking a drink of coffee.

"The girls are having such a rough time, too. We live in a small town Dalton. People talk. Those girls have been teased so much. Hell, I'm not sure what to expect when school starts back next month. Kelly has already said she's not going back," Lana said, sipping her coffee.

"Have you thought about moving?" Dalton asked.

"I hadn't until you made the suggestion," she said.

"You mean you have been considering it?" he said, not bothering to hide his excitement.

"I said I was thinking about what you had said," she said cautiously.

Dalton was elated. Ever since he had realized Lana

was only looking out for his and Katie Mae's best interest he had found out just how much he missed his sister.

"I shouldn't even be telling you this, but Tim has contacted a head hunter."

"A what?" Dalton laughed.

"It's kind of like an agent. You send them your résumé and they do all the leg work for you," Lana explained. "I know I can get on at any of the hospitals in Louisville. We're just trying to see how hard it would be for Tim to find something."

"That would be great," Dalton said, smiling ear to ear. "I know Mom and Dad would love having you guys closer."

"And you?" Lana questioned.

Dalton had expected this question. He looked at his sister. "Lana, growing up we were always close. You always looked out for me. After Mary Katherine died, I lost it. Somehow, I felt as though it was my fault, that I should have insisted she start chemotherapy earlier. Then, when you offered to take Katie Mae, I took it as a slap in the face. That you didn't think I was capable of caring for her, that I might screw that up also. I realize now that was not the case; you were only trying to help. I miss you, Sis, I would love you to be closer. Besides, Katie Mae needs to know her aunt."

"Well, don't you get your hopes up yet, there are a lot of things to consider," she reminded him.

"I realize that, Sis, but considering is half the battle," he said with a wink.

"You could always move up here," Lana reminded him. "Then you could find out if there is any chance of a relationship with Amber."

Dalton grimaced. He would truly love to establish a relationship with Amber, but could he really move? Could he leave behind everything for which he had worked so hard? And if he did, how could he be so sure Amber would want him here? She hadn't even said goodbye to him when she left.

As much as he wanted to explore a relationship with Amber, he knew in his heart there was no way he could leave his beloved Kentucky; his hopes were there, his dreams were there and yes, even though she was dead, Mary Katherine was there. He could not leave. If only Amber lived closer, there may have been a chance. Then things might have been different.

The realization felt like a knife stabbing him in the heart. Dalton had just concluded that there was no hope of a relationship with the woman who had stolen his heart with just one glance.

Chapter Thirty-Six

Amber knocked on Robin's door. Oh let her be here, she thought. She peaked through the window then knocked again. Still there was no answer. Damn.

"Come on Clancy," she said, turning to leave. Just as they stepped off the porch, the front door opened.

Robin answered the door in a red silk robe. Her hair was up in a towel. "Geez girlfriend, can't a person take a shower to cool off on a hot day?"

Amber hurried back onto the porch. "I'm sorry. I didn't realize you were in the shower."

Robin looked at Clancy, who was panting from the heat, put up her hand and shook her head. "Oh no you don't, if you're here asking me to walk you can forget it." She looked over at the thermometer then added, "I just got out of the shower and I'm still sweating. Now come in before you melt."

"Clancy too?"

"Sure, why not? He looks like he's about to drop." Robin went to the cupboard, pulled out a bowl and filled it with water. As she placed it on the floor, she looked up at Amber.

"What do you want to drink?"

"Some water will be fine."

Robin cocked an eyebrow at her friend. "Bowl or glass?"

"It doesn't matter," Amber said absentmindedly.

She studied her friend as she dropped ice into the glass. "It was supposed to be a joke. Earth to Amber."

"What?"

Robin reached up and felt Amber's forehead. "Hey you, how long have you been out in this heat?"

"I'm not sure. Why?"

"Did you run?" Robin asked, sounding worried.

"Yeah, for a bit, but then I decided it was too hot."

"You should have realized that before you started," Robin scolded.

"I'm okay," Amber assured her friend.

"Well, drink some water. You're showing some signs of heat exhaustion."

"I'm fine," Amber repeated, watching Clancy lap up the water.

"You don't look fine," Robin countered. "As a matter of fact, you look as though you could cry any minute."

At that, Amber burst into tears.

"Okay, girlfriend. Let's have it." Robin took a seat at the small white table. She took the towel off her head and ran her fingers through her wet hair while waiting for Amber to begin speaking.

Tears trailed down Ambers face. She reached for a napkin from the table to blow her nose.

"I am so tired of being so emotional," she sniffed.

"Care to tell me what brought this on?" Robin asked. "This must be about more than just the heat."

"Clancy and I cut our walk short because of it. As we were coming past the park I thought I saw Dalton's pickup truck."

"And?"

"I looked and sure enough he was there pushing Katie Mae on the swings. I walked over to say hi and overheard them talking. I didn't want to be rude, so I waited for them to finish."

Robin took a drink of her water and waited for Amber to continue.

"Katie Mae was talking about a woman called Maggie and how much she missed and loved her and Dalton agreed with her. He said he loved her too." With that, she gave way to fresh tears.

"Maybe you were mistaken," Robin said. "You said yourself you only heard half of the conversation."

"That's what I thought at first, because when he saw me he seemed happy I was there."

"So what changed?"

"Well, everything was great," Amber said through fresh sobs. "Katie Mae took Clancy for a walk around the park."

Robin interrupted her. "Wait…you let that tiny little girl walk the beast?"

"He was great with her and walked right beside her," Amber said defensively.

"Clancy?" Robin asked, looking over at the dog that was sprawled out in front of the fan, tongue hanging from his mouth, panting furiously.

"I know, but he was just fine," Amber said, wanting to get on with her story. "Dalton and I sat on the picnic table and watched them."

"And?"

"We kissed," Amber closed her eyes inhaling deeply at the memory.

"It must have been some kiss," Robin said, her eyebrows rising.

"It was incredible."

"Okay, so he's a great kisser. What's the problem? There's obviously chemistry between you two," Robin asked.

"I thought so, too. It was so hot and I don't mean the temperature. I think we would have done it right there if Katie Mae hadn't came back."

"Shit! And me without a video camera," Robin teased.

Amber wiped at her eyes and forced a smile. "Yeah, right."

"So then what?"

"Katie Mae said she was going to tell Maggie and Dalton got upset and ran after her," Amber finished.

"That does seem fishy," Robin agreed. "So then what did you do?"

"I left and we came here," Amber said, finishing her water.

"Amber, you really should have given him a chance to explain."

"What's to explain? It's obvious Dalton is a player. He's no better than Jeff," she said, wiping the new stream of tears. "He has a girlfriend back home and he wants some action on the side. Why are all men pigs?"

Robin shook her head and wiggled her finger at her friend. "Now now, girlfriend. We've been through this before. Not all men are pigs. Some are assholes remember?"

They both laughed.

"You're so lucky," Amber sighed. "Jack is a good man."

"Yes he is," Robin agreed. "My soul mate."

"I want a soul mate. I want someone who looks at me the way Jack looks at you. Like I thought Dalton was looking at me," she said as she released the last of her tears.

Chapter Thirty-Seven

Dalton pulled into the driveway, glad to be home. Katie Mae unbuckled her seatbelt and waited for him to help her down.

"Yay, we're home!" she said triumphantly.

Dalton opened the door, got out and stretched. He helped Katie Mae down out of the truck then went to the back of the trailer.

"Come on out you rotten cat, you're done." He opened the door and watched as the large orange cat ran from the trailer.

"I heard you had a visitor," Maggie laughed as she came up behind him.

"Miss Maggie!" Katie Mae said, running to hug her. "I missed you!"

"I missed you too, Angel," she said, reaching down to hug the child.

"Hello Maggie," Dalton smiled as he hugged the robust lady. "How was your trip?"

"It was incredible. Sally and I went to several shows and we ate way too much." She shook her head and rubbed her plump belly, smiling at the memory.

"Did you bring me anything?" Katie Mae asked excitedly.

"I sure did, little one," Maggie said, patting her on the head.

"Why don't we go sit on the porch," Dalton suggested.

"I have a better idea," Maggie said with a wink. "Let's go inside and I'll whip up some pancakes while you two tell me about your trip."

Dalton and Katie Mae followed her inside and sat at the table while Maggie busied herself at the gas stove.

"I had the batter ready. I figured you two would be along directly." She picked up a bowl and poured batter onto the now warm griddle. "So, how was the drive, any problems?"

Dalton shook his head. "Nope, not a one."

"And the walkie-talkies?" Maggie prodded.

Dalton could tell she suspected something was amiss. He forced a smile. "Like a charm."

"I got to talk on them when I went potty," Katie Mae offered.

"Is that a fact?" Maggie laughed.

"Did Kelly like the horse?"

"Did she ever! She took right to riding. She's a natural," Dalton said proudly.

"Well that doesn't surprise me," Maggie said, flipping a pancake and eyeing him closely. "It runs in the family. How are Lana and Tim doing?"

"Really good, and you know, I think they actually might move back down here," Dalton said, beaming.

"Really?"

"Yeah, apparently Tim has résumés floating around and if he gets an offer they will consider it."

The woman set a plate of pancakes in front of the child. "Why the change, I thought they were happy there?"

Dalton pulled Katie Mae's plate over in front of him and started sawing at the pancakes.

"Seems like Kelly and her friend Julie are having some trouble with some other kids and Lana is getting tired of the small town B.S.," Dalton said, sliding the plate back over to Katie Mae.

"That's a shame. Children can be so cruel. How will Kelly's moving away affect her friend? What did you say her name was? Julie?"

Dalton didn't answer. He hadn't thought about that. He had been so happy at the possibility of Lana moving back that he hadn't given any thought to the consequences. That poor girl had been through so much. How would she handle losing her best friend? He was only half listening to the conversation between Maggie and Katie Mae, but was jolted back to the conversation by Katie Mae's announcement.

"Oh does he?" Maggie set a plate of pancakes in front of him with a smug grin on her face.

"I do not have a girlfriend," Dalton said, giving Katie Mae a stern look.

Maggie turned and poured more batter onto the griddle.

"He kissed her so much," Katie Mae snickered as she took another bite.

"I kissed her one time," Dalton said, defending himself.

"Sounds like some trip," Maggie chuckled and raised an eyebrow. "First, you convince your sister who drives you crazy to move back here, then, you make out in front of your daughter."

"I did not make out. I simply kissed the woman." Dalton stabbed at his pancakes. Catching one, he shoved it into his mouth. He was getting agitated and was wishing that Katie Mae hadn't said anything to Maggie. He loved Maggie, but she could be relentless when it came to finding him a wife.

"They were using their tongues," Katie Mae said, making a face.

"Oh really?" Maggie said, turning off the stove.

"It was really yuck," Katie Mae giggled.

Dalton pushed his half-finished plate away.

"If I'm going to get this kind of abuse I'm going to go to work," he said, getting up and pushing his chair back into place. "Enjoy your breakfast ladies." He stormed out of the room.

Jeez, all of this nonsense over a little kiss, Dalton thought shaking his head, *and for the record, it wasn't yuck.*

He put on his work boots and went outside. Someone had already taken the truck away to unhook the horse trailer. As he walked toward the barn, he pictured himself and Amber on the picnic table. The softness of her touch, the fullness of her lips; he pictured them together, his tongue exploring her mouth. He had wanted her so desperately. If they hadn't been in a public place, he was sure she would have been open to more. She was so sexy, so incredibly lovely and then she was gone.

Why, he thought heading toward the barn. *What on earth have I done wrong?*

Chapter Thirty-Eight

Amber lay on the couch, mindlessly flipping through the channels. The phone rang, but once again, she let the answering machine answer it. She lay there waiting for the outgoing message to finish, then waited for the voice on the other end.

"Amber?" Dalton's voice called out. "Hello, are you there? Listen, I'm not sure what happened that day at the park, but if I did something wrong, I'm sorry. Please call me. I can't stop thinking about you. Please pick up if you are there."

There was a long pause, followed by a click and the sound of a dial tone.

Why? she thought. *Why won't he leave me alone? I don't want to be hurt anymore. I just want to be left alone.*

Once again, the phone rang; once again, Amber let the machine pick it up.

"Mom? Hello, Mom are you there?" called Julie's worried voice.

Amber reached for the phone lying on the floor in front of her. "Yes, baby. I'm here," she said softly. Amber knew she had not been herself in days and even though she knew how worried Julie was, she could not shake the funk that had settled over her like a dark cloud.

"How come you let the machine pick up? You never used to do that."

"I was busy. I didn't get to it in time," Amber lied.

"Mom, Lana wants to know if you want to come over for dinner. They're cooking on the grill tonight."

"No honey, I don't feel like going anywhere today," Amber answered.

"Mom, you haven't felt good for days. Are you sure you're okay?"

"Honey, I'm fine," Amber insisted. "I'm just a little tired that's all. I'm going to go lay down for a while. Enjoy your dinner. I love you baby."

Amber switched off the phone before Julie could object. She retrieved the remote then once again flipped through the channels. Once more, the phone rang; once more, the answering machine did its job.

"Amber, it's Robin. Pick up! I know you're home. Amber, pick up the damn phone!"

Amber waited for the machine to click then resumed her surfing. She didn't feel like talking to anyone. Hell, she didn't feel like doing anything at all. Clancy scratched at the door wanting to be let inside; still Amber continued to lie on the couch.

Her mind wandered back to the day of Kelly's party. She had liked the tall, handsome stranger. The way he looked at her, the longing in his eyes, the way he had held her hand as though he was afraid to let her go. She loved his smile, his perfect white teeth and the incredible blue of his piercing eyes. She remembered the way he looked at her while they sat on the picnic table at the park the next day and the way his mouth felt on hers. His tongue searching out hers, wanting her so desperately.

Then she remembered Katie Mae saying she was going to tell Maggie.

Why? she thought, *why can't I get him out of my mind and more yet, why can't I get him out of my heart?*

The door opened and Clancy ran in, jumped up and started licking the tears that had moistened her cheeks.

"Oh Clancy, get down," she said, pushing him away.

Robin stormed in and stood directly in front of Amber. "Okay girlfriend, spill it," she demanded.

"Spill what? What's up?" Amber asked, sitting up.

"I haven't heard from you in days, you won't answer your phone, I just got a phone call from Lana saying Julie is crying her eyes out because she's so worried about you. So you tell me 'what's up!'"

"I just didn't feel like answering the phone," Amber said with a shrug.

Robin's eyes narrowed. "This is over him isn't it?"

"Who?"

"Don't "who" me. You know good and well "who". It's over Dalton isn't it?" she asked, looming over her friend. "Look at you. You're not even dressed and look at your hair. What's going on here? You weren't this messed up after Jeff died."

"I just can't get him out of my head," Amber said wearily. "It doesn't help that he won't stop calling."

"He's calling you? How did he get your number?"

Amber rolled her eyes. "Duh! Think about it, Lana is his sister, remember?"

"True. Have you told him to stop?"

"No, I haven't spoken to him. After I saw his name on the caller ID, I let the machine get it."

Robin walked over to the machine and hit play. She listened to the pleading voice on the other end.

"Amber this is Dalton are you there? Okay, I was just calling to say hi."

BEEP.

"Hi Amber, this is Dalton again I was hoping to catch you at home. I ... I know I really don't even know you, but I was hoping we could change all that."

BEEP.

Several more messages followed, all seeming a bit more longing than the last. Each time there was more desperation in his voice. When the tape finished playing, Robin sat on the couch beside her friend.

"You know, Amber, I'm no expert but that doesn't sound like the voice of someone that's in love with someone else."

"Then why was he so upset that Katie Mae was going to tell her about our kiss?" Amber asked, confused.

"I don't know, girlfriend, but if you ask me, from the sound of his voice I would say that the man on the other end of that phone is just as miserable as you are."

"Do you really think so?" Amber asked, her voice brimming with hope.

"I'd bet on it. The question is, what are you going to do about it?"

Amber sat thinking. She wasn't sure what to do. What if it were true? What if Dalton wasn't in love with this Maggie person? A frown creased her face. She wouldn't allow herself to be used again. Not this time! No man would ever play her for a fool again. No matter how empty she felt without him, she wouldn't call him, she wouldn't fall into his trap.

Chapter Thirty-Nine

"Amber, are you feeling all right? You barely touched your lunch," Lana asked, concern shining in her eyes.

"I'm fine," Amber insisted. "I just haven't been very hungry lately."

"Maybe you should schedule an appointment; you've been under a lot of stress the past few months."

"I'll be okay. I just need some time I guess," Amber said, pushing her plate away.

"Well, the reason I wanted you to join me is because I wanted to talk to you about something and didn't want to do it on the phone."

Amber braced herself. Dalton had called at least once a day and she had been expecting Lana to take up his crusade.

"It's about Kelly," Lana continued.

Amber was shocked. This wasn't all about her avoiding Dalton? He wasn't asking his sister to help him betray his girlfriend?

Lana's voice interrupted her thoughts. "As you know, Kelly's been having a tough time dealing with things."

Amber cleared her head. "I know, it's hard to believe how much Jeff's actions have affected all of us."

"It will be all right, honey," Lana said, patting Amber's hand. "The thing is: Tim and I are considering moving."

"Oh?" She was shocked she hadn't seen this coming. "I guess that could work. You could just transfer to another school. They do have their choice of schools."

"Amber, you don't understand. We're thinking of moving back home to Kentucky," Lana explained. "Tim has a couple interviews next week and if things work out, we'd like to move within the month so Kelly can start school there. It would be cutting it short, but if things work out, we might be able to pull it off. We have family there and could stay with them until we find a place of our own. And if need be we can take Kelly down early so she can start school on time."

Amber was speechless. Oh my God, she thought, what will this do to Julie?

"That's why I wanted to talk to you, so you could tell Julie before she heard it from Kelly," Lana said, obviously reading Amber's thoughts.

Tears threatened; Amber took a deep breath. She spoke softly. "Thanks for telling me. I appreciate it Lana. I'm just sorry that my situation is making you leave your home."

"Hey, don't you dare blame yourself," Lana said firmly. "You did nothing wrong."

"I know, but he was my husband."

"Yes, but you did nothing wrong," Lana repeated. "You'll find someone someday and this whole mess will be nothing but a bad dream."

"I'd like to think so, but every time I think I've found someone, things just aren't what they seem," Amber replied.

Lana pounced on the opening. "Amber, what happened that day at the park? Dalton told me you ran away."

Damn, you walked right into that, she scolded herself and grimaced. "Like I said, Lana, things aren't always the way they seem. Are they?"

"Amber, I'm not sure what you are referring to. You two seemed to be getting along so well at Kelly's birthday party. What went wrong? I can't help you fix it if you don't tell me what it is."

"Lana, I know about Maggie," Amber said simply.

"Maggie? What does she have to do with this?"

"What does she have to do with this?" Amber asked, raising her voice. "I'm not about to play games. If your brother wants to cheat on his girlfriend, let him do it with someone else."

Amber shoved her chair back, leapt to her feet and stormed out the door.

Lana caught up to her just as she was getting into her car. "Amber wait! You don't understand!"

"What is there to understand?" Amber said, seething.

"Oh, honey, wait! I have something to show you. Please don't leave yet." Lana rifled through her purse. "Please let it be in here."

Amber watched her. Whatever it was, it was not going to change anything. She was not going to allow herself to be hurt again.

Lana smiled when she found what she was looking for. She pulled out a picture and handed it to Amber.

Amber stared at a photograph of Katie Mae with a rather large, older lady. Now it was her turn to be confused.

"Who is this?" she asked, still looking at the picture.

"That, Amber, is Maggie. She's Dalton's housekeeper and Katie Mae's nanny."

"You mean Maggie isn't Dalton's girlfriend?" Amber asked, feeling herself starting to shake.

Lana laughed heartily. "I love Maggie, but I think my brother could do a lot better than that. What on earth made you think Maggie was Dalton's girlfriend anyway?"

"That day at the park, I overheard Katie Mae say she

wished Maggie was there and how much she loved her."

"Of course she loves her. Maggie is the only mother Katie Mae has ever known."

"But I didn't know that, and then Dalton agreed with her. Then later when Katie Mae saw us kiss she threatened to tell Maggie and Dalton got upset," Amber explained.

"Of course he would. Maggie has been trying to get him remarried for years. If she found out he was interested in someone she wouldn't let up. Maggie is a great lady, but when she sets her mind to something, look out." Lana laughed.

Amber paled. "Oh no!"

"What now?" Lana asked.

"I've been avoiding him. He thinks I don't care about him," Amber said frantically.

"Do you?" Lana asked bluntly.

Amber looked up at Lana, and without hesitation, she gave her answer.

"YES! I haven't thought of anything else since I met him. I can't eat or sleep, I've almost picked up the phone a dozen times and told him girlfriend or no girlfriend I want to be with him, but I couldn't. Not after Jeff."

"Well then. I had better let you go," Lana said, stepping aside. "I think you have a phone call to make."

Chapter Forty

Dalton sat on the porch swing. He looked up as the door opened and saw the disapproving look on Maggie's face as she came out. The swing sagged under the added weight as she sat beside him.

"Land sakes, Dalton. You've been moping around here for nearly a week. Why don't you just call the girl."

"I don't know what you're talking about," Dalton grumbled.

"Like heck you don't. I may be old, but I'm not blind, you haven't been the same since you came home. You're walking around like a little lost puppy, even Katie Mae has noticed."

Dalton looked up in obvious concern for his daughter. "Why, what did she say?"

"Now now, don't you fret none about her. The young'un is fine," Maggie assured him, "she just wanted to know why Daddy doesn't play with her anymore."

Dalton felt awful. In his anguish, he had completely neglected his daughter. "Where is she?" he asked, suddenly aware of her absence.

"Jake's sisters are here today. They took her riding."

Dalton's shoulders tensed. "Riding? On Jasper or Molly?"

"Molly," Maggie reassured him.

"That's good, Jasper has been too unpredictable,"

Dalton said, relaxing slightly. He glanced toward the field. Jasper had been unpredictable before, but had developed an even worse disposition since his purchase of Katie Mae's new horse. He had been contemplating getting rid of Jasper, but wasn't sure how Katie Mae would react.

"Did they take the trails?" he asked, suddenly worried.

The old woman laid a hand on his lap. "Dalton, relax. Jake went with them. You know he won't let no harm come to either of his sisters or that little one of yours."

"You're right, I guess I'm just not thinking clearly," Dalton said, his voice trailing.

"I know you're not," Maggie agreed. "You're sick."

"I'm not sick. I'm as healthy as a horse," Dalton said, laughing at the comparison.

"Dalton, you are too sick," Maggie disagreed. "I've seen it before. You, dear boy, are love sick."

Maggie was right and he knew there was no use arguing with her. When she knew she was right she wouldn't give an inch. He sat on the swing beside her. "I just wish she felt the same way."

"Maybe she does, son," Maggie said tenderly. "Call her and find out."

"I have," Dalton said, frustrated. "I've left a dozen messages on her machine and she hasn't returned one of them. The trouble is, I don't even know why. We were getting along so well. Then at the park, we kissed and she didn't seem to mind. One minute she was there and the next she was gone. She literally ran away from me."

"Not even a goodbye?" Maggie asked.

"Nothing. She just ran away. Now she won't even give me the chance to find out what I did wrong." In frustration, he ran his fingers through his thick black hair.

"Is she worth all this heart ache?"

"Maggie, she is a gift from heaven," he said

longingly. "She has jet-black hair, a body to die for and those eyes… She has the darkest eyes I have ever seen, so dark, they draw you in. And she's so genuine, so honest with her feelings. We talked about everything and I do mean everything. It was so easy with her, like I'd known her forever."

"She sounds like a beautiful lady," Maggie agreed. "Well you know, Dalton, if she won't answer her phone you could always go back and knock on her door."

"What? And have her slam it in my face? No thanks," he huffed.

Dalton's cell phone interrupted their conversation.

"Hello? Oh hi, Sis …. No, why would she? ... Why would she think that? Did you tell her the real deal? ... Great! Can I ask a favor of you? Can I bunk at your place for a couple days? … Great, I'll see you tomorrow." He hung up the phone.

"Maggie, will you see to Katie Mae? I have something to take care of." He didn't wait for her answer. He went inside to pack. Within moments, he was back outside, suitcase in hand.

"Dalton," Maggie, said quietly. "Aren't you forgetting something?"

"I don't think so," he said, mentally going over everything he had just packed.

"Don't you think you should wait and say goodbye to your daughter before you leave?" she asked with a kindly grin.

Dalton grinned sheepishly. He walked over and sat on the swing.

"Love can make one act like a school boy, can't it?" Maggie teased.

"I just got carried away, that's all," Dalton replied.

"Care to tell an old lady what the phone call was about?"

"It was Lana," Dalton began. "Seems like somehow

Amber overheard me and Katie Mae talking about missing you and wishing you were there and came to the conclusion that you and I were an item and I was cheating on you. She was hurt by her husband and I guess the whole thing ballooned out of proportion, but, you know Lana, if there's gossip to be had she'll find it."

"Well, it's a good thing for you that she did," Maggie said. "So. Let me ask you this: when you go riding up on your white horse, what are you going to do then?"

"I don't know," Dalton said, once again running his hands through his hair, "I guess I hadn't thought about that yet, but one thing's for sure, if I have my way she'll be coming back with me."

"Well, you'll have plenty of time to worry about that on your drive tonight. Are you sure you don't want to take a nap before you go?"

He jumped up and looked toward the trails. "Heck, Maggie. I couldn't sleep right now if I wanted to."

Chapter Forty-One

"I can't believe you talked me into this," Robin said, slightly out of breath.

"Quit your bitchin', Chickie, running is good for you," Amber teased.

"Yeah, but in this heat?"

"It's better than last week," Amber reminded her. "At least the humidity is better."

"Ain't that the truth," Robin said, wiping the sweat from her face.

"So, what time are you leaving?"

"I'll probably leave around two thirty. My flight doesn't leave until six, but it takes two hours to get to metro and then with the security checks that should give me plenty of time."

"You make sure you give Jack a hug for me and tell him I said hi. I haven't seen him since the funeral."

"You?" Robin laughed, "I'm about to go nuts."

"I wish I was going to California," Amber sighed. "I'd love to get away."

"I'd invite you, but I don't know how much sight-seeing we're going to do." Robin winked.

"I know. I wouldn't dream of tagging along. I'd just love to get away," Amber said, pulling on Clancy's leash to slow him down.

"So, what happened to your moving to Texas?"

Robin smiled knowingly.

"I don't know, I just thought I'd see how things go," Amber replied.

"Things like Dalton?" Robin questioned. "Have you called him?"

A frown crossed her face. "I tried, but the lady that answered the phone said he was out of town for a few days."

"That bites. Did she say when he would be back?"

"No."

"Did you leave a message?"

"No."

"Why not?"

"Oh sure. Dalton this is Amber, sorry I've been such a bitch to you, but it's okay now because I no longer think you are sleeping with your nanny." Amber laughed.

"Hey, it works for me," Robin said, slowing down.

"Easy, Clancy. We don't want to wear Robin out before her big trip," Amber said, pulling on the dog's leash to slow him to a walk.

"That's right," Robin agreed, "I need to save my strength."

"So what are you going to do while I am gone?"

"Go stir crazy I guess," Amber complained. "Julie went away for the weekend with Lana, Tim and Kelly."

"Really? Lana didn't say anything about going away," Robin said, obviously intrigued. "Where did they go?"

"Lana said they wanted to get away, they're driving over to Muskegon to the water park. She just called out of the blue this morning and asked."

"That sounds like fun. Why didn't you go with them?"

"I would have. I even hinted around at it, but didn't get invited."

"You should've just asked. I'm sure they would have

let you go."

Amber shook her head. "No. I made it quite clear I thought it sounded like fun, I wasn't about to invite myself."

"Now I feel bad about leaving you," Robin said, sounding guilty.

"Hey, don't be, I can find something to do."

"Or someone," Robin said, a wide grin spreading across her face as she nodded toward the big black pickup parked in Amber's driveway.

As they neared the house, Clancy's ears perked up and he strained at the leash, barking at the man sitting on Amber's front porch.

Amber nearly stumbled when she saw Dalton. She swallowed hard, trying to quell her nerves. Her legs felt like rubber and her hands were trembling as she struggled to keep a hold on Clancy's leash.

"Oh my God! I can't believe he's here," Amber whispered to her friend.

"Well, I guess I don't have to worry about you," Robin whispered back. "Listen, I'm going to go, I have some things I need to take care of before I leave."

"Okay. Call me and let me know you made it safe."

Robin winked at her friend. "I will. Have fun."

"I will and you too," Amber said, hugging her friend.

"You can count on it," Robin smiled.

Amber turned and smiled hesitantly at Dalton as she approached him. Once again, she swallowed and hoped her voice didn't show her fear. What she was afraid of, she wasn't quite sure. "You came back."

He squared his shoulders and looked at her. When he spoke, his tone was firm. "I had to. You wouldn't return my calls."

"I… I'm so sorry." Amber blushed. She paused, struggling for words. "I thought…"

Dalton put a finger to her lips.

"I know," he said softly. "Maggie said to tell you hello."

Amber's eyes flew open wide with astonishment. "But, how?"

"Lana called me right after your talk yesterday. That's why I'm here."

Amber was amazed. She looked into his bloodshot eyes, then for the first time noticed his unshaven face. Her eyes flew open with shock. "You drove all night just to see me?"

"You have a problem with that?" he asked, petting Clancy, who had jumped up on him.

"No, not at all," she said, and then looked in amazement at Clancy.

"That's unbelievable," she exclaimed.

"What is?" Dalton asked, confused.

"Clancy hates men. I've never seen him take to anyone like this."

Dalton took off his cowboy hat and ran his hand through his thick black hair, smiling. "Well you know what they say, Ma'am, dogs are a great judge of character."

Amber caught her breath. *God he is so fine*, she thought to herself, *and that southern accent...*

"Well, if Clancy likes you then you must be okay," she agreed, returning his smile. "You must be exhausted; would you like to come in where it is cool?"

"What about her?"

"What? Who?"

Dalton nodded toward the house next door. "Do you think we should invite your neighbor? She might not want to miss anything. She's been keeping a close eye on me since I got here."

Amber turned in time to see Karen duck back behind the curtain she was looking around.

"Ohhhh that woman, she is the nosiest neighbor in

the world," she said, unlocking the front door.

"Well then, if it's okay with her, I'd love to," Dalton said, following Amber in to the house.

"Are you hungry? I could fix you something." Amber offered as she unhooked Clancy's leash.

"Why don't I take you out instead?"

"That's fine, but would you mind if I take a quick shower first? I'm all sweaty from my run."

"Oh sure, make me look like the grungy one," Dalton said, feeling his stubble.

"At least you don't stink," Amber said, heading up the stairs.

Clancy looked at Amber then at Dalton, but didn't make a move.

Dalton walked over and sat on the couch. Clancy jumped up beside him, resting his head in Dalton's lap.

"You got yourself a beautiful master," he said, scratching the dog behind the ears.

Amber dried herself off then hurried to get dressed.

Oh my God, I can't believe he is actually here, she thought. *I don't know if it is nerves or if I'm just hungry, but my stomach is in knots.*

She pictured his face. He thought he looked scruffy, but what a hottie.

If I wasn't such a nice girl, I would have jumped his bones right there. The thought made her laugh out loud.

"Shit, Robin's rubbing off on me," she said shaking her head. She put on her lipstick and headed down the stairs. When she reached the bottom, she stopped and stared at the sight. Dalton was on the oversized couch with his head back, sound asleep and there, right next to him, was Clancy, with his head in Dalton's lap. The dog opened his eyes to look at Amber, but made no attempt to get up. Amber stood there for a minute wondering if she should wake him, then decided against it.

He drove all night just to see me the least I can do is make him breakfast.

Chapter Forty-Two

"I still can't believe you didn't wake me," Dalton said, sliding his plate away.

"What, you didn't like my cooking?" Amber teased.

"The only problem I have with your cooking is that I ate too much," Dalton said, leaning back in his chair.

"You are too kind, Sir," Amber said as she picked up his plate.

Dalton got up, pushed his chair in and walked over to the sink to help Amber.

She hesitated. "I've got this."

A chill ran through Dalton as he breathed in her perfume.

"Listen," he said, pretending to be offended, "I didn't get to buy you breakfast, the least I can do is help you clean up."

His arm brushed against hers as he reached for the dishcloth. As he wiped the table, he could still feel the warmth from her arm. He took a deep breath as he stepped up beside her, rinsing the dishcloth, struggling for control.

She smiled, lowering her eyes nervously then reached to set the dish she had been drying into the cabinet. Finishing the breakfast plates, she turned to face Dalton.

"Thank you for your help," she said with eyes full of desire.

It's now or never, Dalton thought, leaning in kissing her ready lips, hoping he wasn't stepping out of line.

She leaned toward him and her mouth parted. He met her tongue with his own. Feeling her body quiver, he reached around and pulled her into him. He wanted her so desperately. Sensing her willingness, he pulled her even closer. He kissed her passionately, their tongues dancing a wild, lustful dance. He pulled away then tenderly kissed her chin.

Slowly, he began working his way down the nape of her neck, kissing, licking, sucking the tender skin ever so softly, and enjoying the soft, kitten-like moans escaping from her slightly parted lips. He worked his way back up to the tender skin just behind her ear, kissing her, making sure not to scratch her with his unshaven stubble. Eagerly he explored her flesh with his tongue. Dalton nibbled on her earlobe as she pressed against him.

"I want you," he whispered into her ear.

Breathless, Amber nodded and took his hand.

"Come with me," she said, leading him down the hall then up the stairway to her bedroom. Clancy followed, but Amber closed the door, effectively shutting him out.

As Amber turned around, Dalton pulled her into him once more. He kissed her fully on the lips, drawing her moist tongue into his mouth. He sucked it then met it with his own.

"I need you," Amber moaned in a raspy tone, full of desire. She pressed her body into the stiffness of his ready member.

Dalton gently guided her backwards to the waiting bed. He lowered her carefully, all the while exploring her mouth with his hungry tongue. He lifted Amber's shirt over her head then reached around and unfastened her bra. He pulled it up, exposing her golden globes, smiling approvingly at the sight of her. His manhood twitched with anticipation. He lowered his head, gently taking an erect nipple into his hot, hungry mouth, once again feeling her shiver from his touch. His hand explored her mound, noting the dampness that had moistened her clothing.

Another soft moan escaped her lips and she pushed against Dalton's hand, writhing under the pressure he was applying. He felt her trembling against his touch as his mouth alternated on her exposed breasts.

"That feels so good," she said breathlessly. With both hands, she guided his head lower, and then lower still.

Dalton looked into Amber's pleading eyes. Smiling, he slowly began working his way to her waiting mound. Her breathing became more erratic. He suspected it had been far too long since she'd had release. Dalton kissed his way down Amber's stomach, making swirling motions with his tongue.

God, she is so beautiful, he thought to himself. *I want her. I need her.*

He reminded himself to go slowly, realizing it had been too long for him as well. He unsnapped her shorts and lowered them to expose her black satin panties. He kissed the fabric that had been dampened by her juices, breathing in the aroma. He blew a hot breath into the fabric and was pleased with the response he received.

Amber tossed her head back, letting out a gasp, her need growing nearly beyond control. Thrusting her hips forward, her eyes met Dalton's begging for release, for him to take her, to finish what he started.

Sensing her urgent need Dalton placed a finger on each side of the thin strap then lowered the black panties. He tossed them on top of the previously discarded shorts. Taking one last look into Amber's lustful eyes, he lowered his head.

Amber pushed into him, grasping the covers in her fists, raising her hips to him, giving in fully to his talented tongue. Dalton gently explored her crevices; licking, kissing, sucking and enjoying the taste of her. He found the node, circled it and felt her stiffen.

She was ready for release.

Amber called out, grabbed the back of his head and didn't let go until the waves of pleasure had subsided. Only then did she release her hold on him. Relaxing, she looked up at him and smiled.

"I want to feel you inside of me," she said in a husky voice, full of want and desire.

Dalton stood, took off his shirt, lowered his jeans and hurried to remove his underwear. Amber's smile deepened as her eyes took in the length of him. Dalton let out his breath as he saw her smile of approval. He climbed back onto the bed, and then slowly lowered himself into her waiting tunnel.

It felt so good that he almost cried out. He moaned and she answered with one in return. He rocked back and forth until he had entered her fully then began slow, long strokes.

Amber wrapped her legs around him, meeting his movements with her own. They picked up the pace; their breathing became heavy. The tension mounted until neither could wait another second. A loud moan escaped from Amber's lips followed by a deep groan from Dalton. They grasped each other firmly, each releasing their tension. Dalton opened his eyes, his brow wrinkled upon seeing tears escape from the corners of Amber's eyes.

"Are you okay?" he asked, concerned.

"I'm fine," she said softly, wiping away the tears. "I just

needed that more than I realized. I'm sorry."

Dalton bent down and kissed her nose. "Don't ever apologize for giving in to pleasure. It's been a long time for me, too." He rolled off her and cradled her in his arms.

Clancy whined at the door, but neither made a move to get up. Lying there in each other's arms was as safe as either had felt in a very long time; neither wanted the moment to end. Silence was their sanctuary. Closeness was their friend. Together they drifted off into a peaceful morning slumber.

Together they fell in love.

Chapter Forty-Three

"I think we've been set up," Dalton said, trying the back door of the large fieldstone farmhouse.

Amber looked under the flowerpot then checked under the doormat.

"I think you're right," she laughed.

"I can't believe her," Dalton said, shutting the screen door. "She tells me I can stay here, and what does she do? She goes off and leaves without leaving a key. I hope the motel in town has a vacancy." He sounded slightly agitated.

"I'm sure there is," Amber assured him. "It's a good thing you didn't bring your cat; I don't think they allow pets."

"What? Oh, Lucky. Nah, he just likes to ride in the horse trailers," Dalton said, checking the window. "This is just like her."

"I think you're right about being setup," Amber repeated.

"How do you mean?"

"Well, this wasn't a planned trip; she just called this morning to see if Julie could go. I all but begged to go, yet they didn't invite me. I think your sister is trying to play matchmaker. You said yourself she knew you were coming up and she didn't mention a word when they picked up Julie."

"Sounds like something she would do. Good ol' Sis, always thinking." He laughed, brightening and took Amber's hand. "We had better go see about a hotel while it's still early."

"Dalton?" Amber said hesitantly, "Would you like to stay at my house? Julie's gone and I have a guest room."

Holy shit! Amber thought to herself. *I can't believe I asked him if he would stay. God, I hardly know him. It's not like he's a psycho though, he's Lana's brother after all. She would've warned me if he was no good. Besides, I enjoy his company and if it leads to more sex, so be it, we're both adults.*

Dalton studied her face. "Are you sure Amber? I don't mind staying at a motel. Honestly it's no big deal."

She looked into his crystal blue eyes, so honest, so trusting. "Dalton, I wouldn't have offered if I didn't mean it. I would really love the company. I mean that."

He pulled her into him and kissed her firmly. "I would love to spend the weekend with you."

Amber pulled back. "Under one condition," she laughed, rubbing his stubble. "You have to shave."

"You are truly stunning," he said, taking her back into his arms.

"Yeah, right," she laughed, trying to pull away.

"What do you mean "yeah right?"" he asked, not letting her go. "You don't believe me?"

Amber found it hard to accept his compliment. Jeff hadn't said anything truly flattering to her in years, even at the end. She hadn't really been fat to begin with, but she had managed to slim and tone considerably. Amber had thought she was looking good, people were telling her she was, but never Jeff, and he had loved her, or so she thought. When he stopped telling her she looked good, it took a toll on her confidence.

Now, this gorgeous man who could have his pick of women was telling her she was stunning. It all made her head spin, but she had to admit she hadn't felt this way in years. Come to think of it, she wondered if she had ever felt this way at all. But how? She didn't know him; she was so scared of being hurt again.

Dalton seemed puzzled by her silence. "Hello? Are you still with me?" he said, running his hand in front of her eyes.

"What? Oh, I'm sorry, I was just thinking," she said softly.

"A penny for your thoughts," he said tenderly.

"It's nothing, really," Amber said.

Dalton relaxed his grip on her and led her to the back deck. "Amber, sit with me." He motioned toward lounge chair on the back deck. As they sat, he began to talk.

"I'm not a stalker or a psycho. I'm just someone who has been waiting for a very long time to meet someone to make my life whole again. I know we've only known each other for a very short time, but I think we have a chance. I can't explain why I feel this way, but I think the reason I haven't met anyone before now is because I have been waiting for you.

"I loved my wife. Her death devastated me. It was a long time before I could even think of dating again. For the last couple of years I have had this overwhelming feeling that something was missing in my life. I don't just mean Mary Katherine. I know I can't replace her. I felt like I was ready to find someone. Not someone to replace Mary Katherine, but someone new to share things with.

"I have been dating on and off for the last two years, but none have worked out. There was always something missing, but with you, it's different. I feel like I've known you all my life; being with you is so comfortable. I want to get to know you better. I know you've been hurt, but I'm not that guy. I won't hurt you. I won't ever let anyone hurt you again. I promise you that."

Amber looked up through a pool of tears. How had

he known what she had been thinking?

"Jeff had me fooled for so long. He said that he loved me when all the time he couldn't stand being around me. I found out after he died that he had been unfaithful our entire marriage. The whole time I was sitting at home taking care of Julie, he was out screwing anything that moved. I don't know what I did wrong," she said, sobbing. "I don't know why I couldn't make him want me."

Dalton hugged her close to him, waited for her tears to subside, then took her face in his hands and kissed her softly on the mouth.

"I don't know what you're husband's problem was," he began, "but I can tell you this, if I had a woman as beautiful and loving as you are, I wouldn't be looking for anything else. And as for his being gone all the time, I would want to spend as much time as possible with you. Please don't take this the wrong way, I'm sorry you lost your husband, but I'm glad he's gone. You see, pretty lady, his loss is my gain. If I came up when you were still married to the jerk, you wouldn't have given me a second thought."

"You're right. I mean, I might have fantasized about you. No, I know I would have fantasized about you," blushing, she continued. "But you're right; I would never have acted on it. No matter how much I wanted to be with you, it would've only been wishful thinking."

"See? I was right; the universe was just waiting until the timing was right. Besides, my horoscope said I would be lucky in love this weekend," he grinned.

Amber's eyes flew open. "You read the horoscope?"

"Of course, every morning with my coffee," he admitted freely. "Why? Does that surprise you?"

"It's just that I read them," she said, rubbing the goose bumps that had appeared on her arms. "I don't read them as much anymore, but I used to read them all the time."

"Horoscopes can be fun, especially when they come true. Why did you stop reading them, if you don't mind my asking?"

"That was the reason," Amber said, still rubbing her arms, "they all started coming true. Like a prediction or something."

"And that's a bad thing?"

"Well, they predicted Jeff's death and it scared the hell out of me."

"That would be frightening," Dalton agreed. "It actually said your husband would die?"

"No," Amber admitted, "but it said, "tragedy would be a blessing in disguise."""

"Well then? It was right. We met, so that's a good thing," Dalton said lightly, grinning. "Now what do you say, Amber Mae? What say we go back to your place, so I can take a shower and get rid of this hobo look?"

Amber Mae, she thought, shivering.

"Oh man," Amber said. "When you say my name and smile like that, I'll never be able to resist you."

He took on a quizzical look. "And that's a bad thing?"

"Not for you," Amber laughed. She stood up, stretching a full body stretch. Her shirt rose up exposing her firm golden brown stomach.

"And when you do that, my dear, I won't be able to resist you," Dalton said playfully.

"And that's a bad thing?" Amber teased.

"Oh no, lady, not at all," he said, taking her into his arms.

Chapter Forty-Four

"I can't believe the weekend went by so fast," Amber said solemnly.

"I know," Dalton agreed. "I wish I could stay longer, but my ranch won't run without me, no matter what Carl says."

"Carl?"

"Oh, he's my ranch foreman. He is as good as it gets," Dalton said, running his hand through his hair.

"He sounds nice," Amber replied.

"Nice," Dalton laughed. "I don't think Carl has ever been described as nice. He is ornery, a jokester, drinks way too much, smokes even more, but nice? Nah."

"Then why do you keep him around?" Amber asked, confused.

"Because he's the best and because he would do anything in the world I ask him to."

"Well then he's nice to a point," Amber said smiling. "Is he the only person you have working for you?"

"Jake works there too." Dalton shifted in his seat. "There are a few others, but Carl and Jake are my main go-to guys."

"Tell me about Jake," Amber said, snuggling up against Dalton on the couch.

"Jake, oh he's a great kid. He's sixteen. He has this way with horses that most people envy," Dalton said, stroking Amber's hair. "Jake has worked for me for nearly two years. His dad ran off and left his mom with three children to feed. Jake's mom is a proud woman; she works her fingers to the bone trying to support Jake and his two younger twin sisters. Jake came around, looking for a job. I can always use an extra hand, so I hired him to load hay.

"Then one day a horse got spooked by a snake. No one could get near her. Up comes little Jake, walks right up to her, settles her down and leads her right to the barn. He has helped with the horses ever since. His mom got offended at first, thinking I was having him work out of feeling sorry for her, but honestly, that boy can get those horses to settle down better than anyone I've ever seen. He comes in the morning before school and then again afterwards. On the weekends and when school is out, he's there most of the time. His two sisters come over to help Maggie and play with Katie Mae. They're really nice girls. Come to think of it, they are probably close to Julie and Kelly's age."

Amber watched as he spoke, moved by the genuine affection and respect in his voice. Suddenly, she realized how content she was just to lay there in the safe confines of his arms. Was this it? Was this what she had been searching for all of her life? Was this what Robin had been telling her about? Letting out a deep, contented sigh, she snuggled even closer.

She tilted her head up to him and her face relaxed. She let her fingers trace the insides of his arm, which was draped casually around her. Their eyes met and held. He leaned down and kissed her full on the lips. She shivered as he brought her closer and kissed the top of her head.

Yes, she thought with finality, *this is most certainly what I have been searching for*.

She reached for his hands, intertwining his fingers with hers. "Dalton, tell me about Maggie."

"Maggie, where do I start? I'm going to marry that woman someday," Dalton teased.

"Very funny," Amber pulled her hand away and crossed her arms, a fake pout playing across her lips.

Dalton traced the outline of Amber's arms. He bent down and kissed her pout away.

"Maggie is the greatest. She cooks, cleans and watches after Katie Mae. She keeps me in line and works way too damned hard," he said with affection. "You'll love her. More important, she'll love you."

"I hope so, I'd love to meet her someday," Amber agreed.

"Why not?" Dalton asked.

"Why not what?" Amber asked, sitting bolt upright, hoping he meant what she thought, yet at the same time afraid he did.

"Why not come down to meet everyone?" Dalton said, his eyes twinkling.

"Well sure… I guess, when?"

"Come with me tonight," Dalton urged.

Amber's eyes flew open. "Tonight? I can't."

"Why not?" Dalton pushed.

"Julie's coming home."

"So? Bring her too. I wasn't expecting you to leave her here. Heck, Maggie would skin me alive if I didn't bring you both. She doesn't have school yet does she?"

"No, not for six weeks," Amber said, running out of reasons to object. Her mind was total chaos.

"Amber? Really, what would stop you from coming with me tonight? I have a big house. If you're worried about Julie, you can have your own room—as long as you sneak into mine every now and then," he said with a wink.

"What about Maggie? What will she think?" Amber questioned.

"Are you kidding?" Dalton laughed. "I'm sure she's been cleaning ever since I left. She'll skin my hide if I don't bring you."

Just then, Clancy ambled into the room, panting and wagging his tail.

"Clancy," Amber said. "What will I do with him?"

"Bring him too." Dalton said, petting the head of the dog that had jumped up after hearing his name.

"What about the house? Robin is out of town."

"What about your cop friend we ran into at Pizza Hut the other night?" Dalton teased.

"Very funny," Amber said, remembering Marty's reaction upon seeing her with another man.

"I thought he was going to shoot me," Dalton laughed nervously.

"Just be glad we were in a public place," Amber said, only half teasing.

"What about the curtain lady?"

"Who?"

"You know, the lady next door that is always peeking out her window?"

"Karen? The Bitch? Oops, sorry," Amber laughed, turning red. "She is the nosiest person I have ever had the displeasure of meeting."

"Yes, but a nosy neighbor is a perfect neighbor," Dalton assured her, reaching for the remote. "Do you really think anyone will come around without her knowing?"

"What are you doing?" Amber asked as he turned on the news.

"I'll bet our having sex is already on CNN," he teased.

"You're probably more right than you know," Amber laughed, "nothing gets past KNN ...Karen News Network."

"Good, give her Lana's number, if anything happens she can call her. Okay? Good it's settled," Dalton said. "Now get your cute little butt up those stairs and start packing,"

Amber's mind was racing, her thoughts pulling her in two directions. On one hand, she wanted to go to be with him, never leaving his side. On the other, she wondered if it was all too soon. Still, what was she waiting for? After being unhappy for so long, didn't she deserve to be happy? To be loved? Dalton had said it before; the universe had brought them together at the perfect time. Who was she to question the universe? She smiled at Dalton's enthusiasm and nodded her head with finality at her decision. She smiled fully. No regrets!

"As soon as Lana gets back with Julie, we can leave. You guys can sleep all the way home. To Kentucky," he corrected himself.

"And when will you sleep?" Amber questioned.

"I'll catch a nap while you're packing and if I get tired on the way down, we can switch off."

"You've got it all figured out don't you?" She smiled. "Do you always get what you want?" she asked, staring into his crystal blue eyes.

"I hope so Amber," he said softly, his expression serious. "I really hope so."

Amber flashed a brilliant smile and kissed him on the cheek. "You take a nap and I will go pack mine and Julie's things."

Dalton watched her run up the stairs then picked up his cell phone, dialed his home number and took a deep breath.

"Maggie, I just wanted to let you know I'm heading back tonight. ... Yeah, I'll be home in the morning. How's Katie Mae? ... Good. Well, when she gets back from Mom and Dad's she can call me. ... Oh, and Maggie, we're going to have company for a while. ... Hello? ... I know its short notice, but if you need anything extra, send Jake to the store, okay? ... Thanks Maggie, you're one in a million. Oh, and Maggie, she's terrific! ... See you in the morning."

He hung up the phone and dialed another set of numbers.

"Carl? This is Dalton. ... Yeah, I'm heading home tonight. ... Hey, I'm bringing a friend with me. Maggie will kill herself getting the house ready, will you have Jake call his sisters to come over and help her? ... Let him know he'll probably have to go to the store for her and tell him I'll take care of all of them in the morning, will you? ... Thanks Carl. Oh, and Carl, I want you to do something for me. Call Mr. Meyers; ask him if he still has that paint horse for sale. If he does this is what I want you to do..."

Chapter Forty-Five

"We're almost there," Dalton announced. "It's just up the road here."

Amber reached around the king cab to wake the sleeping girls. "Julie, Kelly, it's time to wake up and put your shoes on."

Clancy lifted his head up, yawned, then lowered it again.

"Thanks for letting Kelly come too. Those two are nearly inseparable," Amber said smiling.

"Are you kidding? How could I not? Mom and Dad would have had a cow if I hadn't brought her along. You can meet them this weekend," he said, holding her hand. When she stiffened, he added. "Don't worry Amber Mae, they'll love you."

"Oh yeah, Mamal and Papal are the greatest," Kelly said from the back seat.

"I'm sure they are," Amber said, glancing protectively at her daughter. Amber fervently wished for it to be true, but she remembered how uncaring Jeff's parents had been. They were never even remotely friendly to her and Julie never had the luxury of having loving caring grandparents.

That's enough, she scolded herself. *It's not like Dalton has even asked you to marry him. Not yet anyway.* She took a deep breath and let it out slowly. *Baby steps,* she promised herself. The conversation from within the cab of the truck caught her attention.

"Boy, that is a big farm," Julie said, pointing out the window. "That white fence has been going on forever."

"Three quarters of a mile, to be exact," Dalton grinned, turning on his blinker.

"Wow! This is yours?" Julie asked in amazement.

"Yeah, Uncle Dalton is rich," Kelly chimed in.

"I'm not rich," Dalton said, turning crimson.

"Mom said you are, she said you raise Kentucky Derby racehorses," Kelly argued.

"Cool," Julie said, looking around.

They passed under a large wooden plank that read "Sunset Meadows".

It's an omen, Amber thought.

As they traveled down the long driveway, Amber had a sense of coming home, of belonging. Amber's eyes grew wide. "This is your 'little' ranch?"

Dalton smiled, but didn't answer.

"Whoa!" Julie exclaimed as they rounded the corner.

Amber looked at Dalton then back at the house that had just come into view.

"No wonder Maggie has to work so hard," Amber said, looking at the stately two-story house.

A wide porch with white pillars encircled the entire house. Black ceiling fans lined the porch, hovering high above matching rocking chairs. Still, even with its massive size, the home looked safe and peaceful in its cozy, tree-filled setting.

The horse barns were no less breathtaking, surrounded by black arenas, a stark contrast to the white house that governed Dalton's ranch. They pulled up in front of the house, giving them a better view of the distinctly southern home. As they parked, the front door swung open and Katie Mae ran outside. Amber couldn't help but wonder how she kept from getting lost in the massive house.

"Daddy! You're home!" the child shouted as she ran down the stairs.

Dalton jumped out of the truck, scooped up Katie Mae and swung her around. "Hello, Little Bit. How's Daddy's little sunshine today?" he asked, kissing her.

She wrapped her arms around him in greeting. "I'm fine, Daddy. I missed you so so much."

"Hi Katie Mae," Amber said, getting out of the truck.

"Amber Mae! You came to see me!" Katie Mae squealed with excitement. "Did you bring your doggie?"

"He's right there," Dalton said, pointing to the truck.

Katie Mae squinted to see inside the tinted windows. "I can't see, Daddy."

The door opened, allowing Julie and Kelly to exit the truck along with Clancy.

Kelly ran over and hugged her cousin. "Hello Katie Mae."

"Hi Katie Mae," Julie said, also giving the little girl a hug.

Clancy stopped sniffing long enough to lick the child's face.

"He kissed me!" she squealed, wiping her face.

Once again, the front door opened. Amber looked up to see a very large, older lady whom she recognized from the picture Lana had shown her. Her stomach knotted, knowing it was important that this woman like her.

"Land sakes Dalton, aren't you going to invite your guests inside for breakfast?" she yelled, remaining on the porch.

"Good ol' Maggie. One thing is for sure, no one will ever go hungry with her around. Come on into the house everyone," Dalton said, ushering them onto the porch. "Maggie, I'd like you to meet Amber and Julie."

"And Kelly," Katie Mae said, being helpful.

"Katie Mae, Miss Maggie knows me," Kelly laughed.

"And who is this?" Maggie asked, looking down at Clancy.

"That is Clancy. He's Amber Mae's doggie," Katie Mae said holding the leash.

"I see," the woman said, shifting her eyes up to Amber.

Amber took a deep breath.

You can do this, she told herself. *Remember what Dalton told you, her bark is worse than her bite.*

Letting the breath out, she looked Maggie right in the eye. "He gets a little rambunctious now and then, but he really is a good dog."

"Don't worry, Amber. Maggie likes dogs. Don't you, Maggie?" Dalton said, his eyes pleading with the older woman.

Maggie looked around at all the anxious faces. She looked once more at the dog then cast her eyes back at Amber. "Is he housebroken?"

"Oh yes. Totally," Amber assured the robust woman.

"Then we'll get along just fine," Maggie said, turning to go into the house. "Anyone that's hungry follow me."

"She gets a little high-strung when her food gets cold," Dalton whispered, looking at Amber. "She'll be fine once we're all sitting down."

"Will she mind if I go to the bathroom first?" she whispered.

"Amber relax, her bark is worse than her bite, remember? I promise." Dalton laughed, kissing her cheek. "Katie Mae, will you show Amber Mae where the bathroom is for Daddy?"

"Okay, Daddy," Katie Mae said, grabbing Amber's hand.

"Okay girls, let's get some grub," Dalton said, ushering the teens into the dining room.

"Everything smells wonderful," Dalton said, as Maggie came in carrying the biscuits.

"Where's your friend?" Maggie asked, lowering the basket.

"She had to wash her hands Maggie, she'll be right in," Dalton said, fixing Katie Mae a plate.

"Here we are," Katie Mae said as she entered the room, still holding Amber's hand.

"Mmm," Amber said, seeing the feast that was on the table. "I've never had a real southern meal before. Everything smells wonderful."

Casually, she slid into the empty chair beside Dalton. She nearly reached out to pinch herself just to make sure it was all real. She was here. She was sitting next to a man who she had only just met but who she knew she loved. She had been with Jeff nearly fourteen years but never had she felt what she had felt in the time she had known Dalton. For the first time since she was a child, she truly knew what love was. More importantly than that, for the first time ever, she truly knew what it felt like to be in love.

The group sat around the table enjoying their breakfast and making small talk. Dalton watched the tension leave Amber's face. She was virtually glowing. He watched how easily she spoke to Maggie and fussed over Katie Mae. Most importantly, he watched as Maggie's face softened and smiled with acceptance. He was glad Amber was making such a fuss over Maggie's cooking. Maggie could come on a little strong, but appreciate her cooking and she'd love you forever.

Dalton looked over at Julie and gave her a wink. Julie smiled and returned his wink. Dalton reached over and took another biscuit, his eyes met Maggie's and the old woman smiled.

She likes her already, he thought taking a bite. *Now if only I can convince Amber to stay.*

Chapter Forty-Six

So what do you think of the place?" Dalton asked after they finished touring the house.

"I think it's beautiful. Your wife had wonderful taste."

Dalton's brow furrowed. "Does it bother you being here?"

"Not at all," Amber replied truthfully. "Does it bother you? I mean, my being here in her house?"

"I guess I hadn't thought of that," he said. "When Mary Katherine died, everything reminded me of her, but it's been so long that it's my house now."

"I know what you mean. It's the same way with Jeff. I know he hasn't been gone that long, but even when he was alive, he really wasn't around much, so it just feels like my house.

"I used to think it was too big for just me and Julie, but after seeing your place, mine seems small," Amber said, looking around at the huge expanse of a home.

"I know it's big, but I always have room for company. Would you like to see the horse barns?" Dalton asked, leading her towards the front door.

"I'd love to."

"We can go riding after while if you'd like," Dalton offered, leading her toward the front door.

"I haven't been on a horse in years, but I'm game if

you have a slow, gentle horse," Amber laughed.

A mysterious smile crossed his lips as they walked towards one of the barns. "Actually, I have the perfect horse for you."

"That one will do just fine," Amber said, pointing at the small Shetland pony in the front corral.

"Jasper? Heck, he's as rotten as they come. I only keep him around because of Katie Mae. He was her first horse."

"Really? Which one does she ride now?"

"That's hers," Dalton said, pointing toward the big palomino that was grazing in the pasture.

"You're kidding," Amber gasped. "He's huge."

"Yes, she is," Dalton agreed, "but as gentle as a lamb."

"Oh, it's a she," Amber said. "And gentle? Okay, I'll ride her."

"Nah, that's not your type. I have just the horse for you," he said with a mischievous grin.

Amber couldn't help feeling he was up to something. She scanned the barn. "Okay, which one?"

"She's right over here," Dalton said, leading the way.

As they approached, Amber heard a neigh. She looked into the stall and was met by the most beautiful black and white painted horse she had ever seen.

"Oh my God, she's beautiful," she gasped. "She reminds me of the one I used to ride when I was a little girl."

His eyes softened as he studied her. "I was hoping you would like her. She's yours."

Amber stopped in her tracks, eyes wide in surprise. "Mine?"

"Remember when you told me about the painted horse you rode as a child and how you wished you could go back to the happier times?"

"Yes, and I also said it was wishful thinking," Amber

reminded him.

"Exactly." Smiling broadly, he removed the nameplate that until now had been turned around.

"Amber, I'd like you to meet your new horse," he said, handing her the board with the name Wishful Thinking carved into it.

Amber had tears in her eyes. Never had anyone ever done anything so sweet for her.

"I don't know what to say," she said, wiping at the tears that were streaming down her face.

"Say you'll visit often to ride her," he said, taking her into his arms.

Amber melted in his arms and wept. "What did I ever do to deserve you?"

"You were born," he said simply, bending down and kissing her full on the lips.

Amber felt her body respond to him instantly. His hands caressed her back as he held her tight. The painted horse nickered. Dalton pulled back abruptly as giggling filled the barn.

"They're kissing again," Katie Mae said, wrinkling her nose.

Julie and Kelly exchanged glances then started laughing.

"Boy, Mom, your face sure is red," Julie teased.

"We were just talking," Amber said defensively, her cheeks burning hot.

"Is that what you call it?" Kelly said, laughing.

"More like swapping spit!" Julie chimed in.

"Ewww," Katie Mae said, looking up at the older girls. She made a face and wrinkled her nose in disgust. She planted her fists on her hips. "That's yuck! Daddy, spitting is not nice!"

"I wasn't spitting," Dalton said, flustered.

"But you were kissing," she said through her giggles.

"Oh you," he said, running toward the child.

Katie squealed then took off running followed by Dalton and Clancy was right on his heals barking, joining in on the fun.

Kelly and Julie approached Amber.

"You really like my uncle, don't you?" Kelly asked, smiling at Amber.

"Yes I do," Amber said, watching for Julie's reaction.

Julie looked out the barn door toward where Dalton was swinging Katie Mae around. "He's a lot more fun than Dad was. Isn't he, Mom?" she said longingly.

"He's a very good guy," Amber said, putting her arms around both girls.

"Yeah, and when you two get married, Kelly and I will be cousins," Julie said, ducking out of the way.

"Hey! Who said anything about us getting married?" Amber asked, shocked.

"Mom did," Kelly chimed in. "That's why we went to the water park, so that you two could see if you were compatible. Then when you said you were coming down here for a visit, she said you two would be getting married soon."

"This looks like a deep conversation," Dalton said, walking up with Katie Mae riding piggyback. "Dare I ask what you three are talking about?"

"Just girl talk," Amber said, shooting each girl a stern look. "Just girl talk."

Chapter Forty-Seven

Amber broke off the ends of the bean she was holding, pulled out the string, broke it into three sections and tossed it into the pan.

"There, see you're getting the hang of it," Maggie said with approval.

"It's not so hard," Amber said, reaching for another bean. "I've never had fresh green beans before. I always just open a can."

Maggie shook her head, reaching for another bean. "Land sakes child, no wonder you're so skinny."

Amber glanced toward the corral where Dalton was teaching the girls how to use a lasso.

"He sure does love the young'uns," Maggie said, breaking apart another bean.

Amber sighed lovingly. "He has so much patience with them."

"That he does, child."

Amber couldn't help but steal another glance in Dalton's direction. She watched intently as the muscles in his arms bulged as he was twirling the lasso.

"Do you like flowers?"

"What?" Amber asked, directing her attention back to the lady sitting next to her. "Yes, I love flowers. Why?"

"Well, I was thinking, what would really be nice would be some irises and tulips and maybe even some mums planted over there." She extended a heavy arm pointing toward the side of the house.

"I think that would be nice. You should do it," Amber agreed.

"Oh no, not me, child." The woman drew out her arms to display her tremendous girth. "Look at me, if I were to get on my knees in the dirt I would never get back up. I was thinking you should do it."

"Me? You don't plant those flowers until the fall."

"I know child," Maggie said smiling, concentrating on the bean she was breaking.

Amber was wondering if the old woman was losing her mind. "Maggie, I'm leaving next week."

Maggie stopped picking at the bean she was working with, looked into Amber's eyes and smiled. "You'll be back, child," she said simply, then returned to her task.

"What makes you so sure?"

"Because you belong here," Maggie said, reaching for another bean.

Amber had a lump in her throat. How could the old woman have known what she had been feeling?

"You've brought love back into this big old house. I haven't seen that boy this happy since…" she paused, "in a very long time. It's like he's walking on air, and anyone in their right mind can see he's head over heels in love with you." She placed her hand on top of Amber's. "Correct me if I'm wrong, child, but I think you're just as in love with him."

Amber blinked and took a deep breath. "I am," she whispered.

Maggie smiled then returned to the beans. "Have you told him, dear?"

"No."

"And why not?"

"I'm afraid of scaring him away," Amber said, looking toward the corral.

"Child, that boy ain't going nowhere," the woman said, digging in the sack for another bean.

Just then, the orange cat came racing onto the porch followed by Clancy.

"Clancy! You leave Lucky alone," Amber scolded.

Clancy whined then barked at the cat, which had jumped to safety.

"That's enough young man," Amber said firmly.

Clancy plopped down by Amber's feet, but continued to keep an eye on the large orange cat.

"Maggie, what's the story with Lucky? I know Dalton brought him the first time he visited Michigan," Amber said, eyeing the cat.

The older woman chuckled. "Not by choice. He likes to ride in the horse trailers. If the horse trailers are moving, you can bet that cat will be close by. He's more of a pain than anything."

"Then why keep him?" Amber asked, puzzled.

The old woman looked at Amber then glanced over toward the corral, her eyes scanning until they landed on Dalton. Seeming satisfied, she began her story.

"When Mary Katherine got sick, Dalton was beside himself. He was always the strong one, the one that made things better. Only this time he couldn't. All the money and the best doctors couldn't save her.

"Right after she died, while Dalton was still grieving, this pregnant mama cat started hanging around the barn. One day she got too close to one of the horses and got kicked. Well, as she lay there dying, she went into labor and out came this little orange kitten. He was no bigger than this," she said stretching her fingers to show the size. "Well, Dalton sat there and cried like a baby holding that tiny wet kitten. No one said a word as he got up and wiped the blood and mucus from its helpless little body. Dalton fed that kitten with an eyedropper, getting up every couple hours for the next several weeks. Every time he would get up with Katie Mae, he would nurse that kitten as well, refusing all help. I think in some way he had to help that cat. He had to do for it what he couldn't do for Mary Katherine."

Amber had tears in her eyes. That was the most gut-wrenching story she had ever heard.

"He has been through so much," Amber said softly. "It's hard to believe he's still sane."

"Well, you are…"

"I am what?" Amber asked.

"You're sane, and from what you've told me, you have been through just as much."

"I guess you're right," Amber said, wiping her eyes. "You know, it's easy to forget about all the bad stuff when you're surrounded by so much good."

"I know child, I know. That's what I meant when I said you belong here."

Amber smiled at the sight of Dalton showing Julie how to swing a rope. Even from a distance, she could see the smile on her daughter's face and the happiness that radiated from her.

"I think you're right," she said. "I think we both belong here."

Chapter Forty-Eight

"You guys have fun," Amber said, waving at the car pulling away. She turned to face Dalton. "Your mom and dad are great."

"They think you're great too," Dalton said, pulling her close.

"I was surprised they were so eager to take Julie with them." Amber was happy that they had included her daughter. Actually, she was amazed at how readily everyone she had met here accepted both her and her daughter. For the first time in her life, she felt loved, felt like she belonged, like they belonged.

"Why not? Everyone else was going," Dalton reminder her. "Even Maggie."

"I know. It's just that Jeff's parents were never real grandparents to her. They haven't even called her since Jeff died. And here your parents already have her calling them Mamal and Papal."

"Are you kidding? I think they are ready to adopt both of you," Dalton said with a grin.

"Julie's so happy here. I wish it could last forever." Amber realized what she had said and changed the subject.

"That is the most magnificent horse I have ever seen," she said, walking toward the south corral. The big stallion had been turned loose in a corral with a horse that was noticeably smaller. The mare was in season and Crazy Legs was obviously interested. The stallion's erection astounded Amber.

She watched in stunned silence as the big horse reared up and after several awkward attempts, he entered the waiting mare. He screamed a triumphant cry as he pumped his fluids into the mare. After what seemed like an eternity the big horse dismounted, sweat lathered his glistening body and his hanging member still quivered from the encounter. Amber turned to look at Dalton; her body felt like it was on fire, her need growing with every breath.

Dalton cupped her chin with his hand and stared into the depths of her eyes.

"You are beautiful when you're excited," he said, kissing her forcefully.

They both turned as a ranch hand came out of a nearby barn.

"Do you want something to drink?" Dalton asked, leading her in the opposite direction.

"I could use some ice water." Amber struggled to regain her composure as they walked toward the house holding hands. The sight of the horses had left Amber speechless. Yearning.

"After you, my lady," Dalton said, opening the door.

"Why thank you, Sir," Amber replied playfully. "Wow, it's cooler in here."

She lifted her hair to allow the cool breeze from the fan to blow across her neck. With the kids gone and Maggie visiting her sister for the day, the kitchen – normally a theater of activity – was cool and quiet.

"That fan sure feels nice," Dalton agreed, taking a glass from the cabinet, filling it with ice and water and passing it to her. "This should cool you off."

Amber took a drink, tilting the glass a little more than she should have. A shiver ran through her body as the cold water escaped past her lips, trickled down her chin, along her neck and Amber gasped as the cold water invaded her bosom. She set the glass down and reached for a paper towel.

Dalton approached, took the towel from her and gently kissed her tenderly on the mouth. Next, he kissed her chin then continued down Amber's neck retracing the path of the cool water. Amber's eyes were closed, her breathing heavy with anticipation. Dalton stopped when he reached the tops of her breasts. He looked up as if asking permission to continue.

Amber opened her eyes, looked into the depths of Dalton's. She smiled then nodded her head, willing him to continue.

He pulled her shirt over her head, his hungry eyes lingering over her near naked body. He reached around to unhook her bra, allowing her sun-kissed breasts to fall free. Amber moaned as his mouth closed over first one erect nipple then the other, flicking each softly with his tongue.

Placing her hands on the back of his head, she pulled him closer into her. Dalton's mouth explored her breasts, his tongue flickering against her erect nipples, his hands caressing her sun-warmed breasts.

Dropping lower, he began kissing down her taut stomach, tracing the curves of her ribs lightly with his fingertips. When he got to the waistline of her pants, he paused, once again seeking permission.

Amber wanted him more than she had ever wanted anyone. She could not have told him no even if she wanted to. She reached for the button of her shorts.

Dalton touched his hand to hers. "Let me," he whispered.

Amber smiled and nodded, surrendering to his touch.

Dalton gently unsnapped the button, lowered the zipper and slid the shorts down to the floor. Amber picked up one foot, then the other, allowing Dalton to slip off first her shorts then her panties and set them aside.

He was on his knees in front of her, giving him full access to her womanly mound. He looked into her eyes then, shutting his, he submerged his face into her awaiting folds. His hands caressed her buttocks as his tongue found her magic button. Amber hadn't realized just how much the stallion had aroused her.

The first wave hit her so suddenly it caught her by surprise. Once again, she held onto the back of his head, pushing him further into her. She cried out, and then a new warmth escaped from within her folds. He continued lapping up her sweet nectar until her body stiffened again. Amber opened her eyes and looked down at Dalton.

"I need you," she whispered breathlessly.

Dalton hurried to undress, exposing the fullness of his manhood. Turning her around, he entered her from behind, just as the stallion had entered the mare. Her warmth embraced him as they rocked back and forth, her body meeting his every move. Rhythmically they continued until neither could wait any longer. Dalton entered one last time as both their bodies erupted with pleasure. He held her tightly, not wanting the moment to end. Gently, he pulled himself from her then turned her around to face him.

"That was incredible," he said, pulling her to him.

"It was," Amber agreed.

"Why can't it?" Dalton asked, looking into Amber's eyes.

"Why can't it what?" Amber asked, confused.

"Earlier by the horses, you wished it could last forever. Why can't it?"

"I don't understand," Amber stammered, not daring to believe what he was saying.

"Amber, I've loved you from the moment I saw you at the fairgrounds. Then, when I thought you weren't interested in me, I was heartbroken. I felt as though I had lost you. I know it sounds crazy, but do you believe in love at first sight?"

"Do I?" she said with tears in her eyes. "You know, all those years I thought I was in love with Jeff, but never once did I feel the way I feel when I'm with you. I ache when I'm away from you, even for a minute. I think about you every second.

"I love you, Dalton. I was scared at first, but I felt as though I could tell you anything. No, I felt as though I had to tell you everything. Like I had to make you love me. Like I could only be happy if you loved me." Tears streamed down her face. "Do you know when I knew for sure? When I saw the name of your ranch."

"Now I'm afraid I'm the one who doesn't understand," Dalton said.

"Sunset Meadows," she said distantly, gazing off into space. "On one of his good days, my father explained to me how I got my name. He told me I was named after the prettiest amber sunset he had ever seen. He saw it on the way to taking Mom to the hospital to have me. So you see: it's a sign. It means I'm home."

Without another word, Dalton took her hand and led her toward the stairwell.

"Where are we going?" she asked, sniffling.

"I want you," he said softly, "but this time I want to take my time."

Chapter Forty-Nine

"What do you mean you're getting married?" Robin exclaimed, pacing the floor and waving her arms.

"Are you out of your freaking mind, girlfriend? You can't marry a guy you just met!"

Amber smiled. She had expected this reaction. Robin was always looking out for her best interest. Robin sat down next to her.

"How can you be so sure he's the one, Amber? Maybe it's just lust. You know how guys get when they get a great piece of ass: they get all clingy and shit."

"It's not like that," Amber said, shaking her head.

"You mean you two haven't had sex yet?"

"I didn't say that," Amber said, smiling.

"Oh, so you have had sex. How was it?"

"Absolutely wonderful," Amber said dreamily.

"A little wonderful or a lot of wonderful?" Robin pressed.

"It doesn't get any better," Amber sighed.

"So he…?"

"Yes, he does," Amber said, cutting her off.

"Well that's a plus," Robin laughed. "Damn, I'm getting off track. Are you still on birth control?"

"Yes, I have been on the pill for years. You know, Jeff said he didn't want any more children," Amber replied, thinking it ironic another should be born one day soon.

"What makes you so sure he's the one Amber? Really, how are you so sure?"

"I think about him all the time," Amber said, dreamily. "I smile when I hear his voice; just the sight of him takes my breath away. I think about him and he calls. Robin, I'm not crazy. Dalton is my soul mate."

Robin reached over and felt her friend's forehead. "Are you okay, girlfriend? I just thought I heard you use the 'S' word."

"Oh stop," Amber said, pushing her hand away.

"I thought you didn't believe in soul mates."

"It is hard to believe in a soul mate when you don't have one," Amber said, looking at her hands. "Now that I have one, I'm a believer."

"What does Julie think about all of this?"

"Julie is thrilled. She'll be starting a new school and have new friends. Lana is looking for a place nearby so that she and Kelly can go to the same school together. They're already calling each other cousin," Amber laughed. "And both Julie and Katie Mae are thrilled about becoming sisters."

"What does Dalton think about having another daughter?"

"Are you kidding? He loves kids, he has already spent more time with her than Jeff ever did," Amber assured her friend.

"How can you be sure he's not just after you for your inheritance?" Robin asked cautiously.

Amber laughed at the absurdity of that statement. "Did I forget to mention that his house is nearly four times bigger than mine?"

"Holy shit!" Robin exclaimed. "You mean he's rich?"

"I don't think he is hurting, that's for sure."

"Are you after him for his money?"

"Yeah right, I have enough of my own," Amber reminded her.

"True," Robin agreed.

"Anything else?"

"Hmm, we have discussed love, sex, lust and money. Nope, I guess that pretty much covers everything. You have my permission to marry him," Robin said, laughing and hugging Amber.

Amber whisked her hand across her brow dramatically. "Well, I'm glad I have your permission," she teased, feigning relief.

"Not to mention the fact that he is totally friggin gorgeous. I'm just glad you've finally found your Mr. Right."

Amber took on a dreamy expression. "I really did, didn't I?"

"You know what's weird? I think for the first time since I have known you, you seem truly happy."

"I am," Amber agreed.

Robin's smile faded. "Are you going to tell your dad?"

Amber's mood instantly changed. She took a deep breath. "I already did. He was drunk, as always. He wished me a lifetime of happiness, said he would pour me a toast and hung up the phone."

"Why do you let him get to you, Amber?"

"I don't know," Amber said softly. "I guess because he's all I have left."

"You have me," Robin reminded her.

"I know, but he's my dad. He was great until after Mom died. Before she got sick he was always there for me, but after that, he sank into the bottle. I didn't understand then, but now I realize how much losing someone affects a person. Even with all of his faults, he's still my dad."

"Oh Amber, I'm sorry," Robin said, handing her a

tissue.

"It's okay, really," Amber said, blowing her nose. "I'm going to be just fine."

"So, what about selling the house?" Robin asked.

"I've talked to my attorney, Mr. Grether; he's going to take care of everything for me. I am only taking a few pieces of furniture, our personal things and our clothes. Dalton and I picked out new bedroom furniture for our room."

Amber stopped for a minute then repeated what she had said.

"Our room. I really like the sound of that," she said, smiling. "Then Julie picked out a beautiful canopy set for her room. Dalton said he would have it all ready for us when we get back."

"Sounds like you have everything covered, girlfriend."

"Everything but one," Amber said, staring at Robin.

"What's that?"

"Will you be at my wedding? We're not planning anything big. Just a trip to the Justice of the Peace, but I would love to have you there."

"Just let me know when," Robin said, tears streaming down her face. "Just let me know when."

Chapter Fifty

"Amber, darlin', we really need to start," Dalton said tenderly.

"I know," Amber said softly. "I just don't understand why Robin isn't here. She promised me, she knows how important this is to me. I hope nothing happened to her. This is just not like her."

He looked disappointed. "Do you want to postpone?"

She glanced over at Julie, who was sitting next to Kelly and smiled at her. Her eyes met with Lana's, who looked like she was silently willing Amber to go ahead. Maggie sat next to Jake, a tissue at the ready. She looked over at Carl, who surprisingly didn't look half bad cleaned up and without his trademark cigarette hanging from his mouth. She smiled at Katie Mae who was sitting amazingly still next to Dalton's parents, who were smiling approvingly at her.

Really smiling, accepting her into the family.

"No, it's okay," Amber said, looking up into Dalton's relieved blue eyes. "I'm ready."

Dalton took Amber's hand and led her to the front of the room where the Justice of the Peace was standing.

"Are you two ready to begin?"

Amber looked into the old man's kind eyes. His hair, although full, had turned white. He smiled at her, and then glanced over her shoulder. Amber turned just as Robin burst through the door.

"Wait for me," she said, gasping for air.

Amber turned back toward the white haired man. "Just one more minute, please."

The old man nodded patiently.

"I'll just be a moment." Amber squeezed Dalton's hand and searched his crystal blue eyes.

"Go ahead," he said, smiling.

"Where have you been?" Amber asked, more relieved than annoyed. She gave Robin a tight hug. "I was so worried."

"You can yell at me later, girlfriend," Robin said, pulling back. "I was picking up your wedding present."

"Robin! You stopped to shop?" Amber asked furiously. "I was worried sick about you."

"I said I was picking up your wedding present, not picking it out," Robin corrected her and gestured toward the door. "I thought you'd like to have something old at your wedding."

Amber turned to see what Robin was looking at. Suddenly, tears streamed down her face.

"Daddy?"

"Hello, Pumpkin, sorry I'm late," he said, entering the room.

He pulled her to the side and hugged her tightly. He clung to her as he whispered into her ear. "I know I haven't been much of a father to you, but I want you to know I love you, baby, and I do wish you all the happiness in the world."

Amber leaned into the frail man, immediately noting the absence of any alcohol smell.

"Thank you, Daddy," she said, pulling away and wiping her eyes.

The white haired man at the front of the room cleared his throat.

Amber whispered her thank you to Robin, gave her

hand a firm squeeze, and then took her place beside Dalton.

Dalton bent to kiss a tear that had settled on her cheek.

"Dry your tears, Amber Mae," he said with his soothing southern drawl. "It's time for you to be happy."

The Justice of the Peace placed his hand on Amber's. "Are you ready, little lady?"

"I am now," she said, looking up at Dalton. "I am now."

THE END

Acknowledgements

To my wonderful husband and soul mate, thank you for believing in me and encouraging me to follow my dream. To my children and grandchildren, whose humor and antics never cease to amaze me. And, to my best friend Sheila, thank you for unknowingly helping me find my voice.

To my editor, Michelle Johnson, for keeping that voice intact!

SAB

About the Author

Photograph by Hobbs Studio

Born in Louisville, Sherry A. Burton was raised in the small town of Fairdale, Kentucky. Eloping December of 1980 with a Navy man while still in her teens, she has spent all of her adult life moving from state to state counting over thirty-two moves in her thirty years of marriage. Sherry can attest first-hand to the fact that a whirlwind marriage can indeed last. Sherry credits her frequent moves and long separations to her ability to feel her characters' desire to find true happiness.

Sherry has worked as a private nanny and is a certified dog trainer. She is the mother of three adult children and has four wonderful grandchildren. Her hobbies include reading, walking, Pilates, and spending time with her "friends" which is how she refers to the characters she creates. She believes in daily affirmations, positive energy and feels that karma will have the final say.

Sherry A. Burton currently resides in Chesapeake, Virginia, and has several other books in the works, including a sequel to *Tears of Betrayal*.

Other books by Sherry A. Burton

The King of My Heart
Somewhere in My Dreams
(previously released as *The Scars Between Us*)

Made in the USA
Monee, IL
22 February 2022